THE GOBLIN'S GIFT

CONRAD MASON

CORGI BOOKS

THE GOBLIN'S GIFT
A CORGI BOOK 978 0552 57129 6

First published in Great Britain by David Fickling Books
an imprint of Random House Children's Publishers UK
A Random House Group Company

David Fickling Books edition published 2013
Corgi edition published 2014

1 3 5 7 9 10 8 6 4 2

Set in Berling

RANDOM HOUSE CHILDREN'S PUBLISHERS UK
61-63 Uxbridge Road, London W5 5SA

www.randomhousechildrens.co.uk
www.totallyrandombooks.co.uk
www.randomhouse.co.uk

Addresses for companies within The Random House Group Limited can be found at: www.randomhouse.co.uk/offices.htm

THE RANDOM HOUSE GROUP Limited Reg. No. 954009

A CIP catalogue record for this book is available from the British Library.

Printed and bound in Great Britain by Clays Ltd, St Ives plc

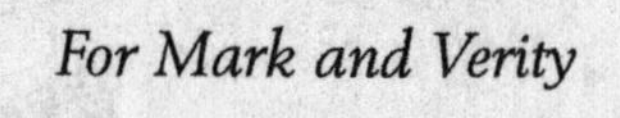

For Mark and Verity

N
TO THE
LONELY ISLE
ELD
THALINTOWN
THE DEMON'S DICE
IMMEL
THE CLAW
TO THE
OLD WORLD
PORTFAYT
THE MIDDLE
ISLANDS
ILLON
NEW
DALPORT
ARLA
TO THE
KING'S ROCK

PORT FAYT
WYRMWOOD MANOR
LIGHTHOUSE
THE LEGLESS MERMAID
DOCKSIDE
MARLINSPIKE QUARTER
CROSSTREE QUARTER
BOOTLES' PIE SHOP
FLAGSTAFF QUARTER
THALIN SQUARE

It's not the pain that he enjoys.

It's the fear.

He straightens his glasses with a thumb and forefinger and inspects the creature squirming on the desk before him. It is pinned to a wooden block, wings pierced with Azurmouth steel so that it cannot escape from the darkened cabin.

A female fairy. Daemonium volans. *Demonspawn.*

There is a grotesque fascination in the way it struggles, tries to lift its wings against the steel of the pins, begs, pleads with him to let it go. Almost unbearably disgusting.

'I'll tell you anything,' it cries. 'Please. I promise.'

'Anything? Truly, you'd tell me anything?'

He is rewarded with a flicker of hope in the creature's eyes.

'Yes, sir. I've lived in Port Fayt all my life, sir. I've seen some things, I can tell you. Just give me a chance.'

He leans over the desk, one hand resting on a green marble paperweight, examining the way the creature's wings protrude through holes cut into the fabric of its dirty dress. So foul. So unnatural.

'But what could you possibly know that might help me?'

'I've seen their fleet, sir. The Fayter fleet. I can tell you about their men and their guns. I can tell you all about Governor Skelmerdale. I can tell you . . . I can . . .' Its voice peters out. The flicker of hope dies.

'Suppose you could. What difference would it make? Do you really suppose the Fayters stand a chance against us? No, my dear. I fear you are no use at all.'

'Kill me then. I'm not afraid.'

It has stopped struggling now and lies, tiny arms folded, glaring up at him. Its body glows faintly against the wooden block.

He raises his eyebrows. He had not expected this. Bravery, from such a despicable creature. He would not have thought it possible. And this bravery has driven away all trace of the fear. The fear that he so enjoys.

'I am impressed,' he admits. 'Most impressed.'

There is a knock at the door.

'Enter.'

Morning sunshine spills into the cabin as a white-jacketed marine ducks his head inside.

'Your honour, a vessel has been sighted to the west of our fleet. A wavecutter, flying no colours.'

The Duke of Garran considers for a moment, then nods.

'Very well. I will attend to it.'

He sweeps his hat from the desk, making the fairy flinch.

'Don't worry,' he tells it. 'You've shown me that you are brave. You're not afraid any more. That's good. Very good.'

Hope returns to the fairy's eyes. Delicious. And in one swift movement, the Duke of Garran lifts the marble paperweight and brings it down.

Once.

Twice.

Three times.

There is not even a scream.

He turns back to the marine.

'Send someone in here,' he says, 'to clean my desk.'

PART ONE
Armada

Chapter One

Joseph Grubb clung to the ratlines, gripping the ropes so tightly they burned his hands.

'What are you waiting for?' came Tabitha's voice from below.

He gritted his teeth and kept climbing, doing his best to block out everything except the regular motion: left foot, right hand; right foot, left hand. *Come on. You can do this.* Back in Fayt, he used to scramble up the stepladder in his uncle's pantry every day. Two weeks ago he'd even clambered onto the rooftops of the Marlinspike Quarter to chase a cat. And now he was climbing to the crow's nest of a wavecutter, swaying on a few bits of rope more than a hundred feet above the deck, so high that the people below looked like colourful beetles. So high that . . . He swallowed.

Not helping.

He paused again, panting, brow prickling with sweat. On his raised right arm a fresh tattoo was scored into his greyish-pink mongrel skin. A swirling blue shark – the mark of a watchman. It was still almost impossible to believe that this was what he was. But the proof was right there, in front of his eyes. The Demon's Watch. Protectors of Port Fayt. Scourge of all sea scum.

Scourge of Mrs Bootle's pies, more like.

The thought made him smile, and he started to climb again.

The crow's nest wasn't far now. As he moved, a spyglass bumped around inside the right pocket of his breeches, balancing out the bouncing of the cutlass on his left hip. Captain Newton had given it to him on the day he got his tattoo. The hand-guard was made of thick, solid brass, and the hilt had smooth oiled leather wrapped tightly around it. There was a small shark carved on the blade, and a word neatly lettered beneath it – GRUBB.

No doubt about it. His days as a tavern boy were well and truly over.

'Hey, tavern boy,' came a shout from below. Joseph chanced a look back over his shoulder. His stomach swam at the altitude, but on the deck he spotted the distant shape of Phineus Clagg – professional smuggler and captain of the *Sharkbane*. His hands were cupped around his mouth, and his long hair and dirty coat flapped in the breeze. 'We ain't got all day, yer know.'

Further down the ratlines, Tabitha's blue-haired head turned to shout at him. 'You want to climb up here? Oh wait, I forgot – you're too fat.'

Joseph didn't wait to hear the smuggler's reply. He closed his eyes and kept going. *Left foot, right hand; right foot, left hand.* The higher he got, the more the breeze buffeted him, forcing him to grip the ropes tighter still. But he couldn't stop now. If he did, Tabitha would never let him forget it.

He opened his eyes and at once they began to water in the wind. One last effort . . . *Right foot, left hand* . . . And finally he was there, hauling himself up through the gap and collapsing onto the platform of the crow's nest. He lay there for a moment, gasping for breath, while Tabitha clambered up after him.

'What's wrong?' she asked, slapping him on the back. 'Don't tell me you're scared of heights!' She was trying to sound casual but Joseph didn't believe it for one second. She crouched on the platform, her eyes wide, her face tinged with green.

'You have to admit, we *are* quite high up.'

Tabitha opened her mouth to argue, then flashed him a smile.

'I s'pose you could say that.'

Joseph grinned back at her. Tabitha acted tough, but she was friendly too. Most of the time. She was always asking him about his old life working for his uncle at the Legless Mermaid, and about the time before, when his parents were alive. She didn't talk about her own much, but for some reason she seemed to enjoy hearing Joseph tell stories about his home with the green front door. He enjoyed it too. It was good to have someone he could share the memories with.

Tabitha nodded out to sea. 'What are you waiting for?'

He scrambled to his feet and grabbed hold of the rail at the front of the crow's nest, trying to ignore the fact that on three other sides there was nothing but a sheer drop down to the deck. The view laid out before him did nothing to calm his churning stomach.

In the distance, Illon rose from the sparkling waters of the Ebony Ocean – the easternmost of the Middle Islands; a hazy green hump like the back of a sea serpent. Its largest bay was cluttered with vessels, anchored with their sails furled, white banners fluttering from every masthead. There were wavecutters and frigates on the fringes, and beyond, towards the heart of the fleet, lay the real battleships – galleons and men-of-war.

In the centre was a ship that could only belong to the Duke of Garran. It towered above the others like a wooden castle, its banner so vast that, even from this distance, Joseph could make out the Golden Sun embroidered on it. It was the biggest ship he had ever seen. But then, this was the biggest fleet he'd ever seen too.

He drew out the spyglass and held it to one eye. He could see movement on board some of the nearest vessels – League marines in their white battle-dress, bayonets gleaming. All humans, of course. It sent a shudder down his spine. The League of the Light had come from the Old World for one purpose alone – to destroy Port Fayt and everyone who lived there. Elves, trolls, fairies . . . and mongrels, naturally. Being half human wouldn't save Joseph when the other half of him was goblin.

Tabitha snatched the spyglass away from him.

'Let me have a look,' she said. 'We're supposed to be gathering information, not just gawping. That's the whole point of this expedition, remember? So we can get back to Fayt and figure out how to beat these dungheads.'

Joseph cast a sidelong glance at her as she sighted down the spyglass, blue hair tied back in a ponytail so the wind wouldn't blow it in her face. Like him she wore a watchman's coat, but with a bandolier of throwing knives slung over her shoulder. *Most* of the time she was friendly. But sometimes Joseph thought she liked those knives better than any real person. Tabitha was the first girl he'd ever met properly. Maybe they were just different from boys.

'No,' said Tabitha.

'Pardon?'

She was lowering the telescope, still staring out to sea. Her face had become greener, and her eyes even wider than before. 'No, no, no. Look!'

Joseph turned back to the League armada. It took him a few seconds to see it, but when he did his blood ran cold. The three closest vessels were moving away from the main fleet, heading towards the *Sharkbane*. They looked like frigates. Fighting ships. Fast ones.

'They've spotted us,' said Tabitha. She leaned over the side of the crow's nest and bawled at the top of her voice, 'Turn about! Three League frigates are closing on us!'

Joseph swallowed. 'Does this mean . . .?'

Tabitha sighed, louder than was necessary. 'Yes, it means we're climbing down again. You first. I don't want you throwing up on me.'

By the time they got down, Phineus Clagg was at the wheel. Joseph had to lean against the tilt of the deck as the *Sharkbane* came about, faster than he would have thought possible for a ship of her size. He and Tabitha hurried towards the stern, dodging smugglers tugging on ropes and shouting out instructions. Hal and the Bootle twins had already gathered around the wheel. All of the Demon's Watch were on board except Newt and Old Jon, who had both stayed behind in Port Fayt.

'Can we outrun them?' asked Hal, adjusting his glasses and peering across the water. He looked anxious. But then, he often did. Before he'd joined the Watch, Joseph had never imagined that a magician could be so . . . jumpy.

'*Can we outrun them?*' Clagg mimicked. 'Course we can, spectacles. Ain't nothing to worry about. This is the *Sharkbane*. The fastest—'

'– ship in the Ebony Ocean,' chorused Frank and Paddy, the troll twins.

'We know,' said Paddy.

'You've mentioned it once or twice before,' added Frank.

Tabitha sprinted up the steps to the poop deck and inspected the League vessels with her spyglass.

'They're gaining on us,' she shouted. 'Those frigates are going faster than a greased fairy.'

'Ain't possible,' said Clagg. He took a long swig from his bottle of firewater and stuffed a fresh lump of tobacco into his mouth, his lazy left eye flicking nervously around the deck. The smuggler hadn't exactly jumped at the chance of helping out the watchmen, but a few ducats and a dangerous look from Newton had been enough to persuade him. He was probably starting to regret it now.

Joseph climbed the steps to join Tabitha. He almost gasped out loud when he saw the frigates. They were much closer than he'd expected, moving steadily, as if unaffected by the waves. In front of every vessel the air shimmered like a mirage, but the ocean was as calm as a glass of water.

'Magic,' he murmured. 'They've got magicians on board.' Spell-casting was banned in Port Fayt – unless you had a warrant, like Hal did – but that made no difference to the League.

Hal appeared next to them. He took the spyglass from Tabitha and examined the enemy ships.

'Ah,' he said at last. 'I fear you may be right. It's elementary brinecraft, applied on a much larger scale than is usually attempted. They're exerting willpower on the waves, reducing tidal movements that would ordinarily disrupt the passage of the vessel. Also I imagine they're performing some sort of aeolian manipulation to increase the flow of wind to the sails. It's rather extraordinary. I've not seen anything like it since—'

'That's fascinating,' cut in Tabitha, 'but maybe we should *do* something about it?'

Joseph leaned over the railing of the poop deck. 'Can we go any faster, Mr Clagg?'

'That's C*aptain* Clagg, matey,' replied the smuggler. He was frowning at the ocean ahead, chewing on the tobacco, his hair and coat flung back by the breeze. 'And no, not without a better wind.'

'Thank Thalin we hired the fastest ship in the Ebony Ocean, eh?' said Paddy, clapping an enormous green hand on the smuggler's back. 'Fastest except for those three frigates, anyway.'

'They're cheating! Stinking magic . . . Ruins all the fun, if you ask me.'

'Hal,' said Tabitha. 'If they're speeding up their ships with magic, why can't you do the same for the *Sharkbane*?'

Hal shook his head. 'I'm flattered, but it's out of the question. Spells that powerful require a team of trained magicians working together, focusing their minds as one. I couldn't do it on my own.'

Frank drew his enormous cutlass and swung it in a practice stroke.

'In that case,' he said, 'we'd best get ready for a fight.'

Chapter Two

There was no need for a spyglass now. The frigates were so close that Joseph could make out cannons poking from the gun ports and groups of white-jacketed magicians standing at each prow, their hands spread out in front of them, smoothing the water ahead. Beyond he could see the movements of marines getting ready to board the *Sharkbane*. Real, battle-hardened soldiers. League soldiers. Soldiers who'd swept through the Old World, taking the Flatland Duchies in little more than a month and defeating the trolls of the Crying Mountains within a week. Soldiers who would kill anyone who wasn't human without a second thought. Butchers, some folk called them – because in battle, their white uniforms were stained with their enemies' blood.

Joseph pulled the cutlass from his belt, its weight reassuring him just a little. Frank and Paddy had been teaching him how to use it, and he tried to run through their lessons in his head to calm himself down. But the advice kept getting jumbled up. He decided to think about something else. There was nothing though – except those frigates bearing down on them. He pressed his fingers more tightly around the leather hilt.

He could make out the names of the enemy vessels now, painted on the prows. As he watched, the two flanking ships, the *Last Redemption* and the *Radiant*, peeled off from the *White Crusader* to port and starboard. Soon they'd come up alongside the *Sharkbane*. Joseph didn't know much about warfare, but he could see that there were enough guns on board the League ships to smash the smuggler's wave-cutter into matchwood.

There was a *CRACK!* from the nearest frigate and Joseph ducked, almost without thinking. Adrenaline coursed through his body.

'Heads down, everyone,' roared Frank or Paddy – in the confusion, it was difficult to tell which. More cracks sounded and musket balls whirred past.

'Snipers,' shouted Tabitha, as if it wasn't obvious by then. She flicked her wrist and sent a knife flashing through the air towards the enemy ship, before ducking down below the gunwale. There was a gleam in her eye and a second knife in her hand. Scared as he was, Joseph couldn't help but marvel at her excitement. Almost as if this was some kind of game, rather than a deadly skirmish they might very well not survive.

'To me!' shouted the other troll twin, and Joseph, Tabitha and Hal scurried to the edge of the poop deck and dropped down onto the upper deck.

Phineus Clagg was hunkered down behind the wheel, his podgy face pale. He had stopped chewing now.

'This is the *Sharkbane,*' he muttered to no one in particular. 'Fastest ship in the Ebony Ocean . . .'

A few of the smugglers were returning fire with pistols, blunderbusses and crossbows. One caught a musket ball in the arm and whirled away, growling with pain. Joseph hurried onwards. The watchmen were gathering by the mainmast, while Clagg's crew milled around them.

'We've got to stop the butchers from boarding,' said Paddy.

'Soon as we let them onto our ship, it's over,' added Frank.

'So we'll split up, help the smugglers fight them off. Joseph and Tabs, we'll stay on the port side. Frank and Hal – you take the starboard.'

There were nods, and the watchmen dispersed, positioning themselves to repel boarders. Joseph hadn't known the troll twins for long, but even he could see that they didn't rate their chances. He lifted his cutlass and told himself he was ready for anything. He didn't believe it though. What good was a sword against musket balls and cannon fire? The thought made him feel faint. He staggered and grabbed the gunwale to steady himself.

The *Last Redemption* was edging up, closer and closer.

'Don't worry,' said a voice to his left. He turned to see Tabitha watching him, doing her best to smile. 'We'll get through this. Somehow we'll—'

The *Sharkbane* jolted, throwing them both off balance. There was a beating and a flapping from overhead, and Joseph looked up to see the ship's sails hanging loose from their yards, as if the wind had gone out of them.

A low, grinding noise rose up from below his feet, and the deck shuddered. Joseph gripped the gunwale tighter.

What in all the sea . . . ?

'Hey, Cap'n Cuttlefish,' Frank shouted. 'What's

happening?' But Phineus Clagg had gone as white as the sails above. His mouth hung open and his tobacco dropped onto the deck.

The grinding grew louder, and with a lurch of his stomach Joseph realized what was happening.

'Sinking!' he yelled. 'We're sinking!'

He leaned over the gunwale and saw the waves bubbling up to meet him.

Cannons flashed on the *Last Redemption*, and a rolling symphony of booms rang out as the cannonballs hurtled towards them.

'Down!' barked Tabitha.

Joseph had no time to duck. But the *Sharkbane* was lower in the water than it had been a few seconds ago, and the cannonballs just tore through the sails, shredding the canvas.

Clagg found his voice at last. 'Not sinking,' he shouted above the chaos. 'She's going down too fast for that. It's like . . . like . . .'

'Like we're being pulled under,' Frank finished for him.

Joseph felt a prickling at the back of his neck. He couldn't help thinking of the Maw, the monstrous sea demon he'd seen rise out of the ocean less than two weeks ago. It still haunted his dreams. And who knew what else lived beneath the waves?

'We got to do something,' Clagg was howling as his crew ran in every direction like headless cockatrices. 'Yer supposed to be the Demon's Watch, ain't yer? So do something. Sky's sake, this is my ship! My dear, lovely ship!'

'Get back!' shouted Paddy. 'Away from the gunwales.'

Joseph didn't need to be told twice. He joined the smugglers and watchmen scurrying towards the main-mast. Soon the whole crew was huddled together in the middle of the deck, weapons facing outwards, waiting for whatever was going to happen. Joseph found himself squeezed between Frank and Tabitha. She didn't look so calm any more.

Cannon fire exploded from the *Radiant*. Everyone ducked as the sails were torn up again and chunks of wood burst from the foremast.

They were practically at sea level now, and Joseph didn't know if it would be safer above the waves or below them. Not that he had any choice in the matter.

'Stick together,' said Frank sternly. 'No matter what.'

Seawater spilled over the gunwales, racing across the deck, surging through their shoes and up their legs. It was freezing cold. Joseph thrust his cutlass back into his belt and took a deep breath, sucking as much air into his lungs as he could. The deck juddered downwards, and suddenly they were all adrift. He gasped as water flooded his clothing, like icy fingers clamping onto his skin.

'Look out!' yelped Tabitha. Joseph floundered out of the way as the mainsail yard came down, smacking into the water and sending up a great gout of spray as it disappeared beneath the waves. Within seconds, the whole ship was gone.

Shouts and screams rent the air as the smugglers and watchmen trod water. Some struck out for the League ships, which towered above them on every side, vast and implacable. But what was the use? There would be no mercy for them there. Joseph had heard the stories. The Duke of Garran's butchers would kill them all, if the sharks didn't get them first.

'Help!' he shouted uselessly. 'Help, please! Help—'

Someone grabbed hold of his ankles. *What in Thalin's name . . . ?* He tried to wriggle free, but the hands were strong and determined, tugging him downwards.

'No! Wait! Let me—'

And then he was under.

Chapter Three

One minute Tabitha was treading water, holding on tight to her knife. The next there were hands around her waist and she was being dragged down below the waves. She tried to stab at her attacker, but whoever it was dodged the blow. A hand closed around her wrist and the knife was twisted free. Tabitha struggled harder but it was no good. A second hand gripped her other wrist and her arms were pulled together behind her back.

As her eyes adjusted to the stinging salt water, she saw figures moving all around them. What in all the ocean was this? Some kind of trick by the League? She glanced down and saw a refracted form below her legs. A fish tail, absurdly oversized, with broad, powerful fins.

Tabitha gasped, swallowing a mouthful of seawater and almost choking in the process. There was only one kind of creature in the Ebony Ocean with the arms and hands of a human and the tail of a fish. *Merfolk*. She craned her neck round and caught a glimpse of a woman's face, long hair drifting out in the water, a necklace of shells . . . And then the mermaid's tail flicked hard like a cracking whip, and they were suddenly moving.

The shapes around them blurred. Bubbles streamed past her face as they shot forward, faster than any land dweller could swim. The mermaid's arms wrapped around her, hugging her in close, and they took on another burst of speed.

Tabitha was feeling faint and sick from the seawater. Her chest and head felt as if they were going to explode, and she found herself wondering which would go first. She had to breathe. If she didn't she was going to pass out. She thrashed feebly, trying to free herself from the mermaid's embrace, but it was hopeless. She didn't have the energy or the strength.

Suddenly they were heading upwards. The water became clearer and lighter, and then there was a thundering of spray all around them, and Tabitha realized they had breached the surface. For one incredible moment they were arcing through the air, the cold breeze biting into her wet, clinging clothes. She saw the waves stretching out on every side, saw gulls in the sky above, saw other doubled shapes moving fast below the surface behind them, each one surely a mermaid holding onto a person.

She almost forgot to breathe, and desperately gulped in air half a second before they hit the surface again with a crash; then there was a muffled quiet as they powered onwards.

They carried on like that, streaking below the surface. Tabitha was furious, but she couldn't break the firm grip of the mermaid. And even if she could somehow get free, what good would it do? She'd be alone, Thalin knew where, in the middle of the Ebony Ocean.

Every time her lungs began to burn with the need for more air, she struggled, and the mermaid, understanding, shot upwards and arced like a dolphin above the surface. Tabitha sucked in as much air as she possibly could, and then they were below again, swimming onwards.

Where are we going?

Tabitha had to admit that the merfolk had saved them from the League. She had to be grateful for that, didn't she? But she didn't feel very grateful. How long had they been swimming for? Hours, maybe. It definitely felt like hours. Above water, she tried to count the other mermaids. Occasionally she saw them breaching too, their captives held tightly, with startled faces and bedraggled hair. Tabitha hoped she didn't look that ridiculous.

Her eyes became accustomed to the salt and she began to see things below the waves. The odd fish, darting away from them as they shot past. A sea snake, coiling through the water. Nothing gave her the slightest clue to where the merfolk were taking them.

They leaped up above the surface again. But this time Tabitha was shoved forward, and suddenly she was tumbling through the air and down onto something grey and hard. Something that definitely wasn't water. 'Aaaargh!' she yelped, going head over heels. She landed flat on her back, staring up at the sky and trying to make the world stop spinning. Behind her, there was a splash as her captor disappeared back into the waves.

Tabitha sat up, rubbing her head. She was on a stony beach, empty except for a slope of scree stretching up ahead of her and a few haggard trees on the horizon.

There were more splashes, and watchmen and

smugglers came crashing down around her like cannonballs, yelping with pain and surprise as they grazed elbows and shins. Soon Hal was fumbling his glasses back onto his nose, the troll twins were wringing out their sodden jackets and Captain Clagg was hunting feverishly through his pockets to check that his bottle of firewater had made it safely. Last of all, Joseph came hurtling down, curled up in a ball with his eyes tightly shut, bouncing from rock to rock and coming to rest next to Tabitha. He was shivering with cold, and his new watchman's coat clung to his bony body.

He ought to count himself lucky, Tabitha reckoned. Not all the smugglers had made it.

She glared at their captors, bobbing out in the deep water. There were between ten and twenty of them, both mermaids and mermen. She'd seen plenty of their kind before, come to trade in Fayt's bay or locked up in the Brig. But these ones were different. Wilder, somehow. They had untamed salt-matted hair and grim faces. They wore tunics woven out of seaweed and bits of old rope, doubtless scavenged from the ocean.

She was about to give them a piece of her mind when she spotted the long pale rods slung on their backs. She had heard about those things. Bonestaffs, they were called, made from the skeletons of sea creatures that lived too deep for any landlubber to ever see. Hal had explained to her once that bonestaffs were really just large, powerful wands. To say that merfolk were good with magic was an understatement – like saying that giants were a bit on the large side.

Captain Clagg leaped to his feet.

'You!' he yelled, then stopped to spit out seaweed. 'You . . . brine-crawling bilgebags! You scaly swabs! My ship – what have you done with my ship?' Tabitha had never seen him look so furious before. Then again, she'd never seen him lose the *Sharkbane* and half his crew before either. He fumbled in his coat pocket and drew out a pistol, the hammer pulled back.

That's all we need.

Tabitha flung herself forward, reaching for the weapon. If Phineus Clagg shot a mermaid, those bonestaffs would be pointed at them in no time. But her foot slipped on a seaweed-covered rock and she came crashing down. There was a click. No gunshot. She looked up to see a dribble of seawater emerge from the the smuggler's pistol barrel.

The merfolk were making strange noises, like a crowd of braying seals. Clambering to her feet, Tabitha realized that they were laughing. At her. It made her shudder. *Of course the pistol wasn't going to go off.* The powder was probably damper than a baby dolphin.

Phineus Clagg cursed and hurled the pistol as hard as he could at their tormentors. It splashed harmlessly into the sea, a good ten feet from the nearest merman. The seal noises swelled in volume.

'What do they want?' asked Joseph. He had sat up now, rubbing at his bruised arms and looking sorry for himself.

Paddy wrung out his sodden tricorne hat and shrugged. 'Beats me. But I doubt it's just a bit of fish and a word of thanks.'

'They have us trapped,' said Hal. 'So whatever it is, I think we'll have to listen.'

Illon is beautiful.

The sand is soft beneath his shoes, golden waves of it extending in either direction, lapped by the blue waves of the Ebony Ocean. Inland, the beach gives way to lush green vegetation: tall grasses and palm trees.

He raises his pistol, closing one eye to sight down the barrel. It jolts in his hands with a satisfying CRACK, *and the bird drops out of the tree as if suddenly made of stone. Its wings twitch on the sand, flashing vivid blue and yellow. Moments later it is still.*

Beautiful, but unprepared. Just like the village his scouts have uncovered on the far side of the island.

Tonight he will have his cooks pluck the bird and roast it for dinner.

And tomorrow, at dawn, they will kill the fishermen and burn their homes.

Two figures are approaching across the sand. One strides, tall, elegant and dressed all in white, a heavy broadsword on her back. Major Turnbull's long blonde hair is loose, fluttering like a flag in the sea breeze. The other stumbles, wrists tied together with a bit of old rope. A scruffy old human with thinning hair, missing teeth and wide, terrified eyes. A prisoner. One of the few captured in the skirmish with the Fayter scout ship.

Worthless.

Perhaps.

'Good day to you,' says the Duke. 'I believe you know who I am. And you . . . you are from Port Fayt, I take it?' He pours gunpowder into the barrel of his pistol.

'No, sir. Begging your pardon, sir. I'm just a smugg— a sailor, sir. From the Old World. Azurmouth.' The man's eyes flicker from side to side, as if in hope of escape. But there is none. Just the smooth golden sand stretching away from them.

'Indeed?' The Duke pulls back the hammer. 'From Azurmouth. And yet you sail on a vessel with the Demon's Watch.'

The smuggler licks his lips.

'I – we came to spy on your fleet, sir, if truth be told. On the League. It was Newton who sent us. Captain Newton of the Watch.'

'I have heard of the man.'

He sights down the barrel again. Another bird has landed in the branches of a tree, even closer this time. It is almost too easy.

'What of the others? Your fellow . . . "sailors".'

The smuggler swallows.

'Our ship was pulled down below. By merfolk, sir. They took Captain Clagg and most of the crew. And the watchmen. I don't know why. You have to believe me, sir.'

Merfolk.

Interesting.

'Well then. That will be all.'

He swings the pistol round, resting it against the man's forehead. At once the smuggler begins to whimper, weeping and begging.

He savours it.

'My friend,' he says softly, 'you are scarcely worth the waste of shot.'

The man's eyes go wide as the pistol is removed. As the Duke lets the hammer go and steps back. There is shock and gratitude in his eyes. Hope.

Delicious.

Even as Major Turnbull slides the sword out of its sheath.

Even as it glints, held high in the glorious sunshine.

Even as it flashes down.

Chapter Four

The merfolk were signing amongst themselves, their hands dancing as they conveyed messages in their silent language. At last one of them swam forward into the shallows – a slim mermaid with short blonde hair sticking up in clumps. She had a bonestaff on her back, and another in her hand.

'Fayters,' she said. Her voice sounded strained, as if this was the first time she'd ever spoken. 'Which of you is king?'

'She means leader,' explained Hal. 'Which of us is the leader.'

Paddy slapped a hand on his brother's shoulder.

'We'll be the king today,' he said. 'So tell us, why are we here?'

The mermaid drew herself up and spoke, her voice ringing out like a town crier's.

'Very well, troll kings. Today we have rescued you from certain death.'

'Now hold on,' said Frank. '"Certain" might be a bit strong, missy. I think we really had a chance back there.'

The mermaid carried on as if he hadn't spoken. 'The men in white have come. You saw for yourselves. They have sailed over the ocean, and they will kill you all. They have many ships and many men.' She gestured to her companions. 'We are here because we merfolk can help you. Together, our people will defeat the men in white. We will pull their ships below. We will smash them to dust. We will turn the very ocean against them. We will—'

'Great,' burst out Tabitha. She stumbled to her feet and strode towards the water's edge, her cheeks burning with anger. 'That's just wonderful. But did you really have to drag us halfway across the Ebony Ocean to explain that you're going to help us?'

A humourless chuckle sounded behind her. It was Clagg, sitting on a boulder. 'There's a catch though, ain't there?' he said.

There were movements among the merfolk. Hunching of shoulders; narrowing of eyes.

The mermaid who had spoken smiled a tight, cold smile.

'A catch,' she repeated.

'Shark pits,' said someone. Tabitha turned to see Joseph standing, his eyes wide. He looked a little embarrassed when he realized that everyone was looking at him, but he carried on anyway. 'I mean, is it to do with the shark pits? You want us to get rid of them?'

Shark pits. Tabitha had never been to one herself, but everyone knew they existed all over Port Fayt. Criminal dens where lowlife went to watch vicious man-eating sharks in combat with merfolk. To the death. Usually it wasn't much of a fight though. It was no wonder these people were upset about it.

'The little grey boy is right,' said the mermaid. 'You take our people like fish from the ocean, for your' – she scowled – '*shark pits*.'

'You have to understand, the shark-pit owners are criminals,' said Paddy. 'We try to stop them but—'

'Silence.' The mermaid glared at him. 'Each new king of Fayt promises an end to these shark pits. It has never come to pass. And now you have taken the greatest pearl in the ocean.' She drew back her arm and hurled the bonestaff she'd been holding. It arced through the air and buried itself in the beach, quivering. In spite of herself, Tabitha was impressed.

'This is the bonestaff of Pallione.' The mermaid folded her arms as if she had said something conclusive. The Fayters all looked blank. She flicked her tail impatiently, sending a gout of spray crashing across the surface. 'Pallione is our king's daughter.'

This time a murmur ran among the smugglers. Hal and the twins exchanged glances. Tabitha hadn't heard of Pallione, but she'd heard of the King of the Merfolk all right. From his seat in the south, he ruled over all the merfolk in the Ebony Ocean. He was said to be older than the sea, and almost as powerful.

And now, apparently, some idiot had kidnapped his daughter.

'What do you want from us?' asked Frank.

'An end to your barbarism. You must close the shark pits down. But first, bring us Pallione; only then will we fight. You must find her. She has hair white as the clouds and eyes green as seaweed. She is beautiful.'

The other merfolk nodded seriously.

There was a burst of laughter. Tabitha turned to see Phineus Clagg doubled up.

'You fish folk are a riot! What can you do to help,

eh? The League've got guns, matey. It'll take a bit more'n a few swimmers with white sticks to—'

Instantly the mermaid had her bonestaff off her back and levelled at Clagg. The air blurred and shimmered, and the smuggler was jerked off his feet, as though picked up by the hand of some angry seraph.

'Wait, no, I didn't mean—'

The mermaid made a circling motion with the bonestaff, and Clagg was flipped upside down. His flask of firewater went tumbling down to land with a clink on the stony beach.

'All right, I've learned me lesson now – no need to—'

The bonestaff jerked to the right, and Phineus Clagg went with it, swooping out over the water like some sort of ugly sea bird.

'Sorry, sorry, sorry, sorr—'

The staff came down hard, thwacking the surface of the sea. Clagg dropped like a stone, splashing into the deep water. Once again the merfolk let out their strange braying seal noises. But this time Tabitha joined in.

'All right,' said Frank as the smuggler surfaced and began to flounder back to shore. 'I reckon you've made your point. We'll go back to Fayt and speak to the governor – I mean, our king.'

'No,' said the mermaid. 'You will stay here on this island, as our captives. Only one of you will go back. The weakest, most insignificant, most valueless among you.' She pointed with her bonestaff. 'Him. The little grey boy. He will go.'

'Me?' said Joseph stupidly.

Tabitha felt her chest tightening. Of course the mermaid was right about Joseph being the weakest. That was obvious. But she'd been a watchman for longer than he had, and she never got to do anything fun. Now this tavern boy had shown up – a tavern boy Newt had made a watchman after barely a day – and he was the one who got to go back to Fayt and deliver the mermaid's message? While the rest of them stayed on this sun-forsaken rock?

'No,' she said, surprising herself.

Everyone, on shore and in the sea, turned to look at her.

'I don't . . . er . . . I don't think Joseph should go.'

'I understand,' said one of the mermen – a big brute with long, wild hair tied back in a ponytail. 'The angry blue-headed girl cares for the little grey boy.' He grinned.

'No,' snapped Tabitha. 'That's not it. I mean, it's just . . . If he's so weak, how's he supposed to deliver the message? Let alone get back.'

She regretted it as soon as she'd said it. She turned to see Joseph looking half confused, half hurt. She felt her cheeks burn.

'She is red!' roared the merman. 'I am right. See? Her face is red!'

'All right,' said Paddy. 'That's enough. Joseph can't go on his own. Tabs neither. They're just children.'

'Very well,' said the big merman, putting on a straight face. 'If that is so, let them go together. The little grey boy and the angry blue-headed girl. Like a man and his wife.' He threw back his head and bellowed with laughter, so hard Tabitha thought he might do himself an injury. In fact, she hoped he did.

'Fine,' she said, stepping forward. Whatever it took to make this bilge-brain shut up. 'We'll go together.'

'Tabs . . .' said Paddy, a note of unease in his voice.

'Then it is decided,' said the mermaid with the spiky blonde hair. 'The two children, or nothing.'

Paddy took Tabitha by the shoulders and leaned down, bringing his big green face close to hers. Out of the corner of her eye, she could see Frank doing the same with Joseph. The tavern boy still looked a little sorry for himself. Why couldn't he see that she was only saying those things to help him? And he knew he was a weakling anyway, didn't he?

So why did she feel so bad about it?

'Tabs, are you sure about this?' said Paddy.

'Of course.'

He sighed. 'Then look after yourself. And take my hat. And my cutlass.'

He pressed them into her hands and at once she almost dropped them. There was no way that cutlass would be any use. She could barely get her hand round the grip, let alone swing it properly.

'Umm – I don't think—'

'No, you're right. Sorry.' He took them back and stood there, looking uncomfortable.

Tabitha realized that he was anxious for them. She felt a sudden urge to say something nice. The kind of thing Joseph would say.

'Don't worry,' she said. She tried to make her tone light and breezy, but that made her sound like a child. She coughed and tried again, going for gruff this time. 'We'll be fine. How hard can it be to deliver a message? I'm more worried about you lot, stuck on this rock.'

'Ah, we'll be all right. Long as it doesn't rain.' They looked up at the grey clouds on the horizon. 'Well. We can't get much wetter than we are already, anyhow.'

'We'll be quick,' she promised. The troll nodded and gave her a punch on the arm – gently, for once.

Tabitha smiled at him and strode down the beach

to join Joseph. He was waiting for her by the water's edge, not quite meeting her eye. She tried to ignore it.

'How do we get back?' she asked. 'I don't see a boat.'

'There is no boat,' said the mermaid. 'We will carry you. As we did before.'

'Oh,' said Tabitha. 'Perfect.'

Chapter Five

There was a sinking feeling in Newton's stomach, and it had been there for days. He took a deep breath. *After all, how much worse can things possibly get?*

'So you're the captain?' he asked. *Please say no*.

The imp nodded eagerly, his big eyes glued to the shark tattoo that adorned Newton's cheek. He looked like he was barely sixteen, and a glance at his red velvet coat and smooth pink hands was enough to tell Newton that he was no seafarer.

'Yes, sir! That I am. The *Dread Unicorn*'s my vessel. Passed down to me by my father. And by his father before him.'

'That so?' Newton looked up at the battered wavecutter rocking in the waves at the end of the quay. He didn't know much about ships, but judging by the state of its hull the *Dread Unicorn* would be more likely to be passed down to the bottom of the ocean before it got to this imp's son. The League's guns would blow it apart within seconds.

'Are you ready to fight?' he asked the imp wearily.

'Yes, sir. Me and my crew, sir. Tell you the truth' – he leaned in closer on tiptoes – 'we're not used to battles really. We're just honest tradesmen.'

'That so?' said Newton again, as if this was a surprise. He glanced at the rabble of sailors lined up along the dock. They looked filthy and dishevelled, each one sporting a sea-green armband instead of a uniform – the mark of Port Fayt's hastily assembled army. Not one of them looked like a soldier though. If he was honest with himself, they looked terrified, as if they all believed, without a shadow of a doubt, that they were going to die.

Right now, Newton was finding it easier not to be honest with himself.

'Let's get you signed up then. And quickly.'

Old Jon began to work his way down the line. His long white hair stirred in the breeze, and he puffed at his pipe as he took names and wrote them down. The elderly elf looked just as placid as ever. It was good to see that at least one person in Fayt wasn't panicking about the League of the Light. It made Newton feel a little calmer himself.

'There's just one thing, sir,' said the captain of the *Dread Unicorn*, jolting Newton out of his thoughts.

'Aye. What is it?'

'I was wondering . . . see . . . we don't have any actual weapons. So, um, are there any we could borrow?'

Something snapped inside Newton.

'Wait here,' he said to Old Jon. Then he turned on his heel and strode off down the quay.

'Whoa, mister. Where are we going?'

He almost jumped at the tiny voice in his ear. His old messenger fairy, Slik, had chattered all the time. But Ty kept quiet when he was told to, and he'd been sitting so still on Newton's shoulder that he'd forgotten the fairy was there.

'Going to see Governor Skelmerdale. I need a word with him.'

''Bout these new recruits?'

He shrugged.

'Hey, watch it! I'll fall off if you're not careful. You don't have any hair to hang onto, remember?'

'Sorry, Ty,' said Newton, carefully keeping his

shoulders still. 'But yes. I reckon if we send them to fight the League, they're doomed.'

'Aye, I reckon so too.'

'Helpful.'

'Well. It's true, isn't it?'

And Newton had to agree.

The dockside was bustling with activity. That was how it normally was, of course, except that today there was an urgency to it. The barrels sitting in rows on the cobbles weren't full of firewater, but gunpowder. The dockside cranes weren't hoisting up crates of dragon scales, but thirty-two-pound cannon and shot. Normally the flags that fluttered above the vessels in the harbour were multi-coloured – the purple and gold of the Cockatrice Trading Company, the red and white of the Redoubtable Company and the dark blue of the Morning Star Company – not to mention the flags of various Old World duchies, independent merchant families and Dockside Militia boats. But today only one colour flew from the mastheads – sea green with a silver shell stitched on. Fayt's new flag – the symbol of a town united against a common enemy.

The governor had made the announcement in Thalin Square less than a week ago. Bunting had still been hanging in the streets from the Pageant of the

Sea. The statue of Thalin the Navigator, founder of Port Fayt, had still been wearing a wreath of seaweed and flowers.

An armada has been sighted, Skelmerdale had told them. He was new to the job, a proud man with a famously fiery temper, tall and thin with dark, stern eyes and white hair cropped short. But that day he'd seemed like a man who had gone for a stroll on a cliff top and had just realized that he'd taken a step off the edge of it.

And this armada is coming from the Old World. It was no surprise to most Fayters. Some of the town's fishermen had already spotted scout ships flying League colours. At first their friends had put the stories down to too much grog. But then more rumours came in, so many that they were impossible to ignore.

The League of the Light is coming. Across the Ebony Ocean. And they are coming for us. For Port Fayt. First there were murmurs, then arguments, then shouting. Everyone knew what the League would do. Each and every Fayter would be hunted down and killed. Perhaps the humans would be spared, but not the trolls. Not the goblins. Not the elves . . . As far as the League were concerned, they were all demonspawn to be stamped out. And that made Port Fayt, home to any creature that arrived on the docks, the town they hated most in all the Ebony Ocean.

Now the governor was marshalling what little forces they had. Within hours they would set sail.

Defeat was certain.

There was a shout from further down the quay, and a figure tore across the cobbles towards them. A dwarf, ragged and bearded, bare feet pounding the cobbles. Blackcoats followed, bayonets glinting in the midday sunshine.

'Deserter!' shouted one.

'Stop him!' yelled the other.

The dwarf glanced back, tripped on a loose cobble and went sprawling. A moment later the militiamen were on top of him, shoving his hands behind his back and hauling him to his feet.

Newton recognized him by his tangled, filthy black beard. Jack Cobley – ex-smuggler. Even crooks had to fight on Fayt's warships. Luckily, Cobley didn't spot Newton as he was bundled away.

'We're all dead!' wailed the dwarf. 'Dead, dead, dead . . .'

If the blackcoats had any sense, they'd leave him behind.

Newton strode on, past a sailor saying goodbye to his wife and children. The youngest clung to her mother's skirts, face red and tear-stained. She was surely too young to understand exactly what was happening, but she could tell that it wasn't good. A tiny goblin girl watched her from a distance, thumb stuck in her mouth, puzzled as to why her friend was so upset. Newton quickened his stride.

Up ahead, a concentration of blackcoats stood guard at a pier in the shadow of the biggest ship in the bay. A war galleon painted inky black from stern to prow and sporting seventy-four of the heaviest guns in Port Fayt – the *Wyvern*. Skelmerdale was bound to be on board. The *Wyvern* was to be the town's flagship, and soon she would be leading the Fayters into battle against the League.

Newton pitied her crew.

The black-coated militiamen tried to stop him, but Newton wasn't in the mood to be stopped. He shouldered through the press, made his way down the pier and climbed up the gangplank onto the deck.

Sure enough, there were many more blackcoats on board, and at the prow, leaning down to inspect a vicious-looking bowchaser gun, was Governor Skelmerdale. He was dressed in a purple velvet jacket and well-laundered breeches, and a long ceremonial sword hung from his belt. The hilt glittered with gold.

Standing next to the governor was a tall elf,

wearing a black coat with silver trimmings. Colonel Cyrus Derringer, commander of the blackcoats. The Dockside Militia. As soon as he spotted Newton, his lip curled and his eyes narrowed. The feeling was mutual. Newton's leg had only just healed from the sword wound the elf had given him the last time they'd disagreed.

'Your honour . . .' he began, trying to keep his voice calm.

Governor Skelmerdale stepped forward and shook Newton's hand briskly.

'Mr Newton. And this must be your fairy.'

Ty bowed.

There weren't many men tall enough to look the captain of the Demon's Watch straight in the eye, but Skelmerdale was one of them. Newton was thrown for a moment by his gaze, direct and bold. As though he had nothing to hide.

Governor Skelmerdale was a leader, that was for sure. *The only problem is, where he's planning to lead us.*

'Your honour, we're not ready.' Newton hadn't meant to blurt it out like that. Particularly to a man so famous for his short temper. But now he'd said it, there was no point in holding back. 'We should wait for the *Sharkbane* to get back with intelligence. We don't know anything about that armada, outside of rumours and guesswork. And look . . .' He swept an arm out, indicating the vessels rocking all around them in the bay. 'This isn't a battle fleet. Most of these ships are merchantmen. Some are barely fit to be called ships at all. Our men are inexperienced, scared and—'

'Mr Newton,' Skelmerdale interrupted. He was frowning slightly, as if Newton were a child who had been sent home from school for misbehaving. 'I understand your concern. And as you say, many of our men are not quite at the fighting standard we would desire. But what do you suggest? Should we wait? While the League occupy our waters? While they sail into our very harbour?' His voice was getting louder, and suddenly Newton realized that the governor was addressing everyone on the ship, not just him. 'No! How could we countenance such a thing? We shall fight. We shall fight until our last living breath.'

'I understand, but—'

'We shall resist, Mr Newton. Until the end. To do otherwise would be . . . *unthinkable*. It would be preposterous. It would be—'

'Governor!' said Colonel Derringer. He was pointing at something in the bay, one hand clamped around the hilt of his sword. 'There's something out there.'

There was a clattering of footsteps on the deck as Skelmerdale and several blackcoats went to see what it was. Newton followed. He peered over the crowd and made out two strange shapes in the distance, poking up from the waves, just rounding the headland and approaching the port.

'Looks like whales,' said a militiaman. 'Two of 'em.'

'It's not whales,' said another. 'It's merfolk. What do they want?'

'They're each carrying something.'

Everyone leaned further over the gunwales, trying to make it out. Someone passed the governor a spyglass and he held it to one eye.

'Aha,' he said.

He turned and passed it to Newton. As he took it, Newton noticed Colonel Derringer scowling at the spyglass. He'd been waiting to receive it himself.

'People,' the governor was saying. 'That's what they're carrying.'

By the time Newton lowered the spyglass, his heart was beating fast.

'Everything all right?' asked Ty, from his shoulder. 'Only you look like you've just stepped in a puddle of griffin bile.'

Newton shook his head. 'They're mine,' he said quietly. 'Tabitha Mandeville and Joseph Grubb.'

'The Demon's Watch,' said the governor.

'Aye. The Demon's Watch. But where are the rest of them?'

Chapter Six

Joseph had put on clean dry clothes, but he was still shivering. It felt as though the cold of the sea had got right into his bones. And if he never took another trip with a mermaid in his life, it would be all right by him.

He and Tabitha sat in the hallway on tall wooden chairs that were probably priceless antiques but weren't very comfortable. The opposite wall was covered in fancy dark green wallpaper, ancient paintings and a fine layer of dust. A clock ticked quietly somewhere. They waited in silence for the governor to call them in.

Joseph had never imagined he would return to

Wyrmwood Manor, let alone so soon. The last time he'd been here, he'd been sneaking around in the dark with the Demon's Watch, trying to avoid blackcoats and rescue old Governor Wyrmwood from his crazy mother. Now, in the daytime, the manor looked more or less the same, except that someone had taken down the portrait of Arabella Wyrmwood, leaving a pale, dust-free square on the wall.

It seemed cruel somehow, even after everything she'd done. As if she had never existed. She'd been so young in that picture. Nothing like the terrifying witch she'd become.

Now there were no more Wyrmwoods left, and the new governor had commandeered the manor as his headquarters. The family home had become the setting for a council of war.

'For the love of Thalin, stop humming,' said Tabitha.

'Am I . . . ? Oh. Sorry,' said Joseph. It was just an old song his mother had taught him long ago. The only thing he had left of her. It helped to keep him calm, running through the words in his head.

Scrub the dishes, scrub them clean, cleaner than you've ever seen . . .

'Just remember, I'll do the talking,' said Tabitha. She was sitting on the edge of her seat, tapping one foot on the carpet and twisting her fingers together over and over.

'It'll be all right,' Joseph said gently. 'Newton's bound to rescue them. He wouldn't just leave them on that rock.'

'I know that,' she snapped. 'I've known him all my life, remember?' She drew in another breath but paused for a moment, considering. When she spoke again her voice was softer. 'It's just – it's not him I'm worried about.'

'Skelmerdale?'

'Skelmerdale.'

Joseph had never seen the new governor before. But Tabitha was right. Whatever Newton wanted, it would be up to Skelmerdale to decide what was done about the merfolk. He was in charge, after all.

Still, he was sure there was something else too. Tabitha was so tense. She'd been acting oddly ever since they left the island.

'Tabs? What you said about me being too, um, weak to get back . . .' Tabitha's body went rigid, and he instantly regretted bringing it up. 'I mean . . . Never mind.'

Tabitha turned to look at him. There was confusion in her big grey eyes. She opened her mouth to say something, then closed it again.

'Look, I'm, er . . . I'm sorry,' she said eventually.

Joseph was so surprised he didn't know what to say. Tabitha looked away quickly, and he felt his face grow hot.

'Well, it's not . . .' he said. 'I mean, I'm glad you're here.'

'Glad?'

'Of course. Imagine if I was on my own . . . I've got a cutlass now, but I don't exactly know how to use it. Not like you with your knives.'

A ghost of a smile hovered on Tabitha's lips. 'I've seen you practising. You're just lucky that old wooden figurehead outside Bootles' doesn't fight back.'

Joseph grinned. 'Hey! You need me too.'

'Well, someone's got to scrub the dishes clean.' She was definitely smiling now. 'And the company's nice, I s'pose.' In an instant she was frowning again, and Joseph felt suddenly awkward. 'I really am sorry. Sometimes I . . . Well . . . It's just—'

There was a rattle of a doorknob, and the door opposite swung open. A portly, pale-skinned elf stepped into the hallway, dressed in the purple and gold livery of the Cockatrice Trading Company. The governor's company.

'His honour will see you now,' he said.

Tabitha rose hurriedly and entered the room, with

Joseph following. It felt like she was as thankful for the interruption as he was.

They came through into the library. At least, it *had* been the library. Old Governor Wyrmwood's bookcases had been cleared out to make space for an enormous table, with a map of the Middle Islands spread out on it and model ships sitting on top. The glass display case containing the ancient Sword of Corin seemed to be the only thing that remained the same.

Blackcoats were stationed around the room, and a cluster of officers stood behind the table, talking earnestly and pointing at things. Joseph saw that Cyrus Derringer, commander of the Dockside Militia, was watching them with suspicion. He swallowed. Then he spotted the shaven head of Newt leaning over the map, and Old Jon beside him. That made him feel a little calmer.

A tall, white-haired man stepped out from among the group. There was something about him – an air of command – and suddenly Joseph felt very safe. This had to be Governor Skelmerdale. And he looked like the kind of person who got things done.

The governor spread his arms wide and smiled. 'Welcome,' he said.

'Your honour,' said Tabitha. She nudged Joseph, bowing low, and he hurried to copy her.

'These are my watchmen, your honour,' said Newt. 'But the last time I saw them, they had a ship and a crew. And where are the rest of the Watch?'

Joseph and Tabitha looked at each other. Then Tabitha took a deep breath and began to explain.

By the time she'd finished, Governor Skelmerdale was leaning on the table, his brow furrowed as he gazed into the distance.

'Your honour,' said Newton. He was keeping his voice calm, but Joseph could tell from the sparkle in his eyes that he was excited. 'This is good news after all. We'll send out search parties. Find this Pallione and bring the merfolk over to us. With them on our side, we'll stand a chance, even if the armada is as big as Tabitha says.'

'Allow me, your honour . . .' said Cyrus Derringer, giving Newt a murderous look. 'As commander of the Dockside Militia, I will be delighted to carry out my duty and find this mermaid for you.'

'It doesn't matter who does it,' burst out Tabitha. 'As long as it gets done.'

The governor held up a finger, and everyone fell quiet. He was still frowning.

'We have lost time over this,' he said. 'But that

can't be helped. We will set sail tomorrow at dawn. To engage the League.'

'Engage the League?' said Joseph. His ears twitched with embarrassment as officers and black-coats turned to look at him.

The governor stepped round the table and knelt down. For a moment his gaze made Joseph feel as if everything was going to be all right.

'Yes, my little friend. You're very young, so I don't expect you to understand. But if we waste time hunting for this mermaid, the League ships will sail right into our harbour before our fleet has even left port. So to save the town we must let your friends go. I am truly sorry. But you must understand that this is war. And in war, we lose people. There is not always a happy ending, like in story books.'

Joseph could almost feel the hope draining out of him.

'But—'

'We will defeat the League though, you may be sure of that.' The governor rose, patting Joseph on the head. 'They may have the advantage of numbers, but we have spirit, and a home to protect. We will prevail.' Joseph got the feeling that the governor wasn't talking just to him any more.

'Your honour,' said Newton. There was a note of

panic in his voice. 'If we set sail now, we can't win. Not without help. We have to—'

'Have faith, Mr Newton. That is what we must do. Have faith.' Skelmerdale raised his voice. 'Go, all of you, and prepare yourselves. Tomorrow, at dawn.' He waved a hand and blackcoats began crowding towards the door, muttering to each other.

'But we're going to find that mermaid, aren't we?' Tabitha said, in a low voice. 'We have to. We can stay behind in Port Fayt and—'

Old Jon's hand fell on her shoulder, cutting her off.

'I'm sorry,' said Newton. He was frowning, and Joseph realized there was nothing the captain of the Demon's Watch could do.

A voice rose behind them.

'Mr Newton,' said the governor. 'A word, if you please.' He was motioning to a corner of the room, by the large windows.

'Wait for me outside,' Newton told Tabitha and Joseph.

'No need,' said the governor. 'The watchmen can stay. The children and the old elf.'

As they followed Newton, Joseph caught a glimpse of Cyrus Derringer lingering by the map table, watching. His eyes narrowed in anger at Newt, before he clicked his boots together and marched out of the room. The door shut with a bang.

Governor Skelmerdale was looking out of the window, hands behind his back, inspecting the immaculate green lawns of Wyrmwood Manor.

'You are not afraid to speak your mind, Mr Newton,' he said. 'I respect that.'

Newton shifted uncomfortably. 'Just trying to do what's best. For Fayt.'

'For Fayt. Indeed. Well, I am sorry to disappoint you. The League's fleet is strong, according to these children. I do not doubt it. But the merfolk do not concern themselves with the business of land dwellers, whatever they may say. They have not gone to war in centuries. Better to show strength in front of my officers than to trust in their help.'

'Can't blame them, your honour. With all the shark-pit owners fishing them out of the ocean, no wonder they don't care too much for us.'

The governor spun round, his eyes full of fire. Joseph flinched at the sight. He'd heard stories about the governor's temper, but it was still a shock to see the rage flare up out of nowhere.

'That's enough. They are not to be relied upon. Do you hear me?'

Newton stood his ground but said nothing. Almost

at once, the fire left the governor's eyes. He seemed suddenly weary.

'You may leave the most important decisions to me, Mr Newton. But I do need someone with your . . . courage.'

'Aye?'

Joseph saw Tabitha's fists clench – which meant she was either anxious or furious. Maybe both. Beyond, Old Jon waited calmly, taking it all in.

'Indeed. Our flagship, the *Wyvern*, needs a captain. And I can think of no more suitable man in Port Fayt.'

Tabitha's mouth began to open. Before he knew what he was doing, Joseph reached out and took hold of her arm. Her temper was almost as bad as the governor's, and if she spoke out of turn, she'd end up in the Brig – or worse.

'Your honour,' said Newton. 'Surely Colonel Derringer would be a better—'

'No. The elf is no good. You and I, Mr Newton, we are both leaders. We understand one another. Colonel Derringer will make a perfectly competent second-in-command, but he cannot inspire the men as you can.'

'You're saying Derringer will be on the *Wyvern* too?'

'Indeed. And take young Tabitha and Joseph with

you. Someone ought to keep an eye on them.' He gave them a friendly wink.

Joseph tightened his hold on Tabitha's arm. If they sailed on the *Wyvern* with Newt and Old Jon, there was no way they could track down the mermaid – even without the governor's permission. Which meant they wouldn't be able to get the watchmen back. But what choice did they have?

'Are you sure, your honour?' said Newton. 'The merfolk—'

'I've already told you, Mr Newton, the merfolk are not like us. We cannot trust them. So what do you say?'

Newton looked at Old Jon, who gave the slightest of shrugs.

'Very well then.'

Governor Skelmerdale stretched out his hand, beaming at last.

'Congratulations,' he said, 'to the commander of the fleet!'

Chapter Seven

Joseph dreamed. It was market day, and he held his father's hand tightly as they threaded through the crowds in the Crosstree Quarter. Stallholders reached out, trying to draw them in with promises of the juiciest shellfish, the sharpest dragons' teeth and the fastest fairies in all the Ebony Ocean.

They stopped at a little stall on a corner – nothing but a rickety table with a red-and-white striped awning. Spread out on the table were long, elegant feathers, each one gleaming with a hundred different colours. When the breeze ruffled them they shimmered red, gold and green.

'Are they griffin feathers?' Joseph asked.

His father chuckled.

'Bless your heart, Joseph, I'm afraid not. Griffin feathers are even bigger than these and you won't get one for less than twenty ducats. No, these are cockatrice feathers.'

The stallholder was a goblin, just like Joseph's father. He leaned forward, taking a puff on his pipe.

'Go ahead,' he said. 'You can touch them.'

Joseph reached out and felt the nearest feather. It was silky and smooth, like his mother's hair.

'Which one shall we have, eh, Joseph?' said his father. 'Which one do you think your ma would like best?'

Joseph stood staring for a long while. At last he picked one out – deep translucent green with flecks of silver and gold.

His father grinned at him and winked.

'Excellent choice, young 'un. Couldn't have chosen a better one myself. And that'll go nicely with her green dress too, won't it?' He counted out three ducats for the stallholder.

Before they left, the stallholder pressed something into Joseph's hand – a tiny red feather with a blue sheen.

'That's from a baby cockatrice,' he said. 'You keep it. And come back soon.'

Joseph held up the feather, twisting it in his fingers so it turned from red to blue and back again.

'What do you say?' said Joseph's father.

'Thank you.'

They were just turning to go when a voice called out behind them:

'Eli.'

Two muscular men were making their way towards the stall.

'Hello, Eli,' said one, grinning.

'Morning, Ben.'

His father's grip tightened on his hand, and all of a sudden Joseph felt nervous.

'This your boy, Eli?'

'Aye. This is Joseph. Joseph, these here are Ben and Geoffrey. We all work together on the docks.'

'Hello,' said Joseph.

Geoffrey leaned down towards him, and Joseph saw that he wasn't grinning any more.

'What's wrong with your skin, boy?' he asked.

'There's nothing wrong,' said Joseph's father. But Joseph noticed his ears twitch.

Ben laid a hand on his friend's shoulder.

'Geoffrey's just joking,' he said, though it hadn't seemed like a joke. 'You're a mongrel, ain't you? Nothing wrong with that. You never told us, Eli.

Little souvenir of a misspent youth, is it?'

Joseph didn't really understand, but his father shook his head.

'This is our boy. Me and my wife Eleanor, we're his parents. Isn't that right, Joseph?'

Joseph nodded.

Ben grinned wider and whistled. Geoffrey just stood, silent, staring at them.

'Well, we can't stick around,' said his father. He pulled out his pocket watch and checked the time. 'Got to get going. See you lads tomorrow.' And Joseph was steered away down the street.

They didn't say much as they walked home to the house with the green front door. And all the way his father kept holding onto his hand, as if Joseph might run away at any minute.

'Pa,' he said at last. 'What's a mongrel?'

Someone was shaking him. His father, of course.

'Wake up. Come on, wake up.'

Joseph tried to roll away, but it was difficult because he wasn't in a bed. A hammock, that's where he was.

Suddenly he was awake.

He opened his mouth and a hand clamped over it. In the darkness, he could only just make out the blue hair on the silhouetted head. Tabitha.

'Get up, Joseph. We need to talk.'

He swung his feet over the side of the canvas and stepped down as lightly as he could. The lower deck was crammed with hammocks, and all around them was the murmur of snoring, mingling with the creaking of the ship. Newton's ship – the *Wyvern*.

He fumbled for his coat and shoes and pulled them on while Tabitha waited.

'Bring your cutlass too,' she hissed.

Why in Thalin's name would he need a cutlass? But by then, Tabitha had already picked it up and shoved it into his hands. On tiptoe, she led the way to the steps and climbed until they reached the top deck, underneath the stars.

A cold breeze whipped across the harbour, rattling the rigging of the fleet and chilling Joseph to the bone. The bay was cluttered with ships rocking gently on the waves. It was so peaceful . . . Hard to imagine that tomorrow these vessels could be in the midst of a battle, smoke billowing, cannons roaring . . . Beyond the *Wyvern*'s stern, Port Fayt slumbered, a few lanterns glowing softly in the night.

Tabitha grabbed him by the arm and pulled him across the deck, down into the shadows behind a cluster of barrels.

'What's going on?'

'We've got to get off this ship,' she replied, as if it was obvious. 'Who else is going to rescue that mermaid?'

Joseph tried to shake off his sleepiness and understand what she was saying.

'What about Newt?' he said. 'We're supposed to stay on the *Wyvern* with him.'

Tabitha rolled her eyes.

'No we're not. Come on. Think about it. He doesn't need us – he's commanding the most powerful warship in Fayt. And what good can we do here? Do you know how to lower an anchor or set a mainsail?'

'Well—'

'Exactly. But if we stay here in Fayt we might be able to find the mermaid.'

'But . . . I mean, have you asked Newt?'

'Of course I've asked Newt. It was his idea.' Tabitha's eyes were shining in the darkness. 'And it's perfect. We're going to be heroes. Don't you see?'

Joseph wasn't sure he wanted to be a hero. But it was true – on board the *Wyvern,* they would only be getting in the way. Here in Port Fayt, they could really make a difference. If they could rescue Pallione . . .

'Are you sure Newt's all right with us going?'

'Of course he is. He's not an idiot. He knows we can do much more good off this ship than on it.'

Joseph thought for a moment. It did make sense. The *Wyvern* would set sail at dawn, with or without them. Of course, if they disembarked, they'd be on their own. They'd have to find the mermaid by themselves, whatever it took. It would be hard – maybe impossible.

But it was worth a try.

'All right,' he said. 'I'm in.'

He almost fell over as Tabitha flung her arms around him in a hug. Once he'd got over the surprise, he hugged her back.

'One other thing,' said Tabitha, moving away again. 'What I said on the island about . . . er . . .'

'Never mind,' said Joseph quickly.

'No, I . . . er . . . I just wanted to say, I don't really think you're weak. I mean, you're not strong exactly, but you're not weak either.'

Joseph could hardly believe what he was hearing. She was trying to be nice again. *Twice in one day*. And Thalin knew, it didn't come naturally to her.

'Don't worry about it,' he managed to say.

'Good.' And suddenly the old Tabitha was back. 'Let's get going then. Quickly now. There's the gangplank. And remember, keep it quiet.'

'Shouldn't we say goodbye to Newt first?'

'Of course not. He's sleeping, isn't he? And he'll need it. He's going into battle, don't forget.'

'Yes. Sorry. You're right.'

Together they crept across the deck and down the gangplank. Joseph pulled on his sword belt and buckled it up. His limbs buzzed with adrenaline. It looked like he was going to need a cutlass, after all.

At the bottom of the gangplank Tabitha turned and strode along the quayside.

'Hey,' hissed Joseph. 'Where are you going?'

'Got to find a place to stay tonight. Come on!'

'What about Bootles'? Or Newt's rooms? They're the other way.' He pointed off in the opposite direction. 'Or why don't we stay on board the *Wyvern* and leave at dawn? Then we could say goodbye to—' He stopped up short, finally understanding. How could he have been so slow? 'Newt *doesn't* know, does he? This was all your idea.'

Luckily it was dark enough that she wouldn't be able to see him blushing. Did she think he was a complete idiot? All right, she'd had him fooled until now. But not any more. He turned and started to climb the gangplank.

Tabitha caught up, grabbed hold of him and tried to pull him away.

'Wait!' she whispered.

Joseph struggled. 'We can't just leave! He won't know where we've gone. At very least we should leave a note so—' His foot slipped off the edge of the plank, and they fell awkwardly. Joseph's heart leaped into his mouth as he saw the dark water looming below. But instead they hit the gangplank, half rolling, half tumbling back down onto the quayside and landing sprawled in a heap on the cobblestones.

'All right,' said Tabitha. 'So he doesn't know. What difference does it make? You agreed with me two minutes ago. Who else is going to find that mermaid, remember?'

'I don't know,' said Joseph. 'But can you get off me?'

'No. Not until you say you're coming too.'

'I . . . No, I can't.'

'Fine.' The weight on top of him lifted as Tabitha got to her feet.

'In that case, I'll go on my own.' And she walked away, without glancing back, without breaking stride.

Joseph watched her, knowing that at any minute the shadows would swallow her and she would be gone. She was heading into Fayt, whether he came with her or not. So should he go too or stay on the ship? He couldn't believe her, putting him in this position. If he returned to the *Wyvern*, she'd be completely on her own. But why should he have to go with her just because she'd got it into her head to be a hero? She was crazy. Crazy and dangerous. Was this what all girls were like?

What would Thalin the Navigator do?

What would Newt do?

What would my father do?

Footsteps sounded on the deck and a gruff voice called out, 'Is someone there?'

Joseph froze. Their tumble down the gangplank must have woken some sleeping sentry. He opened his mouth. He looked at the figure of Tabitha, heading down a side street. Just a few more seconds, and she would turn a corner and disappear from view.

He shut his mouth and scampered after her.

You owe me, Tabs.

As he reached the houses he paused and took one last look at the *Wyvern*, a towering black bulk against the starlit sky.

'Good luck, Newt,' he said quietly. Then he turned and followed Tabitha into Port Fayt.

By the time he reaches the village the real work is done. Even the flames have been doused, leaving only smouldering wreckage and ruin.

They came before dawn, moving through the uphill woodland of Illon, dragging light cannon with them. It would have been easier with cavalry, but victory was never in doubt. The soldiers of the League of the Light are an unstoppable force. A righteous fist, crushing all trace of demonspawn in their path.

He holds a scented handkerchief against his nose as he picks his way through the debris scattered on the cobbled streets. There are bodies all around him but he ignores them. They are of no interest. Once dead, these foul creatures are mere waste to be cleared away. It is the living demonspawn that fascinate him. To get inside the mind of such a creature . . . To understand the darkness that must surely lurk within . . .

There are human corpses too among the rubble. A sad loss, but necessary. He has learned that once tainted by living with demonspawn, even the most upstanding human can fall. And these slaughtered fishermen could hardly be called upstanding.

At last he arrives at the square. A tiny area, as befits the village itself. New Dalport, the only settlement on Illon, the easternmost of the Middle Islands. There was scarcely a need to destroy it, but he believes in doing a job thoroughly. And from the bodies, he can tell that his men have been very thorough indeed.

Majors Metcalfe and Garrick have a table set up, with a map spread out on it. The Golden Sun flutters proudly above, the flagpole thrust into the thatching on the roof of the village hall. Their white uniforms are smudged with soot and blood, and they are drinking grog, taken from the tavern on the square no doubt.

He never drinks.

They put down their flagons and come to attention as he approaches.

'Your grace,' they say, as one.

'Gentlemen. Congratulations. Where is Major Turnbull?'

Metcalfe frowns. 'Somewhere in the village, your grace. Finishing the work.'

The Duke nods. Turnbull has always been the most enthusiastic of his officers where the pursuit of demon-spawn is concerned.

Over the shoulders of his majors, at the corner of the square, he can see a pair of white-coated marines battering on a locked door with their muskets.

'How long before we are done here?'

'An hour, your grace, at most.'

'Good. I believe the Fayters will come soon. They will not allow us to sail into their harbour.'

'Let them come,' says Major Metcalfe. 'We will stand firm against them.'

'Indeed.' He traces a finger across the map, taking in the Middle Islands. Illon. Eld. Immel. And Arla, of course. The largest, where Port Fayt lies.

The Jewel of the Middle Islands.

In the corner of the square, a crack has appeared in the door. The marines redouble their efforts, slamming it harder and harder with their musket butts.

'See it through,' he says. 'And then return to your vessels. We must be at sea by noon. The whole fleet. We

shall show the demonspawn what a force they have to reckon with.'

The door gives way at last and the marines rush inside.

There are screams.

PART TWO
Pallione

Chapter Eight

'How are we going to get in, though?' asked Joseph.

They lay on their bellies on the cliff top, wind rustling the grasses around them, looking down at the Brig. It lay far below, bathed in morning sunshine, beached on the sand like an outsized whale carcass. Its hull was green with mould and its masts had long rotted away. Joseph could just make out the bars that covered the old gun ports. The Brig was a behemoth of a ship. Or at least it had been, before it became Fayt's one and only prison.

'Simple,' said Tabitha, her eyes sparkling. 'We knock. We're the Demon's Watch, remember?' She pushed up her sleeve and prodded her shark tattoo.

Joseph nodded wearily as Tabitha got to her feet and strode off down the coastal path towards the beach. Everything had seemed easy the night before. The hard part had been deciding to leave Newt. Then all they had to do was rescue the mermaid and save Port Fayt. Now, in the cold light of day, he was pretty sure he'd got it the wrong way round, and their troubles were only just beginning.

It didn't help that he'd barely slept. They couldn't go back to Bootles' Pie Shop ('Are you mad?' Tabitha had scoffed. 'They'll send us straight back to Newt!') or to Newt's rooms above a Marlinspike Quarter tavern ('Come on. Think. That's the first place he'd look!'), and they'd no money to pay for a room of their own. In the end they'd had to bed down in an old fishing boat in dry dock under a canvas covering. Now they were tired, grumpy, and stank of rotten fish. Neither of them had admitted it, but so far things weren't going that well.

Joseph scrambled to his feet, following Tabitha. At least they had a plan, of sorts. To find the mermaid, they needed to find which shark pit she was in. To find out which shark pit she was in, they needed to find someone who knew a lot about the shark pits. And to find someone who knew a lot about shark pits, they needed to find a crook.

Which meant they needed to visit the Brig.

Tabitha was reaching the end of the path and Joseph stumbled to catch up. 'Have you been here before?' he asked.

'A couple of times, with Newt. Don't worry about it. We're watchmen.'

'If you say so.' He wasn't convinced though. The first time he'd met Tabitha had been in a grotty tavern called the Pickled Dragon, and on that occasion it had taken her less than a minute to show off her Demon's Watch tattoo and start ordering people around. Unfortunately those people turned out to be militia-men, who laughed at them and then tried to kill them. Joseph would have thought twice about playing the watchman card again. But then, he wasn't Tabitha.

If only Newt were here, Joseph was sure he'd have no trouble getting them in. But no. It was no good thinking like that. They were on their own.

The Brig loomed over them as they approached. Now they were on the sandy beach, Joseph realized how gigantic it was – almost as big as Wyrmwood Manor. He tried to imagine what a ship like that would look like afloat, but it was too hard. It seemed like nothing more than a vast wooden wreck. They said that the pirate Captain Gore was the only person ever to escape the Brig. Which meant there were an awful lot of dangerous maniacs still locked up inside.

A gangplank led up to a wooden door built into the hull, looking just like a door into a house. Above, someone had nailed a wooden plank with the words HOME SWEET HOME painted on it. There were even some decorative shells and bits of seaweed stuck on.

Tabitha hesitated for just a moment before she reached out and knocked.

'Oh. One thing,' she said. 'Don't say anything about the jailer.'

'The jailer? What's—?'

The door creaked a little way open, and a head poked out. It belonged to a troll with pale green skin, a cluster of tarnished silver earrings and a few eyebrow rings for good measure. A trio of scars ran across his cheek, which could have been made by a cat's claws, if the cat had been ten feet tall.

Joseph rested one hand on the hilt of his cutlass and licked his lips. His mouth had gone very dry.

'What?' growled the troll.

Tabitha rolled up her sleeve and showed her tattoo.

'Demon's Watch. We need to talk to a few prisoners.'

'Now?'

'Um . . . yes. Please.'

The jailer muttered something and flung the door open wide. Joseph couldn't help but gasp. Tabitha jabbed him in the ribs, and he shut his mouth at once.

The troll was wearing a full-length, purple satin ball gown.

'Come on then,' he said. 'Haven't got all day.' He clumped off down the wooden passageway, his gown trailing behind him. 'Always something. Why can't they leave me in peace?'

Tabitha threw Joseph a baleful glance as they followed.

At the end of the passage they came into a room unlike any cabin Joseph had ever seen. It was packed from deck to rafters with strange objects, so different and so varied that he didn't know where to look first. There was a jumble of furniture – wooden chairs, stools, even a chaise longue. There were antique paintings on the walls and an enormous mirror covering most of one side of the room, which looked so fancy it wouldn't have been out of place at Wyrmwood Manor. There was a rich red carpet on the floor, and beyond it a whistling kettle on a small stove. In the middle of the carpet was an elegant mahogany drawing-room table with a large, juicy-looking seed cake sitting on it.

Joseph's stomach rumbled at the smell, and he

remembered suddenly that they hadn't had any breakfast yet.

'Sit,' ordered the troll.

Joseph found a wooden chest under the table and dragged it out to make a seat. Tabitha relaxed into a plush padded armchair opposite.

'Is this your home?' asked Joseph. 'It's amazing.'

'Home,' grunted the troll. 'Yes. I am a collector. I love *things*.' He busied himself with the kettle.

'So as I was saying,' said Tabitha, 'we need to speak to some prisoners.'

'Wait,' said the troll. 'Breakfast first.'

There was an awkward silence. Joseph looked at Tabitha, but she just shrugged.

'I like your dress,' said Joseph, before he could stop himself.

The troll whirled round, glaring at him. Tabitha glared too. Joseph felt his ears twitch with embarrassment. What was he thinking? That had obviously been the wrong thing to say.

The troll spoke at last.

'Yes,' he said. 'It is good. I collected it. I love *things*.'

'Um, yes,' said Joseph. 'I like things too.'

'But I don't love *people*.'

Joseph couldn't think what to say to that, so he just smiled as best he could.

The troll finished with the kettle and came over to the table, carrying a mug of something hot and steaming.

'That smells good,' said Tabitha. Joseph noticed that her eyes were flicking between the mug and the seed cake.

'Yes,' said the troll. 'Very good. I collected it from a prisoner. It is called "tea". You drink it hot.'

He picked up a knife and sliced into the seed cake. A little steam rose from it as he lifted a thick, golden slice, and Joseph's stomach rumbled again.

'The cake looks good too,' he found himself saying.

'Yes,' said the troll. 'Very good. Food is one of the things that I like.'

'I like food too,' said Tabitha. She was practically drooling. 'Especially seed cake.'

The troll frowned at her and bit into the cake. Crumbs dropped onto his purple dress. He lifted up the train of his gown and sat down, chewing noisily.

'Yes,' he said through his mouthful. 'Everyone likes cake.'

There was a long silence as the troll ate his cake and slurped his tea. At last he finished the slice, reached forward and cut another one. He began to eat that too.

Joseph stared at their reflection in the enormous

mirror, trying to forget how hungry he was. They made an odd group. The blue-haired girl, the grey-pink mongrel boy and the giant troll in the dress.

'Is it just you?' he asked, to break the silence. 'No guards?'

Tabitha rolled her eyes at the question.

'There were. Blackcoats. They went to fight. Much better on my own.' The troll swallowed the last mouthful of cake. 'Now,' he said, 'we'll go to the cells.' He stomped over to a door opposite the one they had entered by, without waiting to see if they would follow. Joseph and Tabitha hurried after him, Tabitha casting one final longing glance at the seed cake.

The troll led them along a wooden corridor and up some steps, his ball gown swishing as he strode ahead. Someone had entirely removed the interior of the vessel and rebuilt it from scratch, as though it really was a building instead of a ship. There were carpets, pictures on the walls – collected by the troll, Joseph guessed – and a clutter of different lanterns hanging from the ceiling. The jailer had obviously made himself at home.

They climbed down another set of wooden stairs to a barred metal door. The troll fished around beneath his skirts and pulled out a ring of keys.

'You want to talk to some prisoners,' he said,

unlocking the door. 'Good luck.' The door opened with the faintest squeak of hinges, and he led them through.

They were in the hold, and the corridor before them seemed to stretch the whole length of the vessel. On either side there were more barred doors. Hundreds of arms and faces appeared out of the darkness beyond, pointing at them, shouting at them, beckoning them. Joseph suddenly felt very frightened. If it wasn't for the metal holding the prisoners back, there was no telling what they'd do.

He tried not to listen as they made their way down the corridor, but he couldn't help catching an occasional 'mongrel', 'stinking mongrel', 'bilge-brain mongrel', and worse. But most of the abuse was directed at the troll in the dress, who was striding ahead, ignoring the prisoners entirely. Joseph was impressed, and tried to do the same. He was beginning to see how the jailer had come to like things and not people.

'Help! Joseph!'

He spun round, his heart racing. Tabitha had ventured too close to the bars. Now an elf had got hold of her hair and was tugging at it, grinning madly, a string of dribble dangling from his lips.

Joseph leaped forward, grabbed the elf's hand and

tried to pry it away, but another hand got hold of his ear and he was tugged closer to the bars himself.

'Won't bite,' someone was saying. 'Not much . . .'

He yelped, flailed for his cutlass, but couldn't reach it. More hands seized his arms and his head, pulling him closer and closer . . .

THWACK! THWACK! THWACK!

Suddenly the hands had let go, and there were wails of pain from behind the bars. Joseph stumbled away, collapsing in the centre of the corridor, out of reach of the prisoners. He looked up to see the jailer raise a cudgel and bring it down hard on the arm of the elf who had Tabitha. The elf squealed and let go, and Tabitha came tumbling down beside Joseph. Her hair was dishevelled and her big grey eyes were wide.

'Are you all right?'

She frowned, rubbing her head. 'I'm fine.'

The troll growled at the prisoners cowering in the corners of their wooden cells. Then he slid the cudgel down the front of his dress.

'Careful,' he told Joseph and Tabitha. 'Come on.'

Shakily, they got to their feet and followed.

Joseph was starting to feel sick. He hadn't been prepared for what a terrible, desperate place the Brig would be. They passed several large cells with ogres inside, most sitting silently and watching them.

Beyond that, there was a large tank full of greenish water and merfolk, cooped up like salted fish in a barrel. And then there were smaller cells, double-layered like bunk beds, for imps. At the end of the corridor were the smallest cells of all, packed one on top of the other, for fairies – each cage no bigger than the ones for parrots at the market in the Crosstree Quarter. The fairies rushed to the front of the cages as they passed, screaming at them in a high-pitched cacophony.

The troll in the dress came to a halt. 'So?' he said.

'Right,' said Tabitha. 'Um . . . right.'

'There are so many of them,' murmured Joseph. 'How do we know who'll be able to help us?'

Tabitha glanced up at the troll. 'Is there a list we could look at? Of the prisoners?'

The troll wrinkled his nose and frowned, saying nothing. Joseph reckoned that was a no.

'Then we'll just have to ask questions until we get somewhere,' said Tabitha briskly. 'Let's start with the ogres. At least they're a bit quieter than the others.'

'What about the merfolk?' asked Joseph. 'If anyone knows where Pallione is, it ought to be them.'

Tabitha frowned and shook her head. 'Most merfolk only know sign language. Even if they did tell us, we wouldn't be able to understand. Now, are you coming?' She marched back down the corridor with the troll in tow.

Joseph was about to follow when he heard something among the fairy voices. He froze, listening hard. Could it be . . . ?

Yes, there it was again.

'*Grubb.*'

Someone was saying his name.

Chapter Nine

Newton ducked his head as he followed the bosun, climbing the narrow steps to the upper gun deck. In the cramped darkness, Fayters swarmed over each and every cannon, polishing them to a sheen. Colonel Derringer's doing, no doubt. Nothing ever seemed to be clean enough for him.

'Thirty guns on this deck, sir. Eighteen-pounders. Enough to blow any ship out of the water.'

Newton watched a young troll swabbing at the nearest cannon. He couldn't have been more than fourteen years old, but he looked so eager, as if he was actually looking forward to battle. At once his mind turned back to Joseph and Tabitha, vanished in the night. So young and so alone. If he knew Tabs, they'd have gone after that mermaid, trying to rescue her on their own. It made his blood run cold all over again and he forced the thought away.

'How many magicians?' he asked.

'Beg pardon, sir?'

'Magicians. How many?'

Even in the dim light below decks, Newton could see the bosun turn pale. He was a big, jovial man with curly white hair, enormous mutton chops and a beaming smile. But he wasn't smiling now.

'We don't— Well, Mr Newton, as you know, magic is outlawed in Port Fayt, so—'

'Aye. But it's not in the Old World, is it? The League'll have magicians to spare. All trained up too, most likely. All those cannons won't mean a thing if we can't defend ourselves against their magic.'

'I could ask around,' said the bosun stiffly.

Newton shook his head and turned, climbing the steps to the top deck without waiting for the bosun to follow. He'd seen enough. Even if there were magicians on board, they'd hardly be a match for the enemy's Magical Infantry. There'd been a League magician in the zephyrum mines in Garran, twenty years ago. Newt remembered how once, when the miners had tried to fight back, that single scrawny man had dispatched ten or twelve trolls and ogres before he got clonked on the head with a spade.

A blast of fresh air greeted him as he came up onto the deck. Old Jon was leaning against the gunwale, smoking and staring out to sea, long white hair streaking in the wind.

'I've made up my mind,' Newton told him. 'We're going back. We've got to find Joseph and Tabitha. Before they get themselves into trouble.'

Old Jon puffed out a smoke ring.

'I don't know, Newt,' he said.

'We can't go into battle, Jon. The League'll tear us apart. If we sail back to Fayt, at least I can try talking to the governor again, make him see sense. Even if there's a chance the merfolk might fight—'

'Ah,' said Old Jon. 'You don't know why the governor doesn't trust merfolk.'

Newton turned to look at him. As usual the elf didn't meet his eye.

'Tell me.'

Old Jon knocked out his pipe and started to stuff it with fresh tobacco.

'Henry Skelmerdale had a younger brother once. Thomas, his name was. Never had a head for business like Henry did, but he loved fishing. And one day, when Thomas was fourteen years old, he took his dinghy out into the bay not far from port. Cast out his line. A pair of merfolk were watching him, bobbing in the water . . .'

He paused to light the pipe, and Newton waited patiently. There was no sense in rushing Old Jon when he had something to say. The elf puffed at his pipe, and spoke again.

'Now, he'd hardly begun to fish when a storm blew up. Thomas was a fine fisherman but a lousy sailor. He struggled, but he couldn't bring the dinghy in. All it took was one big gust and the hull rolled over with poor Thomas tangled in the rigging. Couldn't get free . . .

'Know what those merfolk did, Newt?'

Newton shook his head.

'Nothing. Nothing but watch him drown. Story goes that Henry was on the docks at the time with a spyglass. Sixteen years old, he would've been.'

There was a long silence.

'Henry Skelmerdale won't go chasing after that princess,' said Old Jon at last. 'Not even if Thomas came back from his watery grave and begged him to.'

Newt nodded, letting the story sink in.

'So what about Joseph and Tabitha?'

'Fayters need you here, Newt. You turn their flagship around, they might lose hope altogether.'

'You're saying I don't have a choice.'

'Aye. That's what I'm saying.'

Newton bit his lip. Joseph had lost his parents when he was little more than a toddler. Tabitha had lost hers when she was just a baby. Someone needed to take care of them. It wasn't right, leaving them on their own.

'She's a tough one, Newt,' said Old Jon gently. 'And I know she don't show it, but she loves you. You're her father. Might as well be.'

'Shouldn't her father go back for her?'

Old Jon gestured around the ship. 'You tell me.'

Newton surveyed the deck. A pair of blackcoats were sharing their lunch, chatting and joking, but every so often one of them would cast a nervous glance east, to the horizon. To where the League fleet would appear. A group of young sailors, each with the sea-green armband of Port Fayt, had gathered around an elderly blackcoat sitting on the steps to the poop deck. It looked almost like an old man with his grandchildren – except that instead of telling tales the old soldier was showing them how to load a pistol.

He sighed. As usual, Old Jon was right. He couldn't let them down. Even if it meant leaving Joseph and Tabitha behind in Port Fayt.

'Don't fret,' said the elf. Sometimes it seemed as though he could tell exactly what Newton was thinking. 'Them youngsters can look after themselves. We wouldn't have stopped that Arabella Wyrmwood if it hadn't been for them. Wouldn't have caught that shapeshifter neither, nor got back the wand he stole. The wooden spoon.'

It was true enough. The thought of them on their own made Newton's stomach squirm, but he had to ignore that. He had to do what was best for Fayt. He had to do the right thing.

'You think they'll get by?'

Old Jon puffed out smoke.

'Tabs can fight. And that tavern boy's got sense. Reckon together they'll get along fine.'

'Sir?'

Newt turned at the voice. It was the bosun, hovering a few feet away as though he didn't want to interrupt their conversation. 'Did you want to inspect the bowchasers, sir?'

Old Jon turned, leaning over the gunwale again and staring out to sea.

Newt sighed. 'Aye,' he said. 'Let's see them then.'

The bosun beamed and strode off towards the foredeck.

Newton lingered just a moment longer.

'Jon,' he said. 'They wouldn't do anything stupid, would they?'

Chapter Ten

Joseph spun round, trying to locate the voice.

'Grubb! Grubb! Over here, you stupid mongrel.'

He crept closer to the cages. There, shaking the bars with his tiny fists, was a fairy. He was glowing in the darkness, his wings twitching with impatience. He wore a tiny waistcoat, jacket and breeches, and he had spiky hair and sparkling eyes.

Joseph recognized him at once.

'Slik!'

The last time they'd met, Slik had been peering out from inside a glass bottle, screaming insults as the troll twins took him away to the Brig. He'd been Captain

Newton's old messenger fairy until he betrayed the Watch and joined forces with a dangerous shapeshifter. In other words, he was probably the least trustworthy fairy in Port Fayt – and that took some doing.

'Mongrel! Am I glad to see you.'

Joseph frowned. So far as he knew, the fairy had never before been pleased to see him. Not when they first met, and certainly not when Joseph and the watchmen had shown up to arrest him.

'Hello, Slik.'

'Come to let me out, have you? About stinking time, if you ask me. I never did anything wrong, see, just sticking up for myself. Folk like us have to do that, don't we? Put-upon folk who aren't treated right. Me a fairy and you a mongrel.'

'Um . . .'

'Well, come on then. Get this cage open.'

'We're not here to rescue you.'

The fairy's face clouded over, and he began to mutter angrily under his breath.

'Maybe you could help though,' Joseph added quickly. 'Do you know a person called Pallione?'

Slik stopped muttering and peered up at him. A sly smile spread across his face.

'What if I do?'

'We're looking for her. It's really important we find her because . . . Well, it's complicated. But if we don't find her, it could be the end of Port Fayt.'

'Pallione the mermaid? The King's daughter?'

Joseph felt his heart beat a little faster.

'That's her! You know where she is?'

'Aye, I know where she is. And what's more, I'll tell you too. Right after you get me out of here.'

Joseph licked his lips and shot a look back down the corridor. Tabitha and the troll were busy talking through the bars to an elderly ogre with a wooden leg. Meanwhile the clamour from the other fairies was drowning out his conversation with Slik.

Should he do it? It would only take a moment. Slik wasn't exactly honest, but it was clear that he really did know who Pallione was. And if he knew that, maybe he knew where to find her, just like he'd said. On the other hand, if they were caught smuggling him out . . . Joseph remembered the cudgel blows the troll had dealt out and shuddered.

'Come on, Grubb,' said Slik. 'Look at me. Look at this cage they keep us in. Barely big enough for a rat. Fairies are meant to fly, mongrel. You know that. And the sugar they give us . . . Don't get me started on the sugar. Infested with weevils, and only a lump every two days. We're criminals? No, Grubb, *this* is criminal. This whole ship. And the worst of it is—'

'All right,' hissed Joseph. 'I'll do it. How do I . . . ? I mean, I don't have a key.'

Slik rolled his eyes.

'Maw's teeth, you don't need a key. This cage is built for fairies, you idiot mongrel. You might be weedy but you're a sight bigger than us. Just pull it open.'

Joseph took another quick glance at the troll to check that his back was turned. Then he curled his fingers around the thin metal bars of the cage and tugged. It was stiff, but he felt it give a little. He tugged harder. And harder. He looked back at the jailer.

'Put your back into it,' demanded Slik. 'I'll tell you if that crazy troll's coming.'

Joseph gritted his teeth and pulled again. This time there was a creak as the metal came loose. He took a deep breath and pulled one last time, as hard as he could. With a rusty screech, the cage door came clear.

Before he could reach inside, Slik had darted out through the gap and dropped down into his pocket, clinging to the fabric and glowing softly. The fairy put a finger to his lips and his light died away almost entirely.

Joseph pushed the cage door back into place and

walked away from the screaming fairies. They'd seen what had happened, but thankfully they couldn't get any louder than they were before anyway.

Tabitha turned to glare at him as he approached.

'Where've you been? Keep up. We got nothing from the ogres. Going to try some of the prisoners further down.'

'Right,' said Joseph, eyeing the troll. 'Actually, I'm not feeling all that well. I think maybe we should leave now.'

The troll's brow wrinkled. Tabitha scowled.

'We can't go. We need to find out where that mermaid is, *remember*? So the merfolk will fight on our side. And so they'll let Hal and the Bootle twins go. That ring any bells?'

'Yes, but, I mean, I'm sure we'll find her anyway.'

He felt sweat prickle on his brow. He had always been a terrible liar.

Tabitha narrowed her eyes.

'What's going on?'

'What? Nothing! I, er . . .' He turned to the troll. 'Would you, um, give us a minute?'

The troll raised an eyebrow, then turned on his heel with a swish of petticoats and strode away to break up a fight between a pair of goblin prisoners.

'What in Thalin's name—?' began Tabitha, but she

stopped as Joseph opened his pocket. Slik winked at her from inside. 'This snotbag? Are you joking? He's got to be the least—'

'He knows,' said Joseph. 'I thought . . . Well, it's a lead, isn't it?'

Tabitha looked for a moment as if she was about to hit him. Then finally her expression softened into an almost-smile.

'All right, it's a lead. Not bad. For a tavern boy.'

Joseph grinned. 'Thanks. And thanks for keeping that troll busy.'

Slik sniggered and made smooching noises from his pocket. Joseph covered him up, his cheeks burning.

'Let's get out of here,' said Tabitha quickly. She turned and called to the troll. 'That's enough for one day. We'll come back later.'

The jailer cracked the goblins' heads together and let them sink to the floor. 'Good,' he said. 'Time for some more tea.'

He led them back through the barred door, locking it behind them. Together they wound their way through the wooden corridors of the Brig, until at last they reached the living room. The cake still sat on the table, untouched except for the two slices the troll had eaten earlier.

'We'll be off now,' said Tabitha stiffly.

'Thanks for all your help,' said Joseph. 'Enjoy your cake.'

There was a sudden squirming in his pocket, and he instantly regretted saying that. Slik struggled upright and popped his head above the edge of the pocket, tiny nose quivering as he sniffed. Joseph moved his hand to conceal the fairy.

'I *will* enjoy it,' said the troll. 'It is good cake.'

The earthy-sweet smell of it was wafting into their nostrils now. Slik leaned past Joseph's hand and Joseph tried to push him back down into his pocket.

'Seed cake,' the troll carried on. 'Very good. Lots of honey in it.'

'Go on,' said Tabitha, her eyes shining with hunger.

Not helpful, Tabs.

'Butter too. Eggs. Seeds. And, most important . . . lots and lots of sugar.'

Slik wriggled free and darted for the cake.

The troll was lightning quick. His cudgel was out in a trice and slamming down towards the fairy. The first blow struck the table, making it shudder. The second smashed the mug, scattering bits of broken pottery and splattering cold tea everywhere. Slik was on top of the cake now, and the troll raised his cudgel a third time.

'No, wait,' called Joseph. 'Not the—'

The cudgel whistled down, and the thud of its impact was muffled by sponge. The cake exploded, golden crumbs flying in every direction.

'GAAAAAAAGH!' yelled the troll, as if it was his own heart he'd just beaten to a pulp. Slik was airborne, licking his lips, his tiny arms wrapped around a large chunk of cake.

The troll's gaze shifted from the fairy to Joseph and Tabitha. The ones who'd let this thief out of his cell . . .

'Run,' croaked Tabitha.

Joseph bolted out of the room, his cutlass banging against his legs as he raced towards the door that led back to the beach. Slik buzzed overhead with his cake and Tabitha pushed past, reaching up with one hand and somehow managing to snag the fairy's legs and tug him down. She crammed him into her coat pocket and fumbled to do up the buttons, ignoring Slik's muffled complaints.

Joseph heard the heavy footsteps of the troll coming after them. He ran faster. There was a swish of air at his back as the cudgel swung dangerously close.

Tabitha threw open the door and leaped down the steps.

The troll was taking aim again. Joseph ducked as the cudgel sailed overhead, thwacking into the wooden wall of the corridor. He sprang forward, out of the door.

The tide had come in, and the bottom of the steps was awash with seawater. Joseph skipped down into it, feeling the waves soak through his shoes instantly. He kept moving, panting, not looking back, dreading the next blow. The blow that would smash his brains out. But no blow came. He stumbled out of the surf onto the hard wet sand. Tabitha was just ahead, running up the beach, each footstep sinking deep.

Joseph chanced a look back. The troll was gone. What the . . . ? And then he saw the jailer standing on the steps of the Brig just above the water, holding his skirts up and frowning at the waves.

'The dress . . .' said Tabitha. She had collapsed onto the sand ahead, gasping for air. 'He doesn't . . . want to . . . get it wet.'

The troll ventured down a step, then thought better of it. He scowled at them. At last he swept back inside and slammed the door behind him.

Joseph could have almost cried with relief. He sank down next to Tabitha, his shoes waterlogged and full of sand, his muscles aching from running.

'You all right?' she asked.

'Just about.'

They lay there in silence except for their panting

and the sounds of Slik gorging himself on his bit of cake inside Tabitha's pocket.

'So where now?' asked Joseph finally. 'Bootles'?'

'Bootles',' agreed Tabitha. 'I don't know about you, but I'm starving.'

Chapter Eleven

Raindrops spattered on the leaf shelter the troll twins had built. The island was tiny, but there were a couple of trees, clinging on for dear life among the barren rocks. A good thing too, because otherwise they would all have been soaked by now.

Again.

Hal sneezed, wrapped his coat tighter around himself and shivered. As if it wasn't bad enough being stuck with Phineus Clagg and his few remaining crewmen, now they had to huddle up together to keep warm and fit under the leafy canopy. Jammed between a pair of sweating, stinking smugglers, Hal could think of places he'd rather be. Quite a lot of them, in fact.

They all watched in silence as the mermaid swam towards them through the rain-pocked sea.

Lunch, on its way.

'Bet you anything in the Ebony Ocean it's fish again,' said Frank.

His twin brother chuckled, but everyone else was too dispirited to reply.

The mermaid reached the shallow water and rose up out of it. Some silver objects flashed in her hands, and she tossed a few to land on the beach.

'There's a surprise,' muttered Clagg, and took a swig from his bottle. He seemed determined to drink away the memory of his lost ship. At the rate he was going, it was incredible that he was still conscious.

'I'll go,' said Hal, before anyone else could offer. He squeezed out from between his smelly neighbours and headed out of the shelter, into the rain. It might be wet out there, but he needed to escape the smugglers' company for a few moments and get some time alone.

He clambered across the wet rocks, down onto the beach. As he passed Pallione's bonestaff, still standing upright in the damp sand, his fingers brushed the wooden spoon in his pocket. Yes, there it was. The most powerful wand he'd ever possessed; but what good was it here? It could only be used to control a single mind. Even if it worked on one mermaid, the others would soon put a stop to it.

He'd been watching out for the merfolk all day, spotting them every now and then, their heads poking up above the water to check that their captives were still in place. As if there was anywhere for them to go. They were well and truly trapped on the island.

He bent down to pick up the silver fish, keeping his spectacles in place with one hand and trying not to think about the cleaning and gutting that would be involved before they could eat it. He was just turning to go when a voice called out to him.

'Human.' It was the mermaid who'd delivered their lunch, bobbing in the waves a few feet out to sea. 'We bring you food, water. What else do you need?'

'A boat would be useful, if you're offering.'

The mermaid looked puzzled. 'I don't understand. You cannot have boat.'

Hal sighed. From what he'd seen so far, merfolk didn't have much of a sense of humour. 'Never mind,' he said.

He was turning for a second time when the mermaid spoke again.

'The men in white have taken the big island.'

Hal's heart sank. 'Do you mean Illon?'

'Yes. The men in white have many ships and guns. Their king is very cruel. The small, fat man with cold eyes. You know him?'

Hal nodded. Everyone in Port Fayt had heard of the Duke of Garran. He tried not to think about what might have happened to the islanders.

'Your fleet has not yet arrived, four-eyed man. But our king will be here soon.'

Hal was confused for a moment. 'Do you mean—?'

'The King of the Merfolk. He is coming with his hosts. Within a day, he will arrive. Let us hope your little grey boy and the angry blue-headed girl bring Pallione quickly.'

'Don't worry. Joseph and Tabs will keep her safe.'

The mermaid threw back her head and howled. Hal guessed it was supposed to be a laugh.

'Pallione does not need protecting, four-eyed man.'

She dived back into the waves with a flick of her silver tail, and Hal was left alone on the beach, raindrops drilling into the sand all around him.

The King of the Merfolk. Hal had read about him at the Azurmouth Academy. Legend said he was older than the tides and had fought off more challengers to his throne than could be counted. No landlubber had ever seen him and lived to tell the tale. So what would he do to the watchmen and the smugglers if Joseph and Tabitha didn't return?

Probably nothing good.

Hal tugged the wooden spoon out of his pocket. He could still scarcely believe how ordinary it looked, warped and chipped from use before it was enchanted. Before it was turned into a wand capable of controlling any mind in the Ebony Ocean. *If the King arrives, maybe it will come in handy after all.* The thought made him shiver.

He thrust the spoon back into his pocket and carried the fish over the beach and the slippery rocks to the green shelter beyond. If only he knew what was happening back in Fayt . . . Surely Joseph and Tabitha would have spoken to Newt by now? And if they'd spoken to Newt, he'd be on his way to rescue them.

Wouldn't he?

He looked at the fish and wrinkled his nose.

They'd better come soon, is all.

Tabitha sat back, licking her lips. She felt a hundred times better with a belly full of pie. She'd never been so hungry in her life.

At once she thought of Hal, Frank and Paddy, stuck

on their little island with no food and no shelter. Outside the pie-shop window it had begun to rain. Whatever they were doing, Tabitha couldn't imagine they were having much fun.

She forced the thought from her mind as Mrs Bootle hurried into the serving room with a big bowl of sugar. The old troll woman set the bowl down on the table and Slik's eyes lit up with greed. He fluttered to the rim and fell in head first, his arms outstretched to embrace the shiny white crystals.

Tabitha caught Joseph's eye. He looked almost as disgusted as she was. It wasn't right, Slik getting rewarded after he'd nearly got them beaten to death by a mad cross-dressing troll. But unfortunately they needed him.

Mr Bootle had found a strong, slender length of cord, one end of which was now tied firmly round Slik's leg. The other end was looped around Tabitha's wrist. She wound it a couple more times, picking up the slack – just to be sure. There was no one in all of Port Fayt she trusted less than Slik. But she had to ignore that. Or at least that's what Newt would have told her, if he was here. Probably. She could make her own decisions, anyway. She was a fully-fledged watchman, wasn't she? With the shark tattoo to prove it.

Mrs Bootle had disappeared into the kitchen, but now she came bustling back with a tray: two mugs of velvetbean and a plate of thick, dark shokel cakes.

'Sugar?' she asked, passing a mug to Joseph.

The tavern boy glanced at Slik, who was now doing the breaststroke through the sugar bowl, slobbering as he went. He shook his head.

'Tabitha?'

'I'll pass, thanks, Mrs Bootle.'

'Oh, will you look at that? I forgot napkins. How could I forget napkins?'

'Don't worry, Mrs Bootle,' said Joseph. 'We don't . . .'

But the twins' mother had already rushed off to the kitchen.

It seemed as if poor Mrs Bootle wasn't entirely with them at the moment. She hadn't even told them off for sneaking away from the *Wyvern* without Newt's permission. Tabitha supposed that was only natural though, if your sons were stranded on an island in the middle of nowhere. If you didn't know whether they were dead or alive.

She wondered if Newton was feeling the same way about her. But then, he was the one in danger, sailing into battle with the League. He wasn't her real father, and he spent half the time ordering her around and stinking of tobacco. Still, she couldn't bear the thought of something bad happening to him.

Mrs Bootle returned with some large red cotton napkins.

'Are you worried about your sons, Mrs Bootle?' Tabitha asked.

Across the table she noticed Joseph stiffen a little. It annoyed her. She thought hard, trying to decide what would be the nicest thing to say. 'I'm sure they'll be all right. I'd be more worried about Hal, actually. He's not as strong as the others and I bet it gets cold at night. There might not be much to eat either. And if there's a storm the twins will be much more—'

'The merfolk will be looking after them,' Joseph cut in. 'And anyway, it's just for a few days. We'll get them back, Mrs Bootle.'

The old troll lady smiled sadly at him.

Tabitha frowned. How come Joseph was the one who took the credit here? She'd been helping to cheer up Mrs Bootle as well. Sometimes it seemed like Joseph was the only one anyone took notice of any more. He didn't have a mother or a father to look after him, but then, neither did she.

An image of her parents – her real ones – flashed into her head. Him: broad-shouldered, dark-haired, handsome. Her: young, beautiful, her long blonde hair shining in the sun. She wasn't even sure if it was really them any more, or if she'd just imagined them like that. Their murderer was dead now, like Tabitha had wanted, but it hadn't made things any better. She still dreamed of them. And these days the watchmen seemed more bothered about Joseph's dead parents than they ever had about hers.

Enough trying to be nice. She turned to Slik, who was lying on his back, kicking his legs in the air, his wings, face and body covered in sugar.

'Right. Where is this mermaid? And if you don't know, I'm going to take you down to the cellar and dunk you in a barrel of Mr Bootle's home-made scrumpy.'

The stupid grin faded from Slik's face, and he sat up.

'Well, if you're going to be like that . . .' he said. 'I'll tell you where she is. Starting to feel a bit sick actually.'

Mrs Bootle headed back into the kitchen as Joseph and Tabitha leaned forward. Slik cleared his throat and settled on the rim of the sugar bowl.

'Pallione was a shark fighter. One of the best too. Only been in Fayt a couple of weeks, and she was the crowd's favourite at Harry's.'

'I know where Harry's is,' said Joseph, his eyes

wide. 'Remember, Tabs? That's where I was kidnapped just before I met you. If we can get in, we can—'

'Slow down, mongrel,' said Slik. 'She's not there any more. Things change in the Marlinspike Quarter, see? Folk are always scrapping over turf. Harry's has got a new owner now. Cove called the Boy King.'

'I've heard of him,' said Tabitha. 'Nasty piece of work.'

'You don't say? A nine-year-old child ruling the biggest gang in the Marlinspike Quarter isn't likely to be all sweetness and light, now, is he? He's more dangerous than a dragon with toothache.'

'Nine years old?' said Joseph. 'How does he . . . ? I mean—'

Slik raised an eyebrow at Tabitha. 'Your boyfriend doesn't know much, does he?'

'He's not my—'

'Whatever you say. Anyway, this youngster's pa used to lead the crew – King Ketteridge, they called him – till one night he got lucky at cards with the wrong crowd. Went home in a box with an axe in his head. After that all the top dogs were squabbling over who should take over, and Lord Wren stepped in. He was Ketteridge's right-hand man. He suggested the old man's son take charge, save them killing each other over it.

'Well, it worked. Each of them bully boys reckoned they'd sooner have a child leading them than one of their rivals. And as it turns out, the boy's got a certain talent for it. Ruthless. Cross him once and you'll feed the fishes. The lads love him. 'Course, Lord Wren's always there with him, making sure he doesn't do anything too crazy.'

Tabitha waved her hand impatiently. 'I've heard all this before. What does it have to do with Pallione?'

'If you'll just shut your trap and listen, I'll tell you. See, the Boy King loves a show. And he doesn't need to go out for it. He has the money and the muscle to get the best performers in Port Fayt brought right in. Musicians, dancers, whatever. And Pallione's one of his acts now. Turns out that besides being a mean shark fighter, she's got one of the best singing voices in the Ebony Ocean. So the Boy King snapped her up. He owns her now.'

'Better than fighting sharks, I suppose,' murmured Joseph.

'So,' said Tabitha, determined to take charge, 'where do we find this show?'

Slik slid back down into the sugar bowl, putting his hands behind his head. The smug grin on his face was spoiled only by the granules of sugar still clinging to his lips.

'I can help you out with that.'

'Too right you can.' Tabitha took a sip of her velvetbean and reached for a shokel cake. Things seemed to be looking up. Now they knew where the mermaid was, they could rescue her, whisk her back to her father and bring the merfolk into battle in no time. Save Port Fayt and their fellow watchmen into the bargain. Simple.

'Can I ask you something?' said Joseph.

'Fire away.'

'Why are you helping us? I mean, we got you thrown into the Brig in the first place. I don't want to be rude, but you sold out the Demon's Watch before – so how do we know you're telling us the truth this time?'

Slik chuckled, as though the question was ridiculous.

'I've got no reason to lie, mongrel. If you go into the court of the Boy King, you're going to get yourselves killed. And I want to be there when it happens.'

Chapter Twelve

'See anything yet?'

Old Jon said nothing, just kept gazing through the spyglass towards the distant green hump of Illon. It was early afternoon, bright but overcast, with a fresh breeze. Good weather for a battle.

Newton strained his eyes but he couldn't see any enemy vessels. They were close, though. They had to be.

He realized he was rubbing at the old red marks around his wrists, and forced himself to stop. He always did that when he felt anxious. And there was a lot to feel anxious about. The troll twins and Hal stranded on a rock somewhere. Joseph and Tabitha trying to rescue a mermaid princess from Thalin knew who. The size of his fleet and how nervous the crews were. And the sight that would soon appear before them – the sails of the enemy ships rising above the horizon, rounding the headland of Illon and closing on them . . .

Stop rubbing.

He let go of his wrist and turned back to his captains, huddled together on the foredeck of the *Wyvern*. Their pale, anxious faces were turned up towards him, waiting to hear the plan. The only trouble was, he didn't have one. At least the *Wyvern* itself was a good vessel, fast and tough, and loaded with cannon. He would have to lead the attack. Set an example. If he was scared he couldn't show it.

And yes, he was scared.

A swarm of fairies swooped out of the sky and landed on the gunwale beside him, clinging on tight against the sea breeze. Ty was their leader. He saluted and his friends all followed suit.

'We've seen the armada, Cap'n,' said Ty.

'And?'

'It's big.'

'Ruddy big,' added one of his friends unhelpfully.

Newt glanced at his own motley fleet, stretched out in a ragged line on either side of his flagship. 'Ruddy big' wasn't how you'd describe it.

'Any clue what their plan is?'

'Reckon they don't need a plan. Other than just to sail right for us and blow us out of the Ebony Ocean. Their flagship's the biggest vessel I ever seen. She's in the centre, and I'm guessing she'll lead. Probably head straight for the *Wyvern*. Anyone needs a plan, it's us.'

Newton cast another glance around at his captains. Most were blackcoat sergeants who didn't know the first thing about sea battles. There was a dwarf privateer. A human merchant who looked familiar. Yes – Newton had seen him a fortnight before at the Pageant of the Sea, dressed in a red lobster costume and playing a squeezebox for a dance. Then later, eyes crossed from too much firewater, hugging his fellow musicians and telling them how much he loved them. He didn't look so cheerful now.

Someone moved at the back of the group, and Newton noticed a trio of imp captains – tough-looking seafarers, but so short they were mostly hidden behind the other captains.

Which gave him an idea.

'You lads at the back. Have you got dhows? The small, nippy ones?'

'Aye, Captain.'

'All right,' he said. 'Here's the plan. Odds are the League'll try and drive a wedge through us, engage us at close quarters where they can bring their guns and men to bear. So we'll let them. Get our whole fleet lined up bow to stern and let fly with broadsides. Except for you three.' He pointed at the imps. 'You bring your ships up behind the *Wyvern*. The dhows are small enough that they'll be good and hidden there. Then, when the enemy flagship comes through, you strike. If we can bring her down, there's a chance of forcing them to surrender. Agreed?'

The captains nodded, and for the first time, Newton could see a little hope in their eyes. He felt himself smiling. Even Cyrus Derringer managed a curt nod. Old Jon didn't seem to be paying attention though. He had lowered the spyglass and was looking in the opposite direction, at something beyond the knot of captains. The old elf's jaw fell open. Newton followed his gaze.

Maw's teeth!

Something was happening beyond the side of the ship. Some strange disruption to the air, as if they were seeing through warped glass. Which could only mean . . .

'Magic!' he roared. 'Battle stations!'

Across the deck, blackcoats unslung muskets and crossbows and drew sabres. Some of the captains readied their weapons, while others stood, gawping like fish on a line.

From the smudged air a form began to take shape. Rigging and a mast – no, two masts. Three. A wave-cutter, and a flag flying above it – the Golden Sun . . . And then, all of a sudden, figures were scrambling aboard the *Wyvern*. White-coated figures. Butchers. Sabres flashed and pistols cracked, sending up puffs of gunpowder.

Already there were howls of pain.

Newton pulled the Banshee from his belt, slotting the three gleaming black pieces of wood together with quick, deft motions. It was the only close-quarter weapon he ever used. He twirled the staff once, checking it was locked in place, then leaped up onto the ship's gunwale, taking a moment to make sure of his balance before running along it and jumping down into the surging mass of black- and white-coated soldiers.

Instinct took over. His staff blurred as he swept it low, knocking a League marine off his feet. He jabbed at a second, forcing him back to the gunwale and then over it, wailing.

Another butcher came at him, sabre slicing, but the blade glanced off the Banshee. Newton shoved his knee hard into the man's stomach, leaving him coughing and retching on the deck. More butchers closed in, but a white-haired whirlwind swooped down on them

– Old Jon, swinging his cudgel with a speed and accuracy most younger elves could only dream of.

Newton spotted Cyrus Derringer beyond, fencing two, sometimes three whitecoats at a time, dodging behind masts and barrels when there were too many for him.

A crossbow bolt whirred past, buried itself in the mainmast. Someone shoved into Newton's back. A pistol went off beside his right ear and a blade hissed past his shoulder. He jerked back into action, smashing the Banshee into the nearest whitecoat with all his strength. Someone had got hold of the other end of his staff and he had to wrestle it free.

Before he could turn, a sabre flashed at him from nowhere and he was recoiling, his staff clattering to the deck as hot pain bit into his arm. He was bleeding, he realized as he sank to his knees. *How serious is it?* He had no idea, but he couldn't worry about it now. He caught a glimpse of Old Jon doing his best to fight through to him, but the press of men was too great. He tried to get to his feet. There was the sound of a pistol being cocked above him, and then the cold metal of the barrel was shoved into his face, forcing him back down again. There was a blade at his chest and another at his stomach. Two muskets appeared, hovering above his head.

'Stay down!' someone was shouting. 'Move and we'll shoot.'

Sweat stung Newton's eyes. He clutched the wound on his arm, and blood oozed between his fingers. He couldn't see past the gun barrels pointing at him and, beyond, the mess of legs and feet as the fight continued.

Something was changing. There were fewer shouts now; fewer gunshots. There was more space around them. The butchers standing over him were relaxing.

So much for his plan. They had lost. Before the battle had even begun. It seemed so sudden – but then, the Fayters had never really stood a chance.

He was hustled to his feet and herded towards the stern. He rubbed his eyes, saw the other captains, Derringer and Old Jon being pushed alongside him, until they were all gathered around the wheel, muskets trained on them.

'Everyone down,' barked a League sergeant. 'On your knees.'

Newton obeyed. No point in arguing at this stage. There were bodies strewn on the deck, beyond the circle of marines guarding them.

A cluster of League magicians stood by the gunwale, talking and smoking, each one dressed in white, with the red fireball of the League Magical

Infantry embroidered on their shoulders. Trained in Azurmouth, no doubt, and far more skilled than the magicians of Port Fayt, who had to practise their art in secret. Hadn't he said they'd need magicians? Of course it made sense to ban magic in times of peace, but in war it was a different matter. Newton had never seen a whole ship made invisible. An invisible apple maybe. But a whole ship . . . If they could do that, what else were they capable of?

He was distracted by a commotion to his left. One of his captains, an elderly troll, was struggling to lower himself fast enough. The League sergeant stepped closer, raising his pistol.

Newton leaped forward before he could think what he was doing. Butchers fell on him – four, five of them – slowing him, shoving him back, and then there was the crack of a pistol shot and a low moan from the Fayters as the old troll fell dead on the deck. A musket butt slammed into Newton's face and he stumbled, fell to his knees again, and then there were more blades and bayonets pointed at him than before.

What are they doing? Have they rounded us up just to kill us?

He licked his dry lips with a dry tongue.

A drummer was playing, beating out a fast martial

rhythm as if they were on an Azurmouth parade ground. As if this was all play-acting. *Thalin knows, it isn't.*

There was a final drum-roll, then silence. The League sergeant opened his mouth.

'Stand aside for his grace, the Duke of Garran!'

The League marines parted and a figure approached, gliding across the deck.

A small man, round and pink-skinned. His white satin coat, white tricorne, white stockings and breeches – all of them were spotless. Unlike the marines, who looked just like the butchers they were nicknamed for, their uniforms smudged with gunpowder, soot and blood.

So this was the man who had ordered the massacre of the Crying Mountains – thousands of unarmed trolls put to the bayonet. The man who had lined the Great Garran Highway with the heads of those trolls, all the way from Azurmouth to Renneth. The man who had sent the few who still lived to work in the darkness of the zephyrum mines. Newton's jaw tightened at the thought.

'You,' said the Duke of Garran. He pointed at Newton with one finger, and Newton saw that he was even wearing white gloves. 'You are the commander of this vessel?'

'Aye.'

The Duke's gloved hand flicked out to the side, and someone stepped forward to place a pistol in it. It was a tall, slender woman, dressed in the uniform of a League officer but hatless, her long blonde hair tied back into a ponytail with a white ribbon. A heavy two-handed sword was strapped to her back – the kind of weapon that might have been common in the Dark Age, and today was anything but. Judging by the long splatter of blood across the side of her coat, she had been using it.

There was something about her – something oddly familiar . . . Newton was sure he'd seen her somewhere before. But where?

'Thank you, Major,' said the Duke. He came nearer, white leather shoes clicking neatly on the deck, pistol dangling at his side. He stopped two paces from Newton, examining him like a fisherman might look at a cod he was about to gut. His eyes were so pale they had almost no colour at all. Newton clamped his hand tighter around his wounded arm to stop himself from lashing out.

'I am disappointed, Mr . . .'

'Newton.'

'Mr Newton. Very disappointed. You are a human, aren't you?'

Newton said nothing. Actually his grandfather had been an ogre, but it only showed in a bit of extra bulk and a strong jawline. He didn't feel like explaining that to this bilge rat.

'You have lost your way,' said the Duke. He raised his pistol, pointing out the other human members of the *Wyvern*'s crew, one by one. 'You have all lost your way.'

There was a pause, then someone called out, 'You're the one who's a hundred miles from home.'

'Go back to the Old World,' called another. 'You cockroach!'

There were murmurs amongst the Fayters, some fearful, others agreeing. Newton just hoped the butchers hadn't seen who'd spoken. Whoever it was, they were brave but stupid.

The Duke didn't look bothered in the slightest. He drew a handkerchief from his pocket and dabbed at a spot of blood that had somehow found its way onto his coat.

'Do you think that we would not kill you now?' he said quietly. He sounded genuinely curious. 'We have done it before. It would not weigh on our conscience to slay all the demonspawn on this vessel, and the misguided humans who fight alongside them.' He replaced the handkerchief and held up his empty gloved hand. 'I myself have killed dozens of demon-spawn with this hand. Trolls. Imps. Dwarves. And may the seraphs give me strength to do so again.'

'That's as may be, your grace,' said Newton, 'but if you kill us you won't last long yourselves.' He nodded out to sea. Several Fayter vessels were bearing down on them now. They must have spotted the League ship, and were coming to help. *Better late than never*.

The enemy magicians fanned out over the deck, watching the approaching vessels. But the Duke of Garran didn't even look round.

'This is nothing we had not anticipated. But we have not come here to kill you. We have come because I wish to speak to your governor. My offer is this. The fleets will remain here, and you will accompany me and my flagship, the *Justice*, back to Port Fayt, where we will discuss terms. Naturally, if you refuse, death will follow. Doubtless we will die too. But you must understand, Mr Newton, that my men and I would welcome such martyrdom.'

'If you say so.'

'Consider my offer. Consider it carefully.'

Newton turned to Old Jon. The elf was frowning, but he gave a short nod. Beyond, Derringer was scowling fiercely.

This wasn't what Newton had expected. What in all the Ebony Ocean did the Duke want? So far as he'd known, the League weren't much for talking. Massacring, yes. But negotiating . . .

He looked up and caught the eyes of the blonde-haired League officer. They gleamed with the cold light of hatred. Her jaw was set tight, and her fingers had curled into fists.

He turned to the faces of his crew and captains, kneeling on the deck, watching the glinting sabres and bayonets of the League. He could practically taste their fear. Most of them had never even been in a battle before.

The body of the elderly troll was sprawled out, his blood already starting to dry.

Not much of a choice.

'We'll do as you say,' said Newton. 'Back to Port Fayt.'

The Duke smiled. But his pale eyes were empty, like twin crystal balls showing nothing of the future.

Chapter Thirteen

The man frowned harder at the piece of paper. He was dressed in rich blue velvet with small golden crowns stitched on each shoulder – livery like that of a trading company official. But his head was shaven, exposing an angry scar where one ear should have been, and his left eye was made of wood and painted to look like a real one, although not very successfully. All in all he looked like a glorified bully boy. Which was exactly what he was.

'You're not on the list,' he said at last.

'I know that,' said Slik. 'But we're not guests, see? Reckon you're short on servants, what with old Skelmerdale dragging all the ships in the harbour out to fight the Duke of Garran. And these two here want to help out in the kitchens, earn a ducat or two. I'm Slik. Cold-eyed Parsons knows me. He'll vouch for me.'

'We already got servants,' said the bully boy.

'Not like these you haven't. The Boy King'll want them. You know how he likes freaks.' Tabitha scowled at Slik, but the fairy carried on anyway. 'Look at that mongrel's skin, all weird and blotchy. And the girl's funny blue hair.'

The bully boy narrowed his one real eye.

'Wait there.'

The door slammed shut, brass knocker jangling.

Joseph hugged his shoulders against the evening chill and gazed up at the building. It didn't look like the headquarters of the most dangerous gang in Port Fayt. It was a large, pale stone merchant's house – just one of a hundred in this street, all identical. It was eerie how quiet it was here. Nothing like the busy Marlinspike Quarter he was used to.

He cast a nervous glance over his shoulder. The street was dark and empty. The Flagstaff Quarter was where the wealthiest merchants in Port Fayt lived, and folk like that tended to stay safe inside their big houses at night. All the same, he was nervous. What if a blackcoat patrol came . . . ?

'They're all at sea, remember?' said Tabitha, who had obviously guessed what he was thinking. 'Slik – I thought you said this would be easy.' She yanked on the fairy's lead, wrapped around her arm and hidden under her jacket cuff.

'No patience, this one,' said Slik. 'He'll let us in. Not nervous, are you?'

'Don't be stupid.'

'*I'm* nervous,' said Joseph.

'Well, I'm not, all right? I just don't trust this fairy.'

Slik shrugged. 'Boo hoo. Not as if you have a choice, anyway.'

'He's right,' said Joseph. 'We couldn't get in on our own.'

Tabitha glared at him, then at Slik. She lifted the fairy up on the back of her hand so that he was level with their faces. Slik grinned at them.

'Listen up, you slimy little sea slug,' she said. 'If you cause any trouble in there, it won't be the Brig any more.' She drew a finger across her throat. 'Got it?'

'You don't scare me.'

Tabitha wrapped her hand around the fairy, so that only his feet and head poked out on either side of her fist. He struggled, but it was no use.

'How about now? One good hard squeeze. That's all it would take. I'd enjoy it too.'

The fairy paled. 'All right, keep your breeches on. I'll behave.'

Footsteps sounded beyond the door. Joseph took a deep breath, clenched and unclenched his fists.

'We'll be all right, Joseph,' said Tabitha. 'Just stick with me.'

He managed a smile. 'Thanks. I will.'

Slik rolled his eyes and pretended to throw up.

The door opened again, and the man with the wooden eye stood back to let them pass. As they entered, two more men stepped out of the shadows and patted them down. Thank Thalin they'd left their weapons at Bootles'. It hadn't been easy persuading Tabitha to part with her knives. Or her watchman's coat, for that matter.

Joseph snuck a quick glance around him. The hallway was large and luxurious, a bronze chandelier hanging high above the white marble floor, its candlelight glowing softly onto blood-red walls. There were portraits, just like the ones in Wyrmwood Manor. Except the people in these paintings were terrifying. Most of them were missing something – front teeth, or an eye or a nose – and every one of them looked like they'd stab you in the face for half a ducat.

Joseph shivered. *We've got to do this*, he reminded himself. They couldn't leave their fellow watchmen at the mercy of the merfolk. Couldn't leave Newt and his fleet to face the League armada on their own.

'All right,' said the doorman. 'Tommy here'll take you down to the kitchens. You'll get a ducat apiece for the evening's work. Cause any trouble and you'll get the hiding of your life. Or worse. Is that clear?'

'Crystal,' said Slik, before Joseph or Tabitha could say anything. 'Reckon I'll stick around and enjoy the party.'

'Reckon you won't,' said the doorman bluntly. 'You can stay with the boy and girl or you can clear off. Parsons doesn't want to see you.'

Joseph thought fast. Better to have the fairy with them, where they could keep an eye on him. 'He'll stay with us,' he said. 'Won't you, Slik?'

'Course I will,' said the fairy, giving him a big grin.

Joseph smiled back, until he remembered Slik's words from earlier. *If you go into the court of the Boy King, you're going to get yourselves killed. And I want to be there when it happens.* The smile died on his lips.

The man called Tommy stepped up behind them and laid his hands on their shoulders. He was tall and thin, dressed in the same blue velvet as the doorman, with a face as pale as a corpse, wispy ginger hair tied back into a ponytail and a long, drooping ginger beard and moustache. He steered them along the dark red corridor, deeper into the house. It wasn't a gentle grip, and the swirling in Joseph's stomach didn't improve when he noticed that the hand on his shoulder had only three fingers.

There was a clatter of pots and pans and raised voices up ahead. They turned a corner, went through a doorway and down wide stone steps, and at last came out into an enormous kitchen. Servants were scurrying in every direction, tasting soup, chopping vegetables or plucking birds at the long table that ran down the middle of the room. Joseph wiped his brow. It was swelteringly hot thanks to three large open fires set into one wall.

Tommy took them across the kitchen, not pausing for a moment. An elf carrying a giant platter of roast meat had to dodge out of his path, and a woman with a pan of white sauce almost spilled it in her hurry to make way.

'Meal's already started,' said Tommy. His voice was thin and nasal. 'But there's room for a couple more serving staff. Put these on . . .'

He pulled costumes off some pegs and handed them to Joseph and Tabitha.

Tabitha frowned. 'Do we have to?'

'Yes,' replied Tommy, in a way that made it clear there was no more to say on the matter. 'The Boy King likes his servants dressed up. And the Boy King gets what he wants. Always.'

Slik sniggered. Joseph's costume was a red and yellow jester suit with an enormous coxcomb on its hood. Tabitha's was a dress sewn together from large purple and green patches with a gigantic ruff at the neck.

'But these are ridiculous. Why do—?'

Quick as a flash, Tommy whipped a silver pistol out of a pocket and pressed it against Tabitha's forehead, two fingers curled around the handle, the third resting on the trigger. Joseph started forward but Tommy's other hand gripped him by the throat, squeezing until he could barely breathe.

The noise died down as the servants stopped to watch.

'Well then, young mistress,' said Tommy, 'I reckon you'll be looking ridiculous.'

Tabitha stayed silent, her eyes wide and her face pale. As quickly as it had appeared, the pistol was put away again; the fingers relaxed around Joseph's throat. The background noise swelled up once more as he gasped and spluttered for air.

'Come on then,' snapped Tommy. 'Haven't got all night.'

They struggled into the costumes, pulling them on

over their clothes. Slik made a big fuss as the dress came down over him, but Tabitha managed to keep the leash concealed.

Joseph caught a glimpse of himself in the curve of a large polished copper pan. Tabitha was right – they looked ridiculous. His costume was too big for him and the coxcomb sagged absurdly to one side. Tabitha's dress pooled around her feet, and the colours clashed madly with her blue hair.

'This way,' said Tommy, and he led them to a table by the wall, crammed with dishes giving off exotic, delicious smells. There was a roasted seagull sitting on a bed of seaweed; a huge platter of rocks with oysters on top; a bowl of baby octopus. Joseph tried to ignore the rumbling in his stomach. It had been a long time since breakfast.

'This is the third course,' said Tommy. 'They're finishing the second now. So you'll be pouring black-wine until they're ready.' He handed them each a large crystal decanter sloshing with dark ruby liquid.

Joseph gazed at his in awe. *Blackwine*. No one in a dockside tavern like his uncle's could afford such an extravagance. Blackwine was imported from the finest vineyards in the Old World, and you could probably feed a family for a year on what this single decanter must have cost. He rearranged his grip, making sure he wasn't going to drop it.

'Now, most important of all: rules. You go in there and you top up anyone whose goblet is getting empty. You do whatever you're told. You don't take the costumes off. You don't speak unless spoken to. You don't, under any circumstances, look the Boy King in the eye. And whatever you do, you don't spill any of that blackwine. Understand?'

'Underst—'

'Not a drop. Those decanters are worth more than your stinking lives.' The blackwine suddenly felt even heavier than before. 'Now scram.'

Tommy ushered them through a thick, studded metal door and slammed it shut behind them, leaving them on their own in a dingy corridor lit by lanterns dangling from the ceiling.

'Come on then,' said Tabitha, and she strode off without waiting to see if Joseph would follow. He hurried after her.

The corridor sloped downwards, gently at first, then more steeply. Joseph's costume was hot and scratchy, and he couldn't stop worrying that he might trip and drop the blackwine. Ahead of him, Tabitha stepped on the hem of her dress and cursed as she stumbled.

Their footsteps began to crunch on sand. The walls were uneven now – the wallpaper replaced by rock, as if they were inside a cave instead of a merchant's house.

Down, down and further down. *Where were they going?*

Sound began to float up towards them – chatter and music. The tunnel grew lighter and the noises louder. At last they came to a corner with light flickering on the wall opposite.

'Are you ready?' hissed Tabitha.

'I think so.'

There was a snort of laughter that could only have come from Slik. 'I don't think you are.'

'Shut it,' said Tabitha. 'Just remember, any trouble and . . .' She lifted her free hand and mimed squeezing it into a fist.

'Good as gold, I'll be.'

Tabitha readjusted her hold on the blackwine and stepped round the corner.

Joseph took a deep breath and followed.

Chapter Fourteen

Slik was right. They hadn't been ready at all.

The room that spread out before them wasn't a room at all. Joseph had expected some kind of ornate, civilized dining hall like the one in Wyrmwood Manor. And he'd been half right. There were tables covered in starched white cloth, laden with food, silver cutlery, crystal goblets and candelabras. But that was where the similarities ended.

They were in a cavern, stretching up so high he could only just make out the tips of the stalactites hanging from the roof. Candles flickered on the tables and moonlight spilled in from a vast opening to their left, looking out onto the deep blue Ebony Ocean.

The tables ran down just three sides of the cavern; in front of the great opening, a square wooden stage had been built, jutting out into the middle of the dining area, with a raised wooden platform in one corner and the ocean as its backdrop. A trio of musicians – all imps – were sitting on the platform playing a rapid dance tune on fiddle, squeezebox and drums.

Joseph gazed around the chattering guests and shivered – not just from the cold air blowing in through the mouth of the cave. These were the most villainous crooks in Port Fayt, their faces marked with scars, tattoos and piercings, their belts loaded with cutlasses, axes and pistols. Men too dangerous even for Governor Skelmerdale's press gangs to touch. Feasting and drinking while Newt and his fleet were out at sea, trying to save Fayt from total destruction . . .

With a jolt, Joseph recognized someone. A lanky troll whose face was covered in white make-up. He was there when Joseph had been kept prisoner in Harry's Shark Pit. *That's the Actor*, the mad elf Harry had told him. *The man runs nigh on every street gang and gambling den in the Marlinspike Quarter.*

Joseph turned to the high table at the rear of the cavern. At once he spotted another familiar face: a large, grim-looking man in black wearing an eye patch and puffing on a pipe. Harry's voice came back to him again: *Lord Wren. Associate of the Boy King. Ain't really a lord of course, my duck, but try telling him that.*

Next to Lord Wren was an enormous chair, the carved wooden back of it towering over even the largest trolls in the cave. And sitting on the chair was the Boy King.

He was human, younger than Joseph, and he was stuffing his face with food. His cheeks were plump; his eyes were small, piggy, and shining with excitement. Everything he wore was gold, from his coat to his stockings. Perched on his head was the biggest tricorne hat Joseph had ever seen, sprouting an enormous golden plume. It was a cockatrice's tail feather. Just like the ones Joseph's father used to give his mother every year as a birthday present – only much, much bigger.

Slik chuckled. 'Fancy, eh? He always wears those stupid clothes. And he throws a fit if anyone touches them.'

Lord Wren leaned in to murmur something and the Boy King nodded, picking his teeth with a lobster claw. His gigantic plume swished against the back of the chair.

'Hey!'

Joseph almost dropped his decanter in shock, and

had to clutch it tighter to his chest. *Those decanters are worth more than your stinking lives.*

An elf had turned round and was shoving his goblet towards them.

'More blackwine!'

'Sorry,' said Joseph, and he stepped forward to pour.

He and Tabitha made their way around the tables, keeping to the shadows as much as possible. Joseph tugged his jester's hood down low. It wasn't as though anyone was going to recognize him, but it made him feel a little safer, all the same.

A dwarf was so drunk that he insisted Joseph keep pouring up to the very brim of his goblet, then lashed out at him when he tried to take the blackwine away. An imp insisted that because Joseph was dressed as a jester he ought to tell a joke, and Joseph had to mumble that he didn't know any and move on. It was worse than a busy day in the Legless Mermaid – at least his uncle's tavern had *some* customers who weren't criminals.

Slowly but surely, he was working his way towards the Boy King himself.

Tabitha nudged him, making him tighten his fingers around the decanter. She beckoned, and he followed her back into the shadows, away from the table.

'You seen anything yet?'

'Seen what?'

She rolled her eyes. 'The mermaid, remember? We're here to rescue her, in case you'd forgotten. It looks like there's a tunnel entrance over there.' She pointed to the far side of the cave, where Joseph saw a dark opening amongst the rocks. 'That could be how the musicians come in and out. And there's a wooden screen over there, by the stage. That must be where they get changed.'

'Right,' said Joseph. 'But . . . I mean, Pallione's a mermaid. She can't walk around like the other performers.'

'Give the boy a medal,' said Slik. 'He's a genius.'

Tabitha scowled. 'Remind me why we need this scumbag again?'

'We can't let him go now,' said Joseph, casting a nervous glance over his shoulder. 'Not in here with all the—'

Someone had got hold of his coxcomb, and before he could react he was spun round and found himself staring into Lord Wren's one eye. The man leaned in, smelling of sweat, smoke and firewater. His patch was made out of a ducat hammered flat, Joseph noticed, and his eye was wide and bloodshot.

'You're supposed to be serving blackwine,' he growled. 'So serve it.'

Tabitha hurried back to the table. Joseph tried to do the same, but Lord Wren was still holding onto his hood.

'I recognize you, boy.'

Joseph's legs went weak and his heart began to pound.

'Yes. I know you. Where do I know you from?'

'I'm a tavern boy,' said Joseph quickly. 'Maybe—'

He was cut off by a roar of applause as the impish band finished their tunes, bowed and shuffled down a ramp towards the cave entrance Tabitha had pointed out. Lord Wren gave Joseph one last look, then cuffed him lightly round the head and strode back to his seat. Joseph willed his heart to slow down, without much success.

The cavern was falling silent, and Joseph saw that the Boy King had wiped his mouth with a napkin and was clambering to his feet. He stepped up on his chair, then onto the table. He struck a pose, one leg extended forward, one hand on his hip and the other up in the air, as if he was some Old World hero about to deliver a speech to his army.

'Ladies and gentlemen,' he said. 'Welcome to the court of the Boy King!'

Applause swelled and feet stamped, dying down instantly as the Boy King raised his hand again. Except not entirely. There was a man near the stage who kept jabbering away to his neighbour, too drunk to shut up. His friends were desperately trying to keep him quiet, but it wasn't working.

The Boy King's eyes narrowed and his face flushed. 'I said, welcome to the court of the Boy King!' His voice was a thin, reedy whine. The voice of a spoiled child who wasn't getting his way.

The drunk man belched and giggled.

No one joined in.

The boy stamped his foot on the table, his plume quivering with fury. He flung out a hand, like a magician casting a spell.

At once, two men in blue velvet livery swooped in from the shadows, grabbed the drunk man and hauled him backwards off his chair. Even through his stupor, the man realized that something was wrong. He yelled out for help, but his friends just looked away.

A fresh burst of applause broke out, mingled with laughter, drowning the cries of the drunk man. In an instant he was gone. Joseph didn't want to guess where, but he was sure they wouldn't be seeing him again. According to Slik, the Boy King had once made a troll crawl around on his belly all day for referring to him as a child. Then had him crawl off a cliff.

The Boy King took up his pose again. 'Now, where was I?' His audience roared with laughter. 'Oh yes. I am the Boy King. And tonight we have entertainment. Splendid, glorious entertainment!' His eyes shone. 'As you all know, I love theatre. And so our next performance is a dramatic display, arranged by none other than . . . *myself*!'

Spittle flew from his lips, but he seemed too excited to notice. He paused for effect, gazing around at the diners. 'I call it' – he threw his arms out wide, and his golden plume danced in the candlelight – '*The Desperate Struggle for the Giant's Knee on the High Cliffs of the Northern Wastes, a Tale of the Great Wars of the Dark Age, retold by the Lord of the Marlinspike Quarter, His August Majesty, the Boy King!*'

Crashing applause echoed around the cavern. Some guests shouted out, 'Hail the Boy King!' and 'Long live his majesty!'

Joseph watched, transfixed. Didn't these people know there was a war on? A League armada bearing down on them, ready to destroy the whole town? And yet here they were, settling down to watch a play.

The Boy King began to strut back and forth along the table.

'Once upon a time,' he declaimed, 'hundreds and

hundreds of years ago, the brave hero Corin led his men into the Northern Wastes to fight the evil sorcerer, Zargath. Because Zargath wanted to conquer the Old World, and he had thousands of ugly, scary trolls and goblins to help him.'

Figures were trooping out of the small cave entrance. Figures dressed in leather and metal, carrying ancient-looking weapons – chipped old blades and shields painted with lurid emblems. They gathered on stage as the boy's reedy voice rose and fell with excitement.

'Corin marched for weeks, and even though the evil Zargath set lots of ambushes and traps for him, he kept going. Finally the wicked sorcerer had no choice. He brought his whole army out to fight, on the cliff top they call the Giant's Knee.'

Servants wheeled a canvas screen onto the stage, behind the armoured figures. It was painted to resemble the edge of a cliff, with grass at the bottom and gulls circling in the blue sky above.

'Behold the Giant's Knee! Taste the salt in the air. Hear the rolling waves of the ocean, far below.'

A sound began to fill the cavern – a high, mournful song without words. It dipped and soared, giving Joseph goose bumps. He craned his neck round, trying to see where it came from.

A small cart rumbled out from behind the wooden screen, pushed by two liveried footmen, up the ramp and onto the raised section of the stage.

The audience all gasped in awe.

On top of the cart was a strange wooden construction, painted grey and hung with seaweed, which was clearly supposed to represent rocks. And sitting on top of the fake rocks was a mermaid with a long silvery tail.

Joseph caught his breath. *Pallione was a shark fighter. One of the best too.* He'd thought nothing of it at the time. But now, that long white hair and those bright green eyes . . . He had seen her before. Surging out of the water, raising a blood-spattered trident in victory. The mermaid who'd saved his life when he was floundering in Harry's Shark Pit, at the mercy of Florence the bull shark.

She looked different now. Her hair was dry and combed, and she was dressed in a costume woven out of seaweed and shells. She had a pearl band holding back her hair, pearl earrings and a pearl necklace. Her eyes shone in the candlelight as she sang.

The King's daughter.

Pallione.

Chapter Fifteen

The fire crackled on the beach, and the sea breeze wafted smoke and the scent of frying fish towards the watchmen.

'Sure you don't want to play?' asked Frank. 'We've got time for a hand or two before dinner.'

Hal made a face and shook his head.

'Suit yourself, grumpy guts,' said Paddy, shuffling the water-damaged cards.

The twins had made a table out of a large flat rock, and Hal had lost count of the number of games they'd played on it. Nothing seemed to dampen the Bootles' spirits. No matter how many hands of Dead Man's Leg they played, or Hunt the Griffin, or Red Flash, they just kept smiling and joking and dealing the cards. Hal had never been too keen on card games, and by now he was trying to decide when to snatch the deck, and if it would be better to throw it into the fire or the ocean.

He peered out beyond the smugglers cooking on the beach, over the dark water. The sun had sunk below the horizon, leaving only an orange tinge in the deep blue sky. But Hal could still make out the merfolk dipping in and out of the waves. By mid-afternoon their guard had doubled, and yet more merfolk had arrived throughout the evening. Hal had watched them in between the card games, and the fried fish, and the endless waiting.

Now the bay was cluttered with heads and flicking tails. Two mermaids streaked through the black water, playing chase. Another arced through the air, disappearing underwater again in a fountain of spray. Most were huddled in small groups signing to each other, sometimes glancing towards their captives on the island.

No doubt about it: the King's army was gathering. Already they had a force that might stand a chance against the League, and it was getting bigger by the hour.

All the same, Hal felt uneasy. What if Joseph and

Tabs didn't bring back the King's daughter? They must have reached Fayt by now. And they must have spoken to Newt. But still, there were no ships on the horizon, and no sign of the mermaid princess. Would the merfolk give up and go home? He seriously doubted it.

'Moping again, Hal?' said Frank, with a wink.

'I'm observing the merfolk, if you must know.'

'That right? Well, there's just one thing I don't get,' said Paddy, laying down a card. 'If this king of theirs is so magical, how come he doesn't rescue his own daughter? I heard he can even bring the dead back to life, just like the Witch Lords did in the Dark Age. So why can't he do a bit of hocus-pocus and save her himself?'

Frank snorted. 'Bring the dead back to life? That's walrus dung.'

Hal leaned forward. *Finally, something interesting to talk about*. 'Merfolk magic is certainly impressive. But to raise the dead . . . That would require an expert of the highest degree. I doubt even Master Gurney at the Azurmouth Academy could achieve such a—'

'Merfolk are different though, aren't they?' Paddy cut in. 'Ma told us that when we were youngsters. They're born magical. Get it from the sea, not from studying at fancy schools.'

'Yes, obviously,' snapped Hal, before Paddy could prattle on any further. 'The magic of the merfolk was one of my principal subjects at Azurmouth. They are natural magicians, but their power is drawn from the ocean. On dry land their "hocus-pocus", as you call it, simply doesn't work. That's why shark-pit owners can keep them locked up so easily once they've managed to fish them out of the sea. It's rather fascinating, in fact. When I was studying at—'

'Oi, you lot!'

Hal turned at the shout, annoyed that he'd been interrupted. Phineus Clagg was stumbling towards them over the rocks, from the other side of the island. The smuggler had run out of firewater an hour ago and had been a little twitchy ever since.

'Well, thank Thalin for that,' said Frank. 'I could feel one of Hal's magic lessons coming on. What's up, Captain Cuttlefish? Found a secret fountain of grog?'

The smuggler came panting to a halt, bent over and wheezing, his lank hair hanging in front of his sweaty red face and his lazy left eye even less under control than usual.

'Come and see for yerselves,' he gasped.

The troll twins rose and followed him, clambering away over the rocks. Hal brought up the rear, lingering to take one last look at the merfolk before he followed.

On the first day Frank and Paddy had led an expedition all over the island, trying to find water or food – and there was nothing. Just rocks, a few patches of windswept grass and some stunted trees. No wonder the merfolk had chosen it. Here the watchmen were entirely dependent on their captors. But now Phineus Clagg, of all people, had found something . . .

The smuggler came to a halt on a high rock and pointed downwards. There was a small pebble beach below, and in the sea beyond it, more merfolk had appeared, milling around among the waves. There were at least as many as on the other side of the island – maybe more. That was nothing though.

In the shallows, the waves lapped at a pile of boulders, each one as big as a crouching ogre. Except the boulders were perched one on top of the other, six or seven impossibly balanced, casting a long, strange shadow across the water. And on top of the boulders . . .

'The King,' whispered Frank.

There was no doubt about it. The merman was perched on the highest rock, staring out to sea. In his right hand he held a bonestaff, the shaft twisted and gleaming with pearls set into the bone. The evening breeze stirred his long white hair and beard. His tail flicked, once. He wore no crown, but that didn't make him seem any less like a king.

If only Master Gurney was here to see this . . .

'Blimey,' said Paddy.

In silence they made their way down across the rocks, pausing when they arrived at the beach. The column of boulders was just a short swim away, and the waters around it were empty of merfolk, who were keeping a respectful distance from their ruler.

'What do we say to him?' hissed Frank.

'Let's ask him if he brought any blackwine with him,' suggested Clagg. 'A king ought to have some decent liquor handy.'

'Mermaids don't drink, walrus-brain,' said Paddy.

Clagg groaned. 'Don't drink? Where's the sense in that?'

Hal stepped forward. 'I'll talk to him. See if I can persuade him to let us go. I'm not sure I trust any of you not to insult him.'

'Fair enough,' sniffed Frank. 'Just don't start talking to him about magic, all right? Don't want him falling asleep on us.'

Hal ignored that and headed across the beach. He felt in his pocket, and his fingers closed around the wooden spoon. He tried to calm his breathing. Did he dare use it? It was incredibly powerful, but then, so was the King.

He took off his shoes, rolled up his breeches and stepped out into the surf, wincing as the cold water swallowed his feet.

'Human,' came a shout from nearby. It was a fair-haired merman, his bare chest covered in tattoos, bobbing in the shallows. His brow was furrowed with suspicion. 'Why do you come here?'

'I wish to speak with the King.'

The merman said nothing. Hal was about to speak again when the water began to tug at his ankles, lightly at first, then suddenly with irresistible force. He fought for balance but it was no good. He fell, water flooding through his clothes, so cold that he was numb at once. He opened his mouth to cry out and got a mouthful of salt water that made him choke. And then he was being dragged across the sea bed, as if by invisible hands, out into the ocean, his back and head bumping against the bottom. His whole body tingled. *Magic,* some part of his brain told him.

He was jerked upwards in a crash of spray, sodden and dripping in the chill evening air, to hover above the waves. He coughed, spluttered and rubbed the salt from his eyes.

When he opened them and cleared the water from his spectacles, he saw that he was floating in mid-air in front of the King. The merman stared at him with his lip curled, as though Hal was a weevil in a ship's biscuit.

Up close the King seemed even more impressive. He was muscled and strong, despite his age, and under his busy white eyebrows his eyes were a vivid green.

'You wish to speak with me, four-eyed man,' he said. His voice rumbled like distant thunder, and his accent was only slight.

'Yes, I, er . . . Indeed,' said Hal. It wasn't quite the commanding response he'd hoped for, but then, it was hard to be commanding when you were soaking wet and dangling six feet above the sea. 'I was hoping you might consider letting us . . . well . . . go.'

A smile twitched at the corner of the King's mouth. 'I see,' he said.

Something tugged at Hal's pocket, and before he could react, the wooden spoon flew out and hovered between them, rotating slowly in mid-air. His heart raced.

'And this wand,' said the King. 'You brought this to persuade me, I take it.'

'I . . . Not exactly . . .'

The wand darted like a fairy, back into Hal's pocket.

'Just as well. My powers are at their strongest, magician.'

'You've been *speaking with the ocean,*' said Hal, before he could stop himself. It was a merfolk expression that Master Gurney had taught him. Every year, each merman and mermaid had to dive down deep, alone, and commune with the sea. It was the closest thing they had to a religion. It took days, sometimes months, but when they returned to the surface their magic was replenished and strong.

Something clicked in Hal's mind.

'That's why you've only just come to— I mean . . .'

He faltered. A cloud had passed across the King's face.

'Yes,' said the merman, and some of the strength and confidence was gone from his voice. 'I was speaking with the ocean when she was taken. I wish it had not been so.' Suddenly his eyes seemed to go a deeper shade of green, dark and threatening, and his voice rumbled again. 'But now I am returned.' He waved his hand in dismissal. 'I cannot release you. Not until my daughter is restored to me.'

Hal nodded. The King's eyes made him want to be as far away as possible. 'I understand. Our friends will bring her back soon.'

'Let us hope so. For your sake.'

Hal opened his mouth to reply, but suddenly there was nothing holding him up any more. He plummeted, hit the waves with a smack, and was dragged away through the water. An instant later he was washed up on the beach like some broken bit of flotsam, coughing and gasping for breath.

The troll twins raced towards him as he sat up. He turned from them to stare at the King, sitting silent on his rock, his strange throne of boulders silhouetted against the evening sky.

It was clear the interview was over. But those last words stayed with him. *Let us hope so. For your sake.*

'Hal?' called Paddy. 'Are you all right? What happened?'

Hal staggered to his feet, trying not to think too hard about what the old merman had said.

Chapter Sixteen

Pallione kept singing, her voice delicate and brittle. Joseph glanced at Tabitha, hoping she might have some idea what to do, but she looked as uncertain as he felt. They couldn't get to the mermaid now. Not with every crook in Port Fayt in the way.

On stage the figures were assembling into two groups. Those on the left wore black armour, their shields painted with skulls and bones. Their helmets hid their faces, but from their size and shape Joseph guessed they were all trolls and goblins. Opposite them were men in silver armour, each of their shields painted white and emblazoned with a golden sword.

Joseph was starting to feel sick.

'Corin's army was only small,' declared the Boy King. He was still swaggering back and forth along the table, his enormous plume bouncing with each stride. 'But he was the boldest, bravest, strongest hero in all the Old World.'

One of the men in silver stepped forward, taking off his helmet and brandishing a sword that had been daubed with gold paint.

'I am Corin,' he said unconvincingly.

'Zargath had a great horde of evil creatures, but he was the evillest of them all,' announced the Boy King. He was all but rubbing his hands together with glee. 'Where are you, Zargath?'

A man stepped out of the group of trolls and goblins, wearing a long black robe and a false beard.

'I am Zargath,' he declared. He didn't sound like a wicked wizard. In fact, he was trembling. Joseph looked back at the figure of Corin and saw that he was trembling too. He began to examine the warriors – the humans in silver and the trolls and goblins in black. All of them were trembling. *What's going on here?*

'Behold,' squealed the Boy King, more excited than ever. 'The two armies face each other.'

There was a hand on Joseph's arm – Tabitha. She caught his eye and nodded towards something at the side of the cavern. Joseph followed her gaze and saw men in the Boy King's livery – blue velvet adorned with golden crowns. They all held muskets and cross-bows, raised and levelled at the stage. At the performers.

'And now!' The Boy King was practically screeching. 'Here! Today! In this very hall! They will fight . . . for our entertainment!'

Thunderous applause from the diners. Pallione's song came to an abrupt end and she turned to glare at the Boy King, the hatred clear in her eyes. Joseph saw that there was a musket levelled at her too.

'What . . . ?' said Tabitha. 'What's happening?'

'LET BATTLE COMMENCE!'

Silence. The armies watched each other, but neither made a move. Pallione's tail flicked and she turned her face away from the stage.

'Please,' said a lone voice. It was one of the humans in silver armour. 'Please don't make us—'

'FIGHT!' shrieked the Boy King. 'FIIIIIGHT!'

There was a whirr and a hiss, and something thunked into the stage behind the trolls. Joseph looked up to see one of the crossbowmen reloading.

A weedy yell came from amongst the black-armoured group, and a goblin rushed forward, wielding a hand-axe. Others joined him, and then both armies were charging, and there was a clatter of metal as they met. The battle had begun.

'Something's wrong,' said Tabitha. Her face was contorted with horror. 'I don't think . . . I mean, is this . . . ?'

'It's not a show,' said Joseph. His voice came out strained and high. 'It's real.'

At the front of the stage, a goblin had got himself trapped between two humans. A sword swung at him, chopped heavily into his shield. *If that had been his arm* . . . thought Joseph, and shuddered. In shock, the goblin dropped the shield and his mace. He looked around for an escape route but there was only one. He leaped off the stage, racing towards the nearest guests.

Three separate musket shots rang out, and the goblin danced and fell, his helmet rolling away under the table. One of the guests picked it up, admiring it and showing it to his neighbour. The goblin lay silent and still. Blood pooled around the table leg.

Gradually, Joseph became aware of Tabitha speaking to him again.

'We have to do something,' she was hissing. 'We have to stop this.'

There were several bodies now, half hidden among the melee. Some were propped up by the press of battle, others trampled underfoot. A human howled.

It was a strange, gurgling sound that seemed scarcely human at all. Blood spattered the nearest diners, and they let out yelps of delighted surprise.

Think, Joseph! They had no weapons. Nothing. 'I don't know what to . . .'

He faltered to a halt. Because suddenly he *did* know. He knew exactly what to do. He took a deep breath and walked towards the Boy King. The one person who could stop the bloodshed.

'Where are you going?' Tabitha asked, but he knew that if he stopped to explain, she'd talk him out of it, or he'd lose his nerve.

The terror of the Marlinspike Quarter was perched on the edge of his seat, eyes as big as cannonballs, a stupid smile painted all over his face as he drank in the fighting and the killing. His golden costume glittered in the candlelight.

He always wears those stupid clothes, Slik had said. *And he throws a fit if anyone touches them . . .*

'You,' the boy yelled at a human, cornered by trolls swinging battle-axes. 'You're not trying. You're supposed to be a hero, not a coward! You trolls, kill him! Teach him a lesson!'

The axes came down. The Boy King laughed, snatched a bunch of grapes and stuffed them into his mouth.

'Your majesty,' said Joseph, lifting up his decanter. 'More blackwine?'

The boy turned, scowling at him. Then he grinned and offered up his crystal goblet.

Joseph began to pour the drink, and the Boy King watched greedily as his goblet was filled with wine. Joseph's right hand shifted to the back of the decanter, raising it higher.

Now or never.

He let go. The decanter slipped forward through his grasp, hit the edge of the table and smashed. Glass scattered over plates, food and cutlery. Blackwine gushed everywhere.

The Boy King leaped to his feet as if he'd been stung by a hornet. Black liquid oozed through his golden jacket and breeches.

'Stop!' he screamed. 'Stop the battle!'

Chapter Seventeen

Silence fell.

Only the guests nearest the Boy King had seen Joseph drop the decanter. But it must have been obvious what had happened, because suddenly a nearby chair scraped, and someone had grabbed Joseph by the neck and was forcing him to the ground. He choked, flailing at his attacker, but someone else got hold of his arm and pinned it down. A pistol jabbed into his stomach, making him gasp. Someone sat on his legs. The man holding his throat had a knife out now, the edge pushing into Joseph's cheek, the point blurring as it hovered close to his eyes.

'Sorry,' he burbled. 'Sorry.' As if that would make any difference. His heart was beating wildly. What in all the Ebony Ocean had he been thinking? He'd wanted to stop the fight, yes. But get himself killed in the process? He'd been a complete bilge-brain. He screwed his eyes shut, wondering which bit of him would be first to feel the terrible pain that was surely coming. Would it be a blow from a fist? A boot? A blade?

But instead the Boy King's voice rang out, loud and clear: 'Don't touch him! Let me through.'

Some of the pressure eased up on Joseph's arm and legs. The blade moved away from his cheek. Cautiously he opened one eye.

The Boy King crouched over him, a peculiar expression on his face. The stain of blackwine had spread now, covering most of his jacket, as though he was bleeding.

'I'm so sorry,' said Joseph. 'I didn't mean to—'

'Shut your trap,' said the boy, 'you filthy, wretched, snivelling *mongrel*.'

There was a chorus of sniggers from the men who'd been holding Joseph down. It was curiosity on the boy's face, Joseph realized. Mixed with a healthy dose of fury and disgust.

'I've never seen a mongrel before. Take off your hood.'

Joseph did so.

'You look funny,' said the boy. 'What's wrong with your skin? It's blotchy.' He poked Joseph's cheek, then flicked his pointed ear.

'My, er, father was a goblin,' said Joseph. 'And my mother was a human.'

The Boy King frowned, thinking. At last his tiny eyes lit up, and a cruel smile spread across his lips.

'What can you do?' he asked.

'I . . . um . . .'

'Come on,' said the boy, and he flicked Joseph's other ear, harder this time. 'Even a mongrel must be able to do *something*.' He pinched the point of the ear and dragged Joseph to his feet, pulling him around the tables. Joseph stumbled along, trying not to trip and fall. Jeers and laughter followed him.

'Clear the stage,' bellowed the Boy King, and the armies clattered away, trooping off into the tunnel they had come from. Joseph was tugged up the wooden steps, wincing at the pain in his ear – and then the boy let go and put one arm around him instead. They were in the centre of the stage, looking out over the diners.

Joseph peered into the shadows, searching for Tabitha. There she was, hovering at the back of the cavern and glaring at him, her blackwine abandoned, her hands curled into fists. She was obviously angry, but Joseph thought he saw a little anxiety in her face too. It was clear she had no idea what to do. Probably for the best. Tabitha could fight, but there was no way she could take on everyone in this cavern.

Just stay there, Tabs . . .

'This mongrel,' announced the Boy King, 'will provide our next entertainment.' More howls of laughter and catcalls. Joseph felt his cheeks burn and his legs go weak. 'And he *will* entertain us. Because if he doesn't' – the Boy King dropped his voice to a whisper – 'we'll see if his insides match his horrible blotchy skin. Do you understand, mongrel?'

Joseph couldn't speak, so he nodded instead.

The guests burst into applause as the Boy King hopped down from the stage and swaggered back to his place at the head of the table. Gradually, silence fell. All eyes were on Joseph. He stood there in the jester's outfit, his cheeks burning, his mind as empty as a cloudless sky.

'Boring!' shouted a very drunk man.

'Do something!' roared an elf, who was just as drunk.

'Get on with it!' yelled a goblin, even drunker than the other two.

'Better hurry, boy,' said a voice from behind, with a soft, lilting accent to it. Joseph turned. Pallione was leaning out of her cart on the raised part of stage, frowning at him. 'Entertain them. Unless you want to get turned inside out. Can you dance?'

Joseph shook his head. He'd spent most of his life in his uncle's tavern, and all he'd ever done there was serve grog, mop floors and wash dishes.

Pallione flicked her tail impatiently. 'Do you know any songs?'

Joseph racked his brain. 'Just one. But it's—'

'Then sing.'

'It's not really—'

'Now.'

Joseph turned back to the audience.

Could he do this?

Yes.

He *had* to.

He opened his mouth and drew in a deep breath.

'*Scrub the dishes, scrub them clean,*
Cleaner than you've ever seen.'

It was his mother's song, but Joseph's voice was nothing compared to hers. In fact he was so scared that it came out even flatter and quieter than normal.

He tried to smile and sang it through again, this time miming scrubbing dishes. He felt ridiculous. Why had he let the mermaid talk him into singing, for Thalin's sake? His eyes met Tabitha's, and her ashen face told him everything he needed to know about how the performance was going. She began to move, creeping closer to the table.

No, thought Joseph, staring straight at her. *Stay there*. Tabitha caught his eye and paused, tense, waiting to see what happened next. She didn't look happy about it though.

The drunken elf tottered to her feet. 'This is bilge,' she announced.

'Yeah,' said someone else. 'Shut it, mongrel.'

A metal plate came spinning out of nowhere, clattering onto the stage. Then a fork flew, bouncing off the wooden screen beyond. Murmurs swelled up from the audience, growing louder and angrier. Above it all rose the shrill giggle of the Boy King.

'Encore,' he called. 'Encore!'

The song was only two lines long – barely a song at all – and he'd already sung it twice.

'Keep going,' called Pallione.

Joseph couldn't think what else to do, so he took a breath to sing it a third time.

And this time, the song sounded better. Much, much better. Louder and more confident, and . . . There was another voice singing with him, he realized. *Pallione's voice.* It danced around the melody, making the song sound alive and rich and beautiful.

The noise from the audience died down. Joseph stopped pretending to do the dishes and just stood, singing. He went through the song a fourth time, the mermaid's voice soaring above his. The guests said nothing any more; just sat in silence and listened. Joseph felt like he might burst into tears with relief.

The fifth round came to an end with a long, reedy note from Joseph and a deep, powerful one from Pallione. Joseph stopped. Waited.

Silence.

And then, at last, applause, filling the cavern. The diners began to cheer.

'Pallione! Pallione! PALLIONE!'

Two liveried footmen hurried onto the raised area and trundled Pallione's cart down a ramp onto the main part of the stage. The applause grew louder.

'PALLIONE!' roared the crowd. 'PALLIONE! PALLIONE! PALLIONE!'

The cart came to a halt next to Joseph, and the two footmen scurried back behind the screen. Pallione scowled at the audience in spite of their applause.

When she turned to Joseph she was still frowning, but her eyes sparkled in the candlelight. A waft of perfume hit his nostrils.

'I know you,' she said. 'You fell into the pit, didn't you? At Harry's. This is the second time I've saved your life.'

Joseph tried to reply, but no words came out. He opened and closed his mouth like a fish, and he felt his ears twitch and his cheeks burn.

Pallione's lips curved upwards. 'No good at fighting sharks. No good at singing. And no good at talking either.'

'Thank you,' Joseph managed to get out.

The mermaid smiled at last. 'It's nothing. I'm joking.'

'Oh, I know. I mean— Well. Thank you anyway.'

She nodded and went back to glowering at the audience.

At the head of the table, the Boy King got to his feet, and the applause came to an end. All eyes turned to the child in gold. His cheeks had gone red, and his plume shook, throwing a huge flickering shadow onto the cavern wall behind him. Suddenly all the relief that Joseph had felt ebbed away. He was scared again. Very scared.

'How dare you!' said the Boy King. 'How DARE you!'

He leaped up onto the table, kicking aside plates and cutlery and toppling a glass goblet which smashed on the ground. Joseph's stomach went cold.

'I commanded the *mongrel* to entertain us. Not *you*, you slimy fish-tailed *sea cow*!'

Murmurs of agreement from the audience. Pallione was staring grimly at the Boy King, as though he was a shark in need of a trident.

'He cheated! And you helped him. After all I did for you, rescuing you from that stinking shark pit!' His face was the colour of a lobster now. 'I am the Boy King,' he shrieked, 'and I will not be made a fool of!' He stamped his foot and pointed at them, his piggy eyes narrowing. 'You will suffer. Both of you. I will devise your punishment myself. I'll rip your ears off! I'll pull your toenails out! I'll—'

A blur of green, purple and blue streaked out of the shadows and onto the table, and the Boy King let out a gurgling cry. More cutlery and glasses fell, clattering and smashing on the ground. Tabitha had one arm locked around the boy's chest. The other held a carving knife pressed against his throat. She forced him down so that he was kneeling on the table. His golden tricorne toppled off, landing on the ground amid the broken glass. The Boy King's hair clung to his head, dark and greasy.

'Nobody touch them,' yelled Tabitha.

'Guurgh,' said the boy. Tabitha pushed the knife closer, squeezing a terrified whimper out of him.

Lord Wren was on his feet with a pistol in his hand. Tabitha sprang forward off the table, taking the boy with her, dragging him through the mess and into the centre of the cavern. All eyes were on her. Joseph felt his chest tighten with fear.

'You let them go,' said Tabitha, much more quietly this time. 'You let them go, and me too. Or I'll cut this little dunghead's throat.'

Joseph started forward but a hand gripped his arm, holding him back. He looked up to see Pallione's green eyes blazing at him.

'Stay here,' she hissed. 'Don't make this worse than it is already.'

Lord Wren was levelling the pistol at Tabitha, fury twisting his face so that he looked like a different person entirely. Then, almost at once, the rage disappeared and he began to smile. Then he chuckled.

'You won't do it,' he said.

'Shut up!' yelled Tabitha. 'I *will* do it.'

'No. You've never cut a throat before. You're a child. You don't know what you're doing.'

'Stay back,' said Tabitha. But her voice wavered. 'Stay back, or I'll— Aaaargh!'

A flash of light darted out of her sleeve, and she dropped the knife.

Slik.

The fairy flew round her back, tugging at his leash and pulling her hand away. The Boy King squirmed out of her grip, stumbling forward.

Clatters and bangs erupted from every table as the boy's guests launched themselves at the girl in the green and purple dress.

'No!' shouted Joseph. He twisted out of the mermaid's grip and leaped from the stage, lunging towards Tabitha. Immediately a troll slammed into him, knocking him flying. As he got to his feet, someone else collided with him, and the air was squeezed out of his lungs. He was on his knees again, and someone was shoving at his back. His hands found the ground and a boot stomped on his fingers, making him yelp with pain.

'Stop!' someone yelled. 'STOP!'

Incredibly, everyone did. Joseph took the chance to clamber to his feet, holding his crushed fingers tightly. At once someone grabbed him and pushed him up towards the boy's table. Tabitha was on the ground in front of it, her blue hair covering her face, arms held behind her back by one of the guests. The leash that had held Slik in place was snapped, and the fairy was nowhere to be seen.

The Boy King had climbed onto the table again. He was pale and wide-eyed, rubbing at his neck where Tabitha's knife had been.

'Enough,' he croaked. 'I've had enough. The revels are finished. All of you go home.'

Lord Wren cleared his throat and glared at Joseph and Tabitha.

'What about these little maggots, your majesty?'

'Feed them to the sharks,' yelled someone.

'Cut them in bits,' called another voice.

'Poison them!'

'Drown them!'

'Stab them and gut them and . . . and . . . eat them!'

The Boy King raised a hand, and silence fell.

'Shut up, all of you,' he said. His voice was quiet, smouldering with rage. 'Lock them away with that ungrateful fish girl. I need to think of something special for them. Something that really, really *hurts*.'

Chapter Eighteen

The wooden door creaked as Newton pushed it open, and the cold evening air made him shiver. Governor Skelmerdale stood on the battlements in a heavy coat, gazing out over the rooftops of Wyrmwood Manor.

'Evening, your honour.'

The governor beckoned but didn't turn round. Newton crossed the flagstones, his old leg injury aching from the climb up the spiral staircase.

As he reached the battlements he was buffeted by wind and his head swam with vertigo. Wyrmwood Manor was high enough as it was, even without the stomach-churning drop down the cliffside below, to

Port Fayt. The town slumbered, quiet and still beneath the deep blue star-flecked sky. The first lanterns had been lit, sending streaks of soft yellow light glimmering across the dark water. At the mouth of the harbour the *Wyvern* rocked at anchor, just where he'd left it. And a little way beyond it, the ghostly shape of the *Justice* bobbed among the waves.

Newton braved a glance at the governor. His short white hair rippled in the wind, and his eyes were watering, but he didn't turn away. He looked so stern, it seemed as though his face had been carved from the same grey rock as the walls.

Tomorrow, the Duke of Garran would come to Wyrmwood Manor. Newton had sent fairies ahead with the news, but he didn't know how the governor had reacted. This silence wasn't especially reassuring.

Of course, he wasn't thrilled about it either. The thought of the League's butchers so close to all the most defenceless Fayters had haunted his dreams the night before. The mothers and the fathers. The children and the elderly. Tabs and Joseph.

He'd wanted to go looking for them as soon as he came ashore, but a squad of blackcoats had been waiting at the docks to meet him and bring him straight here. He just hoped Old Jon was right and they could look after themselves. Old Jon was generally right about most things. If only he was here now . . . But the governor had insisted that Newton come alone.

An imp appeared at Newton's side, wearing the purple velvet livery of the Cockatrice Company and an enormous powdered wig. He held onto the windswept wig with one hand and offered up a silver tray with the other, bearing two delicate glasses of transparent liquid.

'Firewater,' said the governor briskly. 'I'll have none of those fancy Old World wines Governor Wyrmwood was so fond of. I like things plain and simple.'

Newton took a glass and sipped. It scorched his throat, but he held it down. The governor took the second glass, and the imp bowed and hurried away, still clutching his wig.

Skelmerdale knocked back his firewater in one gulp, without so much as a flinch. He fixed his piercing dark eyes on Newton.

'Plain and simple. And this – bringing the Duke of Garran here, into our harbour – this is neither plain nor simple.'

'My apologies, your honour. The man gave me no choice.'

'What does he want?'

'To discuss terms.'

'Bilge.' The governor suddenly drew back his arm

and hurled the glass, sending it spinning out into the night. There was a smash as it struck some unseen part of Wyrmwood Manor.

Newton waited silently for the rage to pass.

'You have heard of this man?' said the governor at last. His voice was calm again.

'Aye.'

'And what do you know of him?'

Too much.

He knew how the Duke liked to set hungry griffins on his prisoners. How he'd once had an elf nobleman strung up in his courtyard and torn apart by magicians. How he wore a red coat to fancy society balls – dyed with the blood of trolls . . .

There were plenty of stories about what the Duke of Garran had done, but none of the man himself. They said he didn't drink. Didn't gamble. Had nothing to do with women. Had no interest in anything besides the persecution of demonspawn.

What did it take to turn a man into such a monster?

And what would such a man do, if he took Port Fayt?

'A little,' he said.

The governor snorted. 'A little. More than a little, I do not doubt. Everyone has heard of him. And I have had the misfortune to meet him too. Make no mistake, Mr Newton. The Duke of Garran appears soft and round and harmless, but it's mere play-acting. On the inside he is a devious, vicious sadist. And you have brought him here. So I will ask you one more time . . .What does he want?'

Newton gazed out at the *Justice* and shook his head.

'I'm sorry. I wish I knew.'

The governor looked for a moment as though he wanted to push Newton over the battlements. *Good luck with that, your honour*. But finally he relaxed and turned back to the town.

'Tomorrow, then. We will find out tomorrow.'

'Aye. Tomorrow.'

Newton didn't like it any more than the governor did. But what choice did they have?

At least we've bought Joseph and Tabitha some time.

He just hoped that was all they needed.

Chapter Nineteen

Tabitha rubbed at the tiny tooth marks on her wrist.

Little scumbag.

She couldn't believe how stupid she'd been. Of *course* Slik was going to betray them. But she'd been so busy worrying about the Boy King that she'd forgotten he was there. If she ever saw that fairy again . . .

Tabitha pulled down her sleeve and looked around, hunting for something to distract her from the pain. They were in a cavern again. But this one was much, much smaller. Big enough for the three of them, a bowl of water and a few rocks, but not much else.

Only a little light filtered through the small barred door. She could see the shadowy shapes of her companions, the glint of their eyes and the long silvery tail of the mermaid. That was about it.

So much for distractions.

'Right,' she said. 'How are we going to get out of here? Any ideas?'

Joseph shook his head. He was still wearing his jester's costume, with the hood and coxcomb pushed back. He'd definitely acted like a clown in the Boy King's cavern. What was he thinking, pouring black-wine everywhere without telling her what he was doing? This whole mess was his fault.

'The door is solid and the lock is new,' said the mermaid. Her accent sounded strange, as though she wasn't used to speaking. 'And in case you didn't notice, I'm a mermaid. I can't exactly run for my life.'

Sarcasm. That's helpful. But Joseph's teeth flashed in a smile. Tabitha suppressed a rush of irritation. Why did he always have to be so . . . *nice* to everyone?

'Thank you for saving me,' he said.

'Don't mention it,' said Tabitha and Pallione, at the same time.

Tabitha shot the mermaid a look. It was difficult to tell in the gloom, but she had a feeling that Pallione was frowning back at her. Thalin knew why. It had been Tabitha who'd attacked the Boy King – probably stopped him from having them executed on the spot.

She was starting to have some serious doubts about this princess.

'I mean, er, thank you both,' said Joseph. 'That is . . . Well, Tabs, remember when I told you about Harry's Shark Pit? It was Pallione who saved me from the shark in there.'

'Is that so?' said Tabitha, sounding colder than she'd intended. 'Well, the important thing is, we're all alive.'

'Why are you here anyway?' said the mermaid. 'And who are you? I'd like to know who's stupid enough to walk into the court of the Boy King, pour blackwine on him and then try to kill him.'

'We're here to rescue *you*,' snapped Tabitha. 'So the least you could do is show a bit of gratitude and help us find a way out of here.'

'Your father wants you back,' said Joseph.

'My father?'

'He sent us to save you. Well, sort of. He captured some of our friends, and if we can get you back to him safely, he'll let them go. And he'll help us Fayters fight our enemies. The League of the Light.'

The mermaid bit her lip.

'My father sent *you* – a mongrel boy and a blue-headed girl-child. Is that all I'm worth to him?' She sounded like she might be about to cry, and for a moment Tabitha almost felt sorry for her. Almost.

'Can we just—?' she began, but Joseph was already speaking.

'How long have they kept you here?' he asked.

Pallione shrugged. 'A couple of weeks. It was worse at Harry's Shark Pit. They locked us up so tight we could barely turn round in the cages.'

'And then there were the fight days. When you never knew who would be coming back with you. If you got any extra room, it was only because your comrade had been—' She stopped abruptly.

Tabitha opened her mouth again, then thought better of it. She could hardly suggest ways to escape after the mermaid had just said that.

'I thought *my* life was hard,' said Joseph.

The mermaid made a sound like a laugh, but without much humour in it.

'And now this. A pair of children come to rescue me. My father rules the very ocean, and this is all he can muster.'

'Funny,' said Tabitha. 'I thought you merfolk didn't

have any magical powers when you're out of the sea. So he wouldn't be able to—'

Pallione waved her hand impatiently. 'That's not the point. The point is, he's too busy with his precious kingdom to care about his own daughter.'

'I've heard stories about him,' said Joseph. 'Is it true he's older than the Ebony Ocean? And that he wrestles sea demons for fun? And—'

'Of course it's not true,' Tabitha interrupted.

'Then what *is* he like?'

'Boring,' said Pallione. 'And strict. Always saying *don't do this* or *don't touch that*.' She paused for a moment, then spoke in a small voice. 'Sometimes, when I was little, he took me to race against dolphins and to find pretty shells on the sea bed. And when I was older, he took me to the harbour to look at Port Fayt. We'd swim up above the surface and watch the big wooden ships coming and going, and the people running around on the docks. Always in a hurry.'

Tabitha snorted. That part was true enough. Pallione scowled at her, confused. She was about to explain when the mermaid spoke again.

'Father used to say that there were good people in Port Fayt, but bad ones too. People who would catch merfolk and be cruel to them. He told me not to swim too close.' There was a quaver in her voice now. 'But what did he expect me to do? He doesn't spend time with me any more, and he doesn't want me to make friends either. He expects me to act like a princess. I don't even know what that means, and . . .'

The mermaid tailed off, glaring at Joseph. He was chuckling.

'What's so funny?' asked Tabitha.

'Sorry,' said Joseph. 'It's just . . . My father used to take me down to the docks at sunset sometimes, to watch for merfolk tails splashing in the bay.' He smiled at Pallione. 'So maybe we were watching you, while you were watching us.'

Tabitha rolled her eyes.

The mermaid just frowned. 'Maybe,' she said. She thought for a few moments. 'That's funny.' She didn't sound convinced.

'Right,' said Tabitha briskly. 'Enough talk. Let's get out of here.'

There was a soft *thunk* as Pallione's tail slapped against the rock she was sitting on.

'No,' she said. 'It's not possible. If it was, I would have already done it without your help.'

Tabitha gritted her teeth. She had known the mermaid less than an hour and was already sick of her. If they hadn't needed the King's help, she'd have been happy to leave Pallione behind.

'Oh really? You said yourself, you can't even walk.'

The mermaid leaned forward. 'Why don't you come over here and say that?'

'Maybe I will.'

There was a scrape of stone as Joseph shifted position.

'I don't know – maybe Tabs is right. We could at least talk about what to do?'

At last the tavern boy was standing up for her, Tabitha thought. Thalin knew, it was the least she deserved. Especially after the stunt he'd pulled with the blackwine.

Pallione lifted her chin. 'Talk, if you must.'

'I say one of us pretends to be sick,' said Tabitha. 'So we yell and scream for help. If we kick up enough of a fuss, someone's bound to come. Then we can whack them over the head and take their keys.'

Silence from her two companions.

'I see,' said the mermaid at last. 'And you don't think they'll guess we're trying to escape?'

Rage boiled up inside Tabitha. She sprang to her feet, her dress swishing as she crossed the cavern in two strides and faced up to the mermaid. Even in the gloom she could make out Pallione's emerald-green eyes and silky white hair. It was true what the merfolk had said. *She is beautiful.* Stuck-up too.

'So you want to die then?'

'Merfolk are not afraid of death.'

'Neither are—'

'Hush,' said Joseph. They both turned to look. He had his pointed ears pressed up against the bars, listening. 'Do you hear something?'

Tabitha and Pallione fell silent.

Footsteps.

Light spilled in through the bars of the door, throwing thick black lines across the cavern. There was a jangle of keys, a scraping of metal as one went into the lock, and a clunk as it turned. Then a creak as the door swung open, and three silhouetted figures stepped inside.

The first two were bully boys with cutlasses hanging from their belts. They stood guard just inside the doorway. The third was a goblin, with a lantern in one hand and a ring of keys in the other. He was dressed in an outfit even more ludicrous than the ones Joseph and Tabitha had on. Large gold hoops dangled from his ears. His yellow coat had purple trimmings and clashed violently with his silver waist-coat, orange breeches and red tricorne hat.

Joseph gasped. Tabitha groaned.

'Well, well, well,' said the goblin. His grin revealed

sharp teeth, and his pale eyes darted from one prisoner to another. 'Long time no see.'

'You know this scum?' asked Pallione.

'Unfortunately, yes,' said Tabitha.

'His name's Jeb,' said Joseph. 'Jeb the Snitch.'

Chapter Twenty

Jeb hadn't changed much. Still smug. Still grinning. Still dressed like a pile of dragon's vomit.

And probably still as reliable as a barrel with no bottom.

Tabitha had never trusted the goblin. Not even in the old days, when he used to help the Demon's Watch by ratting out other crooks. She'd been right as well. In the end he'd betrayed the watchmen and tried to get them all killed by a mad pirate. He was trouble through and through.

'You're Newt's little girl, ain't yer?' said Jeb, stuffing the keys into a pocket. 'What a lovely dress.' He winked at her and Tabitha had to suppress a shudder.

'And you . . .' He turned to Joseph. 'You're the little bleeder who stole that wooden spoon off me. Might've known you'd end up with the Watch. Slimy do-gooder like you.'

'What are you doing here?' Joseph asked. 'Are you working for the Boy King now?'

'Seems so, don't it? Bit of honest work for once, so to speak.' Jeb's grin grew wider. 'Course, this here's so much fun it hardly counts as work.'

'What do you want, greyskin?' spat Pallione. Tabitha had to hand it to her – the mermaid had guts.

Jeb narrowed his pale eyes at her. 'Straight to business, is it? All right then. We're carting you lot off to the banqueting cavern. His glorious highness has decided what to do with you.'

He clicked his fingers at one of the bully boys and the man stepped outside, returning a moment later trundling a wheelbarrow.

Pallione eyed it with obvious distaste.

'That's for rotten vegetables. Not a princess.'

'Is that so?' said Jeb. 'Maybe yer should've thought of that before crossing his supreme excellency. No fancy carriages for you, my dear.'

'What . . . er . . . What *has* he decided to do with us?' asked Joseph. Tabitha saw that he was wringing his hands.

'Don't want to spoil the surprise,' said Jeb. 'But let's just say it involves a big fire, some fiddly harnesses and a rather unusual use of a spit. Lord Wren says it were one of Zargath the Sorcerer's favourite execution methods. So yer won't be disappointed.' He sniggered, and the bully boys joined in. 'Now, don't want to keep his majestic royalness waiting, do we?'

The bully boys took hold of Pallione, one snatching her tail and the other grabbing her arms from behind. The mermaid struggled and cried out, but she wasn't strong enough, and they dumped her into the wheelbarrow. Tabitha tensed, ready to fight, but Jeb produced a pistol from his coat pocket and levelled it at her. It was a strange-looking thing with four different barrels clustered together, all made of metal.

'Don't look so surprised, my dear. This little beauty was made by a friend of mine. So's yer can kill four men instead of just one.'

Tabitha shrugged, doing her best to stay calm. 'I'm surprised, all right. Surprised that you *have* any friends.'

Jeb chuckled and ran his tongue over his sharp teeth. His ears twitched.

'Well then. This here's going to surprise you even more.'

The goblin spun round in a whirl of yellow coat-tails.

BANG!

The nearest bully boy jerked and slumped against the open cell door, hands clawing at his throat, blood foaming down his blue velvet jacket.

Tabitha's brain was working in slow motion, trying to keep up with what her eyes were seeing. Had Jeb just shot his own man? And now he was turning, aiming the smoking pistol at the other bully boy as it whirred, rotating and locking the second barrel into position . . .

Quick as lightning, Pallione snatched the cutlass from the dying man's belt and swung it to point at Jeb's throat. The goblin twisted, levelling the pistol at her instead. The last bully boy seized the moment, turned tail and shot out of the cell, his boots pounding and echoing down the corridor.

'You stupid fish girl,' snarled Jeb. 'Now he's going to raise the alarm, ain't he?'

Tabitha sprang forward, piling into Jeb and knocking him flying. His lantern skittered away across the cavern floor, along with the pistol. She scrambled to hold the goblin down but he lashed out, catching her a stinging blow on the mouth and knocking her sideways.

'Stop,' said someone. Tabitha looked up to see Joseph holding the pistol with both hands, aiming it at Jeb. The weapon shook. But at this range even he couldn't miss.

'You bilge-brains,' groaned Jeb, climbing to his feet and dusting off his hat. 'Can't you see I'm trying to help you escape?'

Tabitha would have thought she was dreaming if her jaw wasn't hurting so badly. There had to be some mistake. Jeb the Snitch was helping them? What next – talking fish? Modest magicians? 'What's going on?' she demanded.

Jeb gave an elaborate sigh. 'Do you want me to explain,' he said, as though he was talking to a child throwing a tantrum, 'or do you want to get out of here in one piece?'

Somewhere in the distance there were shouts, and running footsteps.

'They're coming,' said Jeb. 'And I know the way out.'

Tabitha looked at Joseph, but he was just gawping. *No help at all.* She tried to think it through. Should they trust Jeb the Snitch? She'd rather stick her head in a shark's mouth. But then again, she wasn't too keen on the sound of Zargath's favourite execution method either.

A door opened and closed, and the footsteps grew louder.

'Come on!' snapped Pallione. 'We don't have a choice. Or do you want to be roasted to death?'

'Fine,' Tabitha snapped back. 'But only until we get out of here. And he's pushing the wheelbarrow.' She picked up the lantern, which was somehow still lit, and marched out of the door.

Jeb replaced his tricorne hat and winked at her. 'You won't regret this, darling.' He took the wheelbarrow handles and trundled Pallione into the corridor. The mermaid clung onto her cutlass, leaning out of the wheelbarrow to check that no one was coming. Joseph followed, the pistol still trained on Jeb.

There was no time to lose the dress. Tabitha lifted her skirts and led the way down the tunnel at a trot. The floor was sandy, the walls rough and rocky, lit by flaming torches set in old-fashioned brackets. Even here it was obvious that the Boy King had a taste for the dramatic. The wheelbarrow rumbled behind her, Jeb panting and puffing as he heaved it along.

'Been scoffing a lot of seaweed lately, have we?' he muttered.

'Mind your own business, you despicable goblin,' retorted Pallione. 'Or you'll get a faceful of tail.'

'Quiet, both of you,' Tabitha told them.

They twisted and turned, following directions from Jeb – who seemed to have the layout of the caverns inside his head. Tabitha hated to admit it, but they would have been lost without him. Once or twice they heard footsteps and shouts in the distance, but only for a moment.

A cold breeze began to whistle down the passageways, and the flickering torches were replaced by natural moonlight. Tabitha shivered. Finally she was glad of the extra layer the dress provided.

They turned a corner and were met by a blast of freezing air. Ahead was a short flight of steps leading up to a barred door, the starry sky twinkling beyond it.

'Ain't been used in dragons' years,' said Jeb, setting down the wheelbarrow. 'Good job we can unlock it, eh?' He reached into his pocket and drew out the ring of keys, jangling them and grinning. He picked out the right one and passed it to Tabitha. 'Now, who's going to help carry this fat fish girl?' He ducked just in time to avoid a vicious swipe from Pallione's tail.

Tabitha unlocked the door and heaved it open. It was practically rusted shut, and it took all her strength to budge it. Then she lifted the front of the wheelbarrow and helped Jeb heave it up the steps. Joseph brought up the rear, his eyes wide, coxcomb sagging from side to side as he cast anxious glances behind them.

They came out onto a steep hillside street, still in the Flagstaff Quarter, judging by the fancy houses. Tabitha could see most of Port Fayt spread out below, the harbour front glimmering, staining the black sky with a haze of lantern light. High up to her left was Wyrmwood Manor, where the governor had held his council of war. She closed her eyes and sucked the cold night air into her lungs. She hadn't realized until now how musty it had been in the caverns.

'Where now?' asked Joseph.

'To the docks of course,' said Pallione, pointing her cutlass downhill. 'And quickly. You came to rescue me, didn't you? Just take me to the water and I can swim back to the King's Rock.'

'All very well for you,' said Jeb. 'But we need to get out of this town too. That's if we don't want to be burned alive. Better wait till dawn, when we can find a ship.'

Tabitha felt herself getting angry again. 'Shut your trap, Jeb. You can't tell us what to do. Why in all the Ebony Ocean are you here, anyway? You were working for the Boy King ten minutes ago.'

In the darkness she saw his teeth flash in a smile. 'That gold-coated turd? Not on your life. Thought you knew by now – Jeb the Snitch only ever works for himself.'

Pallione slapped her tail against the side of the wheelbarrow. 'What difference does it make? Why don't you let me go?'

'She's right,' said Joseph. 'We need to get her out of Port Fayt. It's the least we can do.'

Tabitha ground her teeth in frustration. For a tavern boy, Joseph had a lot of opinions. He'd been in the Watch for barely a fortnight, and now he seemed to think he knew everything. Well, he didn't. He didn't know what he was talking about.

'We can't go down to the docks,' she explained. 'We need a ship, and there won't be one at this time of night. Besides, we can't just let the mermaid go. We need her father to know it was us who rescued her. Otherwise he might not release Frank and Paddy and Hal, and he definitely won't help us fight the League.'

'You didn't rescue me,' said Pallione. 'I rescued myself. With help from this horrible greyskin.'

'That's not—'

'Are we going to stand around jawing all night,' Jeb interrupted, 'or are we going to get out of here? The Boy King's bully boys'll be after us soon enough, and I don't fancy sticking around for them.'

Tabitha turned on him. 'We're getting out of here all right, but you're not coming with us.'

Something in Jeb's smile changed. It was suddenly sinister, not cheerful. 'Oh, I'm coming, my dear. Unless you want me to send the Boy King straight to Bootles' Pie Shop . . . See, unlike that little brat, I know you're a watchman. So I know just where to find you. And those nice old trolls.'

Tabitha's heartbeat quickened, and she snatched the pistol out of Joseph's hand. *Still three barrels left unfired*. That meant she could kill Jeb. Three times over. But she couldn't do it – not in cold blood. Another tide of helpless anger surged up, threatening to engulf her. *What would Newt do*? If only he were here, he'd—

No. He wasn't here. And anyway, it didn't matter because they didn't have a choice. Jeb was the slimiest, least trustworthy scumbag in all of Port Fayt. But right now, they had to take him with them. She held up the lantern so she could see his pale eyes, but they gave nothing away.

'I don't understand,' said Joseph. 'Why do you want to come?'

'Got my reasons.'

'Yes, but what are th—?'

Shouts from the caverns below. Joseph flinched

and Tabitha tightened her grip on the pistol until her knuckles were white. The Boy King's men were getting closer. And Jeb the Snitch kept smiling.

'We'd better get to Bootles',' she said. 'And quickly.'

The mermaid scowled at her, but Tabitha ignored it.

'Right you are,' said Jeb, picking up the handles again. 'Knew yer'd see sense.' They set off, the wheelbarrow rumbling on the cobblestones as they hurried down the street.

Tabitha tried to calm her beating heart. Tomorrow they'd be out of Port Fayt. They'd take Pallione back to her father, free the Demon's Watch and bring the merfolk over to their side. They'd be rid of the mermaid and, better still, rid of Jeb. She couldn't wait. They'd already had their fingers burned with that two-faced fairy Slik, and she wasn't about to let this slimy goblin make fools of them too.

What in Thalin's name was he doing helping them?

It niggled at her, like a cut finger dipped in seawater.

The tavern is almost empty. After all, this is a town at war.

He pushes back the hood of his cloak and takes a seat in the gloom amid the clatter of tankards and the soft glow of the lantern light. The Legless Mermaid smells of firewater, of fish and sweat. The stool he sits on is roughly made and encrusted with filth, and the table is no better. It is probably for the best that it is so dark inside.

An impish child in an apron scurries up to him, small and pink-skinned, with a big nose and slightly pointed ears. Daemonium Minus. *A textbook specimen. There is a hunted look in the child's eyes, but it is not scared of him. It should be.*

'What can I get you? We've got eels for dinner. And for grog, how about Lightly's Finest Bowelbuster? Mr Lightly's the landlord, you see.' He nods towards a big aproned man behind the bar, swathed in fat, his face ruddy, his eyes small and cruel.

He smiles. Now he understands that hunted look.

'Grog,' he says, and the word feels foul in his mouth.

As the imp leaves, he takes in the other customers, few as they are. Mostly old, broken things, not fit to go into battle with the Fayter fleet. A dwarf so fat he can scarcely imagine it is able to walk. Daemonium Crassum. *An old goblin woman, uglier than a demon's backside.* Daemonium Cinereum. *A pair of elves, drunk and bleary-eyed, arguing over a game of dice.* Daemonium Pulchrum.

He licks his lips, savouring the squalor of it all. He has seen many demonspawn before. But still their proximity sends a little thrill through his body. These twisted creatures, so like humans – and yet, so unlike them. Major Turnbull told him not to come tonight. Told him to stay aboard the Justice, *where he'd be safe. But he couldn't resist a little excursion in secret.*

The imp hurries to his table and sets down a dull, battered old tankard. He raises it to his nose and sniffs. A strange, spicy odour, mingled with the sharp scent of strong firewater. Disgusting. He lowers it again, untouched.

The child is still waiting – for payment, he supposes. He draws out his pouch and hands it a half-ducat. As the imp takes the money, he studies its face. Its overgrown eyes, misshapen nose, too-pink skin.

'Are you happy, imp?' he asks.

'Beg pardon?'

'Are you happy here in Port Fayt?'

A faraway look comes into the child's eyes.

'I used to work for a carpenter. Mr Boggs. But then he was . . . Then he died. Now I work here, for Mr Lightly.'

'You didn't answer my question.'

'No. Sorry, sir.' The imp thinks for a moment, trying to decide what to say. When it speaks, it's in a lowered voice, so no one else can hear. 'It's a hard life, sir. But better here than the Old World. I'll bring your change.' And it hurries away with the half-ducat.

Better here indeed. But not for long.

'Oi, mate.'

He turns and sees that one of the elves is staring at him – or at least trying to, through a haze of grog.

'Wanna play dice?'

This place is turning his stomach. He rises, eyes fixed on the door.

'Hey! I said, wanna play dice? You deaf?'

He pauses a moment. Inside his cloak, his fingers curl around the hilt of his sabre.

'I said, ARE YOU DEAF? Stuck-up walrus.'

Its friends snigger.

He closes his eyes and draws a deep breath before opening them again.

'I heard you the first time,' he says quietly. 'Wretched creature.'

'What?'

Five years he spent, studying fencing at Taggart's School of Blades. The best academy in the Old World. With his left hand, he brushes aside his cloak. With his right, he draws the sabre. It flashes in the lantern light. Four steps, he estimates. On the first he locks eyes with the elf. On the second, he draws back his sword arm. On the third, he kicks aside the stool standing between them. And on the fourth, he lunges, throwing his whole body into it. Then pulls back, fast and clean.

The elf slumps to the floor. So drunk it didn't even have time to look surprised.

The clatter of tankards has ceased. All conversations cut short. Every degenerate human and demonspawn in the tavern stares at him.

He runs a thumb along the blade, wiping away the few drops of blood he has spilled. Then he slides it back into its scabbard and pulls his hood up over his face.

'Goodnight, gentlemen,' he says. 'I'll be seeing you all again. Very soon.'

PART THREE
Of Seraphs and Demons

Chapter Twenty-one

Mr Bootle peered out at them, the light of the lantern throwing his green face into craggy relief. In his nightgown he looked a bit like an oversized ghost, and the wide eyes and gaping mouth added to the impression. Joseph couldn't blame him. It wasn't every day a mermaid in a wheelbarrow turned up on your doorstep.

They trundled Pallione into the pie shop, and Mrs Bootle set about putting food on the table. The mermaid princess insisted that she should be put onto a chair like everyone else, and the elderly trolls carried her between them and delicately set her down. There were pies, gravy and smashed-up patatas for Joseph,

Tabitha and Jeb, and raw fish for Pallione. She pulled it apart with her fingers and wolfed it down, casting suspicious glances at her companions.

Tabitha's food went untouched. She sat frowning, the multi-barrelled pistol resting beside her plate, pointed none too subtly at Jeb.

'All right,' she said, as soon as the Bootles had disappeared into the back rooms. 'Time for you to explain. What are you doing here?'

Jeb burped and pushed his plate away, licking gravy from his fingers.

'Can't an honest goblin lend a hand to some old friends? What's the world coming to?' He winked at Joseph.

'Very funny,' said Tabitha. 'And by the way, there are man-eating sea demons I'm better friends with than you.' She fingered the hilt of her favourite knife, sliding it a little way out of its sheath, then back in again. Joseph thought she seemed a little calmer now that she'd got her bandolier back. She'd slung it on the moment they got through the door.

'All right. Cards on the table,' said Jeb. He leaned forward, pale eyes darting left and right, as though checking that no one was listening in. 'Truth is, I want the same as you. Get this mermaid back to her father.'

Tabitha snorted. 'You'll have to do better than that.'

Jeb spread his hands. 'Think about it. Her pa's the most powerful cove in all the ocean. Who wouldn't want to be the one to bring his daughter back?'

Pallione spat a half-chewed morsel of fish at him. 'If you think my father will reward you, you are mistaken.'

'I wouldn't be so sure, fish-tail. You merfolk are honourable types. Especially fogeys like yer old pa. I reckon he'll give me my due.'

'We don't need you,' said Joseph. This was the goblin who'd got him thrown into the shark pit. The one who'd tried to have the entire Demon's Watch killed. And now he wanted to help them?

'Now, that's where you're wrong, mate,' said Jeb, wagging a long grey finger. 'How d'you reckon you'll be getting out of Port Fayt? Stroll down to the docks and hop on a ship?' He threw back his head and cackled with laughter. 'Face it, yer haven't thought this through. Skelmerdale's taken nearly every vessel in the harbour to fight the League. But I can get us one. Which means you *do* need me.'

Joseph glanced at Tabitha, who was busy scowling at the Snitch. He had a nasty feeling the goblin was right.

'Tomorrow morning we'll head down to the docks,' said Jeb. 'I know a captain who'll take us, for a price. Then fish girl will have her pa back, you watchmen'll have whatever it is you get out of doing the right thing, and I'll have my reward.'

'I'm not going on your stinking ship,' said Pallione. 'I'll swim. I'm sick of dry land.' She glared at the wheelbarrow sitting in the corner, as if this was all its fault.

Joseph leaned across to Tabitha, keeping his voice low.

'What do you think?'

'What do I think? I think I don't trust him. I think I'd rather trust a pirate with a sack of ducats.'

'Me too. But we *do* need a ship, don't we? And the Boy King will be after him as well as us. Maybe we're in this together.'

Tabitha rolled her eyes. 'Joseph, we're not on his side, remember? He's scum. We should probably just kill him.'

Joseph didn't know what to say to that. Tabitha glared at him, then at last gave a long, loud sigh. 'Fine. You can help us with the ship. But until then, we'll be watching you. Try anything and you're dead, understand?'

Jeb grinned, and his eyes twinkled. Something about that smile gave Joseph a very bad feeling indeed.

* * *

Wind rattled the door of Bootles' Pie Shop, and the night cold seeped into the serving room. Joseph was alone. He pulled the blanket tighter around his shoulders and edged his stool closer to the dying embers of the fire.

Of course, he wasn't really alone – it just felt like it. His three companions lay huddled on a heap of straw in the corner of the room. He'd been looking forward to one of the big soft beds in Mr and Mrs Bootle's guest rooms, but Tabitha had insisted they stay down here in the serving room for the night. That way, if the Boy King did track them down, it would be easier to escape. Not to mention the fact that they could keep an eye on Jeb the Snitch.

Joseph had been on watch for an hour now. One more hour to go, and then he could wake up Tabitha and get some sleep himself. But he wasn't tired. Not even close. His fingers drummed lightly on the ancient blunderbuss resting across his knees, in time with the snores coming from the corner.

The mermaid had been rescued. Now all they had to do was get her back to that rocky island, and the Demon's Watch would be free. They'd join up with Newton again, and the merfolk would fight with them against the League. But all the same, he couldn't relax with the Snitch lying there. He kept running it over in his head, trying to work out how to get rid of the goblin. Maybe they could leave him locked up at the pie shop . . . But that would put the Bootles in danger. Besides, they needed that ship.

Joseph sighed and glanced over at the sleeping Pallione. She looked peaceful for once, her white hair spilling over the straw in a plait, her tail flicking occasionally, like the wagging of a dog's tail. Joseph had always thought his life had been tough, but he'd never been locked up like an animal and made to fight in front of hundreds of baying Fayters. That quaver in her voice when she spoke of her father – that was the only sign of weakness he'd seen in her.

She must miss him. Though it seemed like she'd never admit it.

Tabitha had rolled over to face the mermaid – as if they were friends, deep in conversation. In fact she'd hardly said a word to Pallione since they got back to Bootles'. After dinner she'd sat by the fire on her own, sharpening her knives and scowling at Jeb the Snitch as he scoffed the leftovers. Once or twice, Joseph could have sworn she'd been glaring at him too. Meanwhile Pallione had plaited her hair and told Joseph stories about her father. She couldn't stop talking about him, even though most of that was complaining about how little attention he paid her. Joseph would have given anything to be able to speak to his own father again.

He held his hands closer to the embers, hoping for a little extra warmth.

His mother had let him plait her hair when he was very little. She'd taught him early one morning, at the velvethouse where she worked, while the hot velvetbean was brewing. He'd had to stand on a stool to reach.

'First the left one goes into the middle,' his mother told him. 'Then the right one. Then start over again. Keep going.'

Joseph couldn't believe that such a simple thing could make a plait so neat. Then the other velvethouse maids had come bustling into the room, and his mother had lifted him down from the stool. They crowded around him, cooing over him and making a fuss. They meant well, but Joseph was young, and he was scared. He'd called out for his mother, and of course she appeared at once, her face a picture of concern.

'It's all right, Joseph,' she told him. 'It's all right.' And then Joseph had known that it really *was* all right, if his mother said so.

But then, later . . .

It was lunch time, and Spottington's stopped serving velvetbean for an hour so the maids and the owner could eat. Joseph's mother had put him on the stool and told him to wait there while she fetched them some bread and cheese.

As soon as she was out of the room, the maids crowded around him again.

'Poor dear,' said one. 'It must be hard.' Joseph didn't know what she meant. 'Here.' She pressed a half-ducat into his hand. 'Your ma must be having a tough time on velvethouse wages. You buy yourself some sweets.'

'If only you had a papa,' sighed another of the maids.

Joseph had shaken his head. 'I *do* have a papa,' he said.

The maid laughed. 'Of course you do. Everyone does. I meant, well . . .' Her eyes flicked to her feet, as though she was unsure what to say. 'I meant one who lives with you and your ma.'

There was a commotion behind the maid, who turned to see that Joseph's mother had returned. The bread and cheese trembled in her hands. Her face was red and flustered. It was the first time Joseph had ever seen her like that.

'Joseph's father lives with us,' she said to the maid, and there was anger in her voice, barely suppressed.

'He lives with us, and he's alive and well, and he works, thank you very much.' She hurried over to Joseph and made him open his fingers. 'Give that back, Joseph.'

He'd done so at once. He had no idea why she was so cross. He'd told her he was sorry, feeling as if he was about to cry.

At once the anger fled her face, and she knelt down in front of him.

'No, Joseph. You mustn't be sorry. You mustn't ever be sorry.'

'Oi!'

Joseph almost leaped out of his stool. His fingers closed around the blunderbuss and he swung it to his shoulder, taking aim.

Jeb the Snitch was standing by the fireplace in front of him, one finger against his lips. His yellow coat was rumpled from sleeping in it, and a bit of straw stuck out from behind one ear.

'Watch it,' the goblin hissed. 'You'll wake up the fish girl. And that vicious little friend of yours.'

'What do you want?'

Jeb shrugged. 'Just a little chat.' He pulled up a stool beside the fireplace, rubbing his hands and trying to warm them on the near-cold embers. Slowly Joseph lowered the blunderbuss.

'What was that you were singing, eh?' asked Jeb.

'Singing?'

'Aye. Under yer breath. Something about scrubbing dishes, weren't it?'

'It's nothing. Just a song I learned when I was young.' He hadn't realized what he was doing.

'Learned it from your ma, did yer?'

The words hit Joseph like a punch to the face. 'How did you know that?'

Jeb just smiled, firelight glinting off his pointed teeth.

'So. Been a while since our paths have crossed, mongrel, ain't it? And now you're a watchman, are yer?' He nodded at the shark tattoo on Joseph's arm. 'You done good for a tavern mongrel, that's sure enough.'

Joseph shrugged.

'And now yer still off adventuring, taking what's not yours. What happened to that black velvet package anyway? No, don't tell me. Heard it turned out to be a wand. That skinny magician of yours has it now, I'll bet. What a waste. Thalin knows how many ducats I could've got for it.' He sighed, picked up a poker and prodded the coals, sending orange sparks dancing.

Joseph tightened his grip on the blunderbuss. 'Why are you here, anyway?' he asked. 'Really.'

'I already told you, mongrel. Ducats. It's always about ducats with me. Or whatever it is them fish folk use instead. Reckon they'll have something worth my while.' He cast a glance at the mermaid, who was frowning in her sleep. 'Poor lass, can't stop talking about her pa. All lost without him. 'Course, you'd know about that, wouldn't yer?'

Joseph's ears twitched. He racked his brains, tried to remember if he'd told the Snitch about his parents.

He hadn't.

'Thing is, you can't see your pa again so easy, can yer? But I wonder what you'd give if you could.'

'What are you saying?'

The goblin held his hands up. 'Nothing, nothing. Just wondering, is all. Let's say your pa was still alive, and—'

'He's not.'

'Is that so?' Jeb's pale eyes sparkled. 'Think about it. Six years ago a blackcoat came to your home, told yer ma that old Elijah had been murdered. Killed by humans, just for being a goblin. You ain't seen him since. But you ain't seen his body neither.'

Silence.

Joseph stared at him. The room was spinning, and he felt sick. 'Shut up,' he said. 'Don't talk about my parents.'

'Just trying to help, mate.'

'No you're not.' He raised the blunderbuss, his hands trembling so that it shook all over the place. 'My parents are dead. How do you—?'

'Recognized that song you were singing,' said Jeb. 'That bilge about scrubbing dishes. You sing it all the time, in case yer hadn't noticed. Just like your ma did. And there ain't too many mongrels like you in Port Fayt.'

Joseph tried to think clearly. 'So you knew my father. So what? It doesn't mean he's alive. You're just trying to—'

'What's going on?'

Joseph must have been speaking louder than he realized, because Tabitha was wide awake and on her feet. Her hair was dishevelled and she held a knife in one hand and Jeb's revolving pistol in the other. Both were pointing at the Snitch.

'This bilge rat was . . . He was . . .'

'Calm down.'

Joseph closed his eyes and drew in a deep breath. If Tabs was telling him to calm down, he must have crossed a line. He gestured at the Snitch with his blunderbuss. 'He says my father's alive.'

'Aye,' said the goblin. 'It's true.'

Tabitha's eyes widened for just a moment. Then she relaxed.

'So what? He'll say anything to get what he wants. You know that.'

Joseph felt a strange surge of emotions. Anger at the Snitch, but also at Tabs. Relief, but disappointment too. He took another deep breath.

'I know,' he said. 'You're right. I mean, of course I don't believe him.'

'Whatever you say, mate,' said Jeb. He stretched and yawned. 'Reckon I'll turn in, anyhow. Been a long day.' He gave Joseph a wink and headed back to his bed on the straw.

Tabitha sheathed her knife and headed for the empty stool. 'My turn to take watch,' she said, as though nothing had happened. 'You get some sleep.'

Joseph handed her the blunderbuss. He was still shaking. He found an empty space in the corner, lay down and pulled a blanket over himself.

'Actually, Joseph. You don't, er . . . You don't have to go and sleep right away,' said Tabitha stiffly. 'We could talk a bit. If you like.'

Talk? Joseph didn't think she'd ever wanted to talk before.

'I – I can't wait to get out of here,' she said. 'Back to Newt and the others.' She cast a glance at the mermaid, still sleeping peacefully on the straw. 'How about you?'

'Me too.'

'I keep thinking about them, stuck on that rock. And Newt, going into battle. Do you think they'll be all right?'

'Me too.'

She glared at him suddenly.

'I mean . . . yes. Sorry. What was the question?'

The truth was, he didn't want to talk. He wanted to think.

There was an awkward silence.

'Well then,' said Tabitha briskly. 'Goodnight.' The dying fire was reflected in her grey eyes. It might have been a trick of the light, but for a moment Joseph thought they were filmed with moisture. She turned away at once, holding onto the blunderbuss like a little child with a doll.

''Night,' he said. And he closed his eyes, grateful to be alone with his thoughts.

Of course he didn't believe the Snitch. He wasn't an idiot. But still the goblin's words ran round and round his head.

Let's say your pa was still alive . . .

Even if it wasn't true, the Snitch knew *something*. He'd recognized the song Joseph's mother sang; the one she'd made up herself. The only people who knew it were Joseph, his mother and his father.

Then again, everything was a trick with Jeb. Each time he seemed to be helping, he was really just helping himself. So what did he want from Joseph? Why tell him his father was alive? Was it just to hurt him?

He sighed and turned over. If only he could ask more questions . . . But he couldn't. Not with Tabitha there. She'd get angry and tell him he was being ridiculous.

Anyway, she was right. The Snitch was a liar.

Wasn't he?

Chapter Twenty-two

The door opened and men in white began to file into the library of Wyrmwood Manor. First a young magician, red fireballs embroidered on his shoulders. Then two officers with swords jangling on their hips. They looked so ordinary, just like the humans who lived in Fayt. Except for those white uniforms.

Next came the slender, fair-haired officer whom Newton half recognized, with the heavy two-handed sword strapped to her back. Last of all, the Duke of Garran, delicate and precise in his movements. He removed his tricorne as he entered and smoothed down his grey hair with pink fingers. He looked relaxed. Peaceful, even.

On the inside he is a devious, vicious sadist.

Newton cast a quick glance to his side. Morning sunlight filtered through the windows, glinting off the silver on Colonel Derringer's lapels. The elf looked calm, smiling as usual, one hand resting on the hilt of his sword. Governor Skelmerdale didn't look calm at all. He was seated in front of the map table on a straight-backed wooden chair, hands glued to the arm rests, glaring at his guests with all the welcome of a dragon that had just spotted a would-be hero trying to steal its treasure.

Newton cleared his throat, ignoring a twinge of pain from his stitched-up arm wound. The League was here now, and they had to keep this civil. If anyone lost their temper, nothing good would come of it.

'Welcome to Port Fayt, your grace,' he said.

A blackcoat came forward from the side of the room, placing a second straight-backed chair for the Duke to sit on. He did so, resting his hat on his knee and re-arranging his cuffs. His strange colourless eyes swept around the room, appraising everyone and everything in sight.

'Your grace,' Newton continued, 'allow me to introduce Governor Skelmerdale.'

'We are acquainted,' said the governor. His voice sounded strained, as if it was all he could do not to leap out of his chair and stab the other man with a paper knife.

'Indeed,' said the Duke of Garran. 'On my last visit, I believe you told me that Port Fayt would never submit to the way of the Light. That we of the League are murderers. You see' – he brushed invisible dust from his hat – 'I told you I have a good memory, Mr Skelmerdale.'

'Governor,' replied Skelmerdale.

'I beg your pardon?'

'I am *Governor* Skelmerdale.'

Newton cleared his throat again. 'Shall we get down to business, your grace?'

The Duke of Garran gave a curt nod.

'Well, Mr Skelmerdale. My position is this. Port Fayt will submit to the way of the Light, whether you like it or not. Your colleague here has sent fairies to spy on our fleet. No doubt he has conveyed to you the gravity of your situation?'

'Indeed.'

'However, the League is prepared to make allowances. All humans in Port Fayt will be free to stay and live here under our protection. You, Mr Skelmerdale, may even remain as governor, despite your rather unfortunate temper. There will be no battle. No bloodshed. No—'

'What about the other Fayters?' said the governor.

'Others?'

'The trolls. The imps. The dwarves.'

'The elves,' added Derringer.

A cloud passed over the Duke's face. He examined his fingernails. 'You know what will happen to them. We must bring light into the darkness.'

Newton tensed, in case he had to grab Skelmerdale and hold him back. But instead the governor let out a snort of laughter. 'You came all the way here to tell us this?'

The Duke sighed and massaged his brow. 'Must you be so foolish? Look around you.' He swept out a pink hand, taking in the whole room. 'Imagine this library, burning. The books. The furniture. *The people.* And if you are stubborn, Mr Skelmerdale, this will happen to all of Port Fayt – humans and demonspawn alike.'

'You're forgetting something,' said Colonel Derringer. 'We might win.'

The League officers smiled. All except the tall blonde woman. Her mouth was set in a hard line, just like on the *Wyvern*, when her coat had been stained with blood.

'Please,' said the Duke of Garran. 'Don't let your imagination run away with you.' His gaze settled on something. He got to his feet and stepped lightly across the room to the podium with the glass case on top. 'May I?' Without waiting for an answer he lifted the lid and drew out the sword from inside. Its long, slender blade gleamed in the sunlight. The white starstones sparkled in the silver hilt.

'The Sword of Corin the Bold,' said Newton. 'It belonged to Governor Wyrmwood.'

'Indeed?' The Duke stepped into the centre of the room, swung the blade once, twice, experimentally. He tossed it into his other hand and flicked his wrist, slicing the air and sending dust motes dancing. Newton was surprised by the Duke's skill. He had thought this was a man who got others to do his fighting for him.

The Duke of Garran brought the blade to rest, point down on the carpet, hand resting on the hilt. He sighed.

'Such a pleasure,' he said dreamily. 'There is nothing in all the Old World so fine as a good sword. Don't you agree?' He looked at Newton expectantly.

'Indeed,' said Colonel Derringer stiffly, as if it was he who'd been asked.

'The balance. The weight. The singing of the blade,' the Duke went on, ignoring Derringer. 'A true joy.'

'Don't use them,' said Newton. It wasn't right,

talking like this to the enemy. And talking about fighting at that.

'Ah,' said the Duke. He was smiling strangely, as if he knew something Newton didn't, and was enjoying it. 'Too many bad memories, perhaps?'

'What do you mean?'

'Nothing at all.'

The strange smile was gone, and he took the sword by the hilt and passed it over, blade dangling downwards. As Newton grasped it, the Duke locked his other hand around Newton's wrist, pulling back the sleeve.

'As I thought . . .' he said.

Newton felt his face getting hot. The marks on his wrists, still red and raw after all these years, were plain for all to see. Everyone was leaning in, Fayters and League alike. He caught the eye of the fair-haired woman. She was watching him with a curious expression.

'Manacles,' the Duke explained. 'Your captain here has spent time in our zephyrum mines in Garran. A long time, judging by these marks.' He looked up into Newton's face, pale eyes studying his features. 'It's no work for a human, labouring in the darkness, hunting for the magical metal. But then, you're not really human at all, are you? There is ogre blood in your veins. *Daemonium Turpe*. I can see it in your face. Such a shame, because otherwise you seem to be a fine specimen of humanity.'

Newton felt his grip tighten on the hilt of the Sword of Corin. *Stay calm*. What was it he'd said to himself earlier? *If anyone lost their temper, nothing good would come of it*.

The Duke smiled, and Newton's knuckles went white around the hilt.

'A fascinating twist of fate. Corin the Bold would never have dreamed that such a creature would one day hold his sword. A mongrel like you, if you'll forgive the expression. A refugee from the mines. I wonder what he might say . . . Little enough, I imagine. In the stories, Corin was never a man of words. He was a fighter. A killer. A slayer of trolls and a scourge of goblins. A man who—'

Suddenly there was nothing but rage, blotting out everything else. Newton slammed his left palm into the Duke's chest, sending him staggering backwards. Pain stabbed at the wound in his arm but it didn't matter. He spun the blade upright, brought it slicing down at the man's head. He was going to kill this cockroach. This scum. But instead of hitting home, there was a clash of metal and his blade juddered, the vibrations shaking his arm and somehow coursing through his whole body, so hard that he almost let go.

Standing in front of the Duke was the tall woman with the blonde hair, in a fighting stance, her huge blade drawn and locked against the Sword of Corin. A curl of hair had escaped from her ponytail and hung in front of her face, and she glared at Newton from behind it – steel in her hands and steel in her eyes. She shoved, and Newton had to step back to regain his balance. He hadn't expected such strength from her.

Who was she?

'I don't believe I introduced Major Turnbull,' said the Duke of Garran. He was fussing with his coat where Newton had touched it, making sure that it was still perfectly white. 'Of course, it's possible you've met before. For many years Turnbull lived in Wyborough, in Garran. Above the mines.'

Wyborough. Turnbull. The names stirred distant memories.

Suddenly Newton saw the woman's face differently. Not the face of an adult, but of a little girl, blonde and smiling, her hair in pigtails. That was how he'd known her. Governor Turnbull of Wyborough had overseen the mining of zephyrum. And this woman before him was Alice. The governor's daughter.

He felt dizzy.

She couldn't have been more than ten years old the last time he saw her. Clinging to her mother's skirts and sucking her thumb as she watched her father inspect the miners.

She wasn't sucking her thumb now, that was for sure.

Out of the corner of his eye, Newton saw that the Duke was smiling. Again the urge welled up to attack him, stab him, hurt him . . .

There was a hand on his shoulder.

'Mr Newton,' said Governor Skelmerdale gently. 'Put up that sword.'

Slowly the rage washed out of him, like bathwater down the drain. He was left with something else, cold and hard. *Anger*. The memory of the mines burned inside him, impossible to ignore now the Duke had reminded him. He stepped back, lowering the sword as he did so, the pain in his arm subsiding to a dull ache.

'I'm sorry,' he said tightly.

Skelmerdale nodded and turned to the Duke of Garran. 'Is there anything else you wish to discuss? If not, I suggest you go back to your ships at once. There will be no agreement, unless it is for the League to return to the Old World in peace.'

The Duke of Garran shook his head, no longer smiling. 'I'm afraid that will not happen.'

Alice Turnbull sheathed her sword in one fluid movement. Newton felt a shiver run down his spine. She'd been a shy child, but happy. Whatever had happened to her since then, there was no trace of the quiet little girl left in those cold eyes.

One of the League officers opened the door, and the men in white began to leave the room.

Only the Duke of Garran remained, motionless.

'I am very sorry to hear this,' he said quietly. 'I had hoped you would see sense.' He turned to leave, then paused and turned back, looking thoughtful. 'Forgive me, but . . . it is strange for the people of Fayt to possess such a sword. A sword that has slain countless demonspawn. A sword that stands against the darkness.'

'It's just a sword,' said Newton coldly. 'A tool. It could kill you just as easily as it could a troll or a goblin.' His heart was racing again, his voice getting louder, and Governor Skelmerdale's hand was on his arm once more. He didn't care though. Not now. He levelled the sword, pointing it at the Duke. 'I'll prove it too. I'm coming for you, your grace. With this blade here. The Sword of Corin.'

'I do not doubt it,' said the Duke. 'But be assured I will be ready.'

He bowed low, replaced his tricorne on his head

and left the room. His footsteps receded down the corridor as the door swung shut.

'Put that sword down!' roared the governor, making everyone in the room flinch.

Newton lowered the blade. The rage was gone again, passing as quickly as a spring shower. And though the anger remained, there was something else too – a dull, throbbing pain of regret. This wasn't like him. 'I'm sorry, your honour. I – I shouldn't have let him—'

'No, you shouldn't.' Skelmerdale's eyes blazed for a moment longer. 'But what's done is done. There was never a chance of another outcome, in any case. Back to your ships.'

There was a shift in the room, as blackcoats and captains made their way towards the door.

'You two, wait,' said the governor, indicating Newton and Derringer.

'Your honour,' said the elf, coming smartly to attention.

'Aye,' said Newton. He could guess what was coming.

'Mr Newton. Thalin knows, I understand anger. But this is too much. If you cannot control yourself, how can I rely on you to lead our fleet? A commander must think only of what is best for his men.'

Like when you refused to seek the help of the merfolk?

But there was no point in saying it out loud. Besides, the governor was right. Newton was not to be relied on. Not any more.

'From henceforth, Colonel Derringer, you will take charge of the *Wyvern*, and of the fleet. Captain Newton, you will act as the colonel's second-in-command. Is that understood?'

Derringer smirked, his eyes shining like the silver on his uniform.

'Understood, your honour,' said Newton.

It didn't matter. Commander or not, he was going to kill the Duke of Garran.

And he was going to enjoy it.

Chapter Twenty-three

The mermaid still slept. Even her snoring was annoying. Any louder and Tabitha was going to grab hold of that slimy fish tail and drag her onto the flagstones.

She rubbed her tired eyes, hunched over the table and took another swig of velvetbean, the warmth of it seeping down her throat. The morning had dawned bright but cloudy, as if uncertain which way it would go. With any luck they'd be on a ship by noon, and Jeb the Snitch would be walking the plank. If he thought he could outwit them he was as crazy as a crate of crabs.

The door to the back rooms opened and Joseph

emerged, frowning, dabbing at his ears with a threadbare towel. He looked clean but exhausted, as though he hadn't slept either.

Tabitha watched him sit down opposite her and pour a mug of velvetbean. He was being so odd lately. Ever since they'd rescued Pallione. What was he doing, listening to the mermaid drone on about her father after dinner – then not even caring when she'd tried to talk to him in the night?

She wished he hadn't seen her crying. Then again, considering the way he was acting right now, he probably hadn't even noticed.

'Sleep well?' she asked. She'd meant to sound casual and friendly, but instead her voice was wooden.

Joseph blinked and looked up at her. 'Hmm? Oh. Yes, thank you. Sort of.' He stirred sugar into his velvetbean. 'You?'

'Not with that mermaid snoring all night. Didn't she keep you up?'

He shrugged.

Tabitha swirled the last of the velvetbean around her mug, choosing her words carefully. 'Don't you find her a bit . . . you know . . . annoying?'

Joseph looked puzzled. 'I think she's nice.'

'You think everyone's nice,' she snapped. *Careful, Tabs*. 'Sorry. What I mean is, she keeps complaining and arguing about everything. And we've got a job to do, remember?'

'I suppose.' He cast a glance at the sleeping mermaid, then turned to check that the door to the back room was closed. Jeb was still in there with Mrs Bootle, looking for clothes. Joseph leaned in, a strange, pleading look in his eyes. 'You know what the Snitch said last night? About my father . . .?'

Tabitha blinked, thrown by the change of subject.

'I've been thinking about it,' he went on. 'I never told him who my parents were, but he knew. And he knew my mother's song. So he probably knows more. Even if my father isn't—'

'Joseph,' said Tabitha. It was all she could do not to grab him and knock his head on the table. 'Don't be stupid, all right? He's the Snitch. He knows a lot of things. And I already told you, he's the biggest liar in Port Fayt.'

'But what if it's true? What if my father *is* alive? What if he wasn't killed after all?'

His eyes were wide, and it was making her feel uncomfortable. She tried to make her voice stern and commanding, like Newt would have done.

'Forget it, Joseph. Right now, all that matters is getting the princess back to that island. We've got more important things to worry about than—'

'More important things?'

'Well, I mean, I don't— Look, you can't believe a stinking goblin snitch like Jeb. He'd sell his own grandmother for a swig of grog.'

Joseph's ears twitched. 'What do you mean, "stinking goblin"?'

'All right, sorry. That's not what I meant. I was just—'

'Look, what if it was your father? Imagine he was alive. Wouldn't you—?'

She shot up, her stool scraping backwards across the flagstones.

'He's not. And you don't know what you're talking about.'

Joseph shrank back, instantly defeated. 'I'm sorry,' he said.

Tabitha felt her cheeks heating up.

'I— No, that's not . . . I—'

The door swung open with a bang and Jeb the Snitch swept in, scowling. His fancy clothes were gone, and in their place he wore a yellowing shirt and a dirty old coat several sizes too large for him. He was barely recognizable without all his finery. Mrs Bootle appeared behind him, one eyebrow raised at the outfit.

'Is this supposed to be a joke?' said Jeb. ''Cos it ain't funny, and I ain't wearing this.'

In all her life, Tabitha had never been so relieved to see the Snitch.

'Yes you are,' she told him. 'And be grateful for it too. This way there's a chance the Boy King's men won't recognize you. Anyway, it's a lot more sensible than the stuff you normally wear. Thank you, Mrs Bootle.'

The old troll woman did her best to smile. Tabitha could tell she wasn't happy about having the Snitch in her pie shop.

'All right,' she said hurriedly. 'Let's wake up the mermaid and get out of here.'

Joseph nodded, but said nothing.

There was no noise except for the trundling of the wheelbarrow on cobblestones as they strode down Mer Way towards the quayside. The street was as empty as the grey sky above, and it gave Tabitha the chills. Shop shutters were down, doors and windows bolted shut. There were no buskers, no beggars and no one trying to sell them things. Fayters were all either at sea fighting the League, or at home hoping for good news.

And it's up to us to make the good news happen, she thought. *Up to us to bring the merfolk into the war and beat the Duke of Garran*. There was just the small matter of getting out of Port Fayt to deal with first. She felt for her knives, stowed in her bandolier under a big brown coat.

They probably shouldn't be on Mer Way at all, but for some reason she'd insisted. Actually, she knew exactly why. Just before they'd set off, Joseph had suggested they keep to the back streets and Pallione had agreed. That was when she'd decided. It would be quicker and therefore better to go down Fayt's biggest street. Now that they'd found Mer Way empty, Tabitha was ready to admit to herself that in truth she'd just wanted to do the opposite of what the tavern boy and the annoying mermaid had wanted.

She glanced sideways at Joseph. He looked like he was barely with them at all, just frowning into the distance as he tramped along. He'd hardly said a word since they'd left Bootles'. Still moping about his father probably, though Thalin knew why. He was dead, just like Tabitha's parents. Simple as that. How Joseph could even consider believing Jeb the Snitch was beyond her.

The goblin was pushing the wheelbarrow on Tabitha's right-hand side. He was sulking too; had been ever since he'd left his mad clothes behind at the pie shop. But they couldn't take any chances with this.

If they were recognized by one of the Boy King's bully boys, it was all over.

The bundle in the wheelbarrow shifted, and Pallione's voice floated out from under the sackcloth covering:

'Aren't we there yet?'

Tabitha rolled her eyes. 'No. Just keep quiet.'

The mermaid's head poked out from under the sackcloth, her hair in disarray, her eyes blazing. 'It stinks under here. Everything stinks in this dump of a town. We should go faster.'

'We're trying not to draw attention to ourselves, remember? So stay down.'

Pallione groaned and disappeared again. For a moment Tabitha almost felt sorry for her, being forced to ride in a dirty old barrow that was barely big enough for her. But it was hard to sympathize with an ungrateful princess who kept trying to order you around.

'Streets are empty,' she said casually. No one answered. She was fed up with this. Fed up with having to be in charge all the time, and not getting a word of thanks for it. She had no idea how Newt did it. *Please, Thalin, let him be safe, wherever he is. Let him not be in a battle* . . . But the last thing she needed was to start worrying about him too.

They wheeled to a stop at the end of Mer Way,

where the docks spread out in front of them and on either side. The harbour was even emptier than the rest of the town. Usually you could barely see the open sea for all the masts and sails. But today, Tabitha could count the number of vessels rocking at anchor on her fingers. In the distance, a huge white ship was sailing away from Fayt, and a little closer another vessel followed, black-hulled, still large by normal standards, flying the sea-green flag of Port Fayt. If Tabitha didn't know better, she would have sworn that was the *Wyvern*.

Jeb gave her a nudge, bringing her attention back to the quayside. Nearby, a few off-duty sailors lounged on overturned crates, watching them. Tabitha felt very exposed.

'You lot wait here,' muttered Jeb. 'Back in a brace of shakes.'

Before Tabitha could protest, he had darted over to the sailors and begun speaking to the biggest of them, a troll with a weather-beaten face and fists the size of cannonballs.

'You can let me go now,' said Pallione. 'Into the sea.'

Her head was poking out again, and Tabitha quickly covered it.

'You want to get us killed?' she hissed. 'Stay under, for Thalin's sake.'

'Tabs,' said Joseph, grabbing hold of her sleeve. His face had come alive, and his eyes had lost their glassy look. He pointed along the docks.

Tabitha caught her breath. A gang of men with muskets was swaggering towards them. There were six of them and they walked side by side, spread out loosely between the sea and the store fronts so that no one could get past. They looked like scruffy reprobates. Definitely not blackcoats, and they weren't wearing the sea-green band of the Fayt navy either.

'What's going on?' asked Pallione.

'Shh. Whatever you do, don't move.' Tabitha's right hand fumbled inside her coat for a knife. 'We won't run,' she murmured. 'That way they'd definitely chase us. We'll just walk away fast and take a side street. Clear?'

Jeb strode back towards them, rubbing his hands.

'Well, that's that. Got us a ship for tomorrow morning. Had to call in a little favour, but it's—'

He froze, staring at something beyond them. Tabitha looked up and saw six more men approaching from the opposite direction.

Trapped. Like merfolk in a net.

Chapter Twenty-four

'Well, strike my colours and call me Nancy. If it ain't old Jeb the Snitch. How are you, my dear?'

The voice was a grating, high-pitched whine. It seemed to suit its owner, who stepped forward from the surrounding circle of bully boys. He was an elf, tall and spindly, with dirty grey curls sprouting madly from under his tricorne hat. His coat was made of some strange, rough material stained with blood, and a cutlass rested on his shoulder. On his other shoulder perched a messenger fairy, wearing exactly the same outfit as his owner.

'And you,' said the elf, turning to Joseph. The

tavern boy seemed to have recognized him, and wasn't looking too happy about it. 'Now, you *are* a sight for sore eyes, my duck. The young fellow who got my sweet Florence near killed and gave us the slip. How things have changed, eh? Last time I saw you, old Jeb here was trying to kill you. Now it seems you're the best of friends. How lovely.' He smiled so widely that Tabitha began to wonder if he was entirely sane.

'Harry—' Jeb began, but the elf held up a finger, cutting him off.

'And you, my darling,' he said to Tabitha. He swept off his hat and bowed low, the fairy on his shoulder mimicking him perfectly. Tabitha kept her hand curled tightly around the knife inside her coat. 'I don't believe we've had the pleasure. Folk call me Harry. Formerly of Harry's Shark Pit. Of course, those days are gone now.'

His smile turned into an equally exaggerated frown, the sides of his mouth curving down as low as they would go. 'No pit for old Harry any more. No sharkies neither. The Boy King took them, see? Took them for his show. Harry works for the boy now, my ducks. And the boy is looking for something. He's sent us all out, see, combing the streets. Poor lad's in a right tizzy, my dears, and no mistake.' He reached up to tickle his fairy under the chin. 'Then this little darling spotted you trundling down Mer Way, and I thought to myself, why not ask my old friends if they happen to have seen anything, eh?'

Tabitha shot a glance at the wheelbarrow, and saw that the sackcloth was quivering, as though Pallione was shaking with fear. She stepped in front of the elf.

'Whoever he's looking for, it isn't us,' she said. 'So we'll be on our way if you don't mind.'

The elf's eyes narrowed, and he leaned down towards her. Now Tabitha could see what his coat was made out of.

Shark skin.

'Interesting choice of words, duck,' said Harry. '"Whoever", is it? Believe I said he was looking for some*thing,* not some*one*. But as it happens, you're right. The boy's looking for a mermaid, name of Pallione. Ring any bells?'

Tabitha could have kicked herself. She shook her head stiffly, not trusting herself to say anything.

Harry stepped past her. The mermaid's quivering stopped as he walked slowly around the wheelbarrow, inspecting it. Suddenly he brought the cutlass down hard against the wooden sides. There was a hollow thunk but Pallione didn't move.

'Strikes me,' said Harry, 'if I was planning on kidnapping a mermaid – and believe me, I've stolen a few in my time' – the bully boys sniggered – 'a wheelbarrow wouldn't be a bad choice to cart her off in. What do you think, Jeb, my sweet?'

Jeb shrugged.

'How about you, dearie?'

Joseph nodded, then changed his mind and shook his head, blushing deeply. *Perfect*. He couldn't keep a secret to save his life.

'Well then,' said Harry. 'Maybe we should look inside?'

Tabitha felt the wind go out of her sails. He knew. Harry *knew*. He was just toying with them.

'What do you want?' she asked.

The elf turned his mad gaze on her.

'What do I want?'

'In exchange for leaving us alone.'

A faraway look came into Harry's eyes and, for a moment, Tabitha allowed herself to hope.

'What do I want? I want my shark pit back, dear. Want to see my sharkies prowl those waters again. To see the fighters trembling as they go out to meet them. See the deadly dance, just one more time. The cut and thrust. Darling Florence and Marjorie and Lucille biting down on a nice chunk of merfolk flesh.

Those tails twitching their last. Blood spreading through the—'

Pallione erupted from the wheelbarrow, throwing aside the sackcloth and rearing up above the elf. In that instant, Tabitha saw how wrong she'd been about the mermaid. She'd been trembling, all right. But not with fear.

'You!' roared Pallione. 'You *filth*!'

Harry just had time to raise his cutlass before she fell upon him, tipping the wheelbarrow with her. He stumbled and made a strangled sound as the mermaid's arms locked around his neck, crushing his windpipe, tighter and tighter. His hat toppled to the ground and his fairy took to the air, squawking with terror.

'Thalin's sake!' shouted Tabitha. 'Let him go!' She waded in, grabbed hold of Harry and tried to tug him away from Pallione. Joseph leaped forward and joined her. But they weren't strong enough. Harry's face was going purple. His fairy darted around their heads, jabbering and shaking his tiny fist at them.

The bully boys had their muskets raised now, trying to work out whether to shoot or not.

'Let go,' Tabitha begged, staring into the mermaid's eyes. But Pallione seemed too angry even to notice her.

Jeb dived in, grabbed hold of the wheelbarrow handles and tugged. Pallione overbalanced, loosening her grip just enough for Harry to break free and stagger forward, pushing Tabitha and Joseph aside. He turned at the edge of the pier, and his face would have been comical if it hadn't been such a terrifying colour.

Before he could say a word Tabitha stepped forward once, twice, and planted her boot squarely in his chest. A quick shove and the elf dropped like a stone over the edge of the pier, his mouth still open in shock. His fairy dived after him, squealing.

'Come on!' shouted Tabitha. She barged into Jeb, took the handles of the wheelbarrow and put her full weight into it, driving the mermaid towards the line of bully boys.

'No!' howled Pallione. 'Take me back. I'll kill him!' She leaned over the side, quick and elegant as a leaping dolphin, swept Harry's fallen cutlass up off the ground and flung it hard. It went spinning into the surf, a few feet from the shark-pit owner. 'Turn round!' she bellowed. 'Turn round now!'

But Tabitha wasn't turning round for anyone.

At the sight of the wheelbarrow and the furious mermaid careering towards them, the bully boys scattered. There were two or three musket shots, but too late. They were through.

Tabitha cast a glance backwards, saw Joseph and Jeb following. Joseph's face was white as a sail. He had his cutlass out and his skinny legs were pumping away as fast as they could go. Somehow Jeb had got hold of a musket and a pistol. He let fly randomly behind him.

A few of the bully boys had already pulled themselves together and were chasing after them as Harry's voice rose up from the water, a high-pitched squeal: 'I'm coming for you, you sacks of scum! I'm going to gut you and skin you and turn you into coats. You'll all be coats! All of you!'

They thundered over the cobbles, past a few surprised sailors, and veered wildly into a side street. Tabitha's arms burned with the weight of the wheelbarrow, and she knew she might drop it at any moment. She wished Frank or Paddy were here . . . A troll would have no trouble running with this infuriating mermaid. Pallione was facing her, holding onto the sides of the wheelbarrow and scowling ferociously.

'I told you to take me back,' she snarled. 'I could have killed him. I could have got out of this horrible town for good, and instead I'm still stuck here in this filthy wheelbarrow with *you*.'

Tabitha almost tipped her out on the cobblestones.

'Your fault . . .' she puffed, 'we're running . . . in the first place . . .'

'We're losing them,' shouted Joseph, from behind.

Tabitha looked back to see the tavern boy hot on her heels and Jeb half a street behind, firing at their pursuers. The bully boys were darting from cover to cover, returning fire, and it was slowing them down.

'Go left here,' shouted Jeb, tossing his smoking weapons aside. 'Then second right.'

'You're not in charge, all right?' yelled Tabitha. 'If anyone's in charge it's—'

A musket ball thunked into a cart by the roadside, sending splinters flying and shutting her up instantly.

The truth was, she didn't know where to go. And right now, following the Snitch's directions seemed like a better idea than doing nothing.

Another musket ball ricocheted off a shop sign above them, making it swing crazily.

'You're not going to listen to him?' demanded the mermaid. 'He's a crook!'

That decided it. No fish girl was going to tell her what to do.

She steered left, hard.

'What are you doing?' squealed the mermaid.

'Getting you out of here,' hissed Tabitha, through gritted teeth.

'But—' said Pallione, then shut her mouth and tightened her grip on the sides of the wheelbarrow as they bounced over bumpy cobblestones. Tabitha took the second right, like Jeb had told her. A dark alleyway, where the overhanging buildings were so close they almost touched. A dead end.

'I *told* you,' yelped the mermaid.

'Quiet,' snapped Tabitha. Her heart was pounding like a drum, her arms ached and sweat stung her eyes. She wiped it away with her sleeve.

Joseph raced into the alleyway behind them, gasping for breath. 'Where now?'

And then she saw it – a gap between the houses, just wide enough for a wheelbarrow to squeeze through. 'There.' They raced in and stood in the darkness, panting. Footsteps sounded on the cobbles behind them and Jeb flung himself round the corner.

'Told yer,' he said, with a wink. 'No one knows these streets better than the Snitch.'

Tabitha ignored him.

They waited, uncomfortably close to each other, listening to the shouts of the bully boys on the main street. They were ankle deep in rotten vegetables and bits of old rubbish, and judging by the smell, Tabitha reckoned that more than one person had used their hiding place as a privy. Flies buzzed around them, but Tabitha didn't dare swat them away.

A minute passed. Finally the voices and the footsteps receded into the distance.

Tabitha let out a breath she didn't know she'd been holding.

They were safe.

That was, if you ignored the fact that the biggest gang in Port Fayt was out to get them. And that their only allies were a backstabbing goblin and a stuck-up mermaid. And that Joseph seemed more worried about his dead parents than about all the real, live people who wanted to kill them.

Safe. Well, that was one way of looking at it.

'Come in.'

The cabin door opens and Major Turnbull enters. He sits back in his chair and examines her by the lantern light. It throws half her face into shadow, turning its beauty into something more sinister. Those cold blue eyes, and the cruel curve of her lips . . .

He has heard it said that a gang of elves attacked her mother during the Miners' Rising, when Turnbull was just a little girl. That she hid in a cupboard and saw it all. He wonders if the story is true. It might explain the fiery rage with which she hates all demonspawn.

Hatred is one thing. But anger – too much anger can

be dangerous. It is essential to remain calm. That way, no mistakes are made.

He drums his fingers on his green marble paperweight, takes a sip of blackwine and swills it around his mouth. The White Valley '73. A fine vintage.

'So,' he says quietly. 'It is done.'

Major Turnbull nods once. The Duke of Garran reaches across his desk, taking the crystal decanter and pouring a goblet for his guest.

'You have excelled yourself, Major. The finest magicians in the Academy could do no better work.'

She shrugs.

'I dare say there'll be a colonel's commission when we return to Azurmouth. Provided, of course, that nothing goes wrong.'

She stays silent. He takes another sip of blackwine, savouring its complexity.

'Tell me. How did you conceal the spell? They don't teach arts like that at the Academy. A room full of people watching, and no one sees a hint of – what do you call it? – ah yes: a tremor.'

He drains his goblet and sets it down, watching the lantern light glitter through the facets of the cut glass and enjoying the silence.

'On second thought, don't tell me.' As if she would. 'A magician should never reveal her secrets.'

He smiles, but of course Turnbull does not.

'That will be all. It was a delight to speak to you, as ever.'

Major Turnbull nods, polite but silent, and leaves, closing the cabin door behind her with a creak and a soft click.

He sets down his empty goblet and takes Turnbull's untouched blackwine for himself. As he sips, his gaze wanders over the sketches pinned to his cabin wall. Every single variety of demonspawn, catalogued for his benefit by Dr William Silverbell's best draughtsman. His eyes alight finally on the merperson. Daemonium Piscarium.

The charcoal illustration shows a frowning mermaid, one hand grasping a bonestaff, her long tail curving away below. He recalls the relevant entry in The Authoritative Compendium of Demonspawn. *A lesser form, to be sure, but far from irrelevant. If they were to side with the Fayters, the consequences could be . . . unfortunate.*

He will not let it happen.

The Duke of Garran rises and pads across the cabin floor. He puts on his reading spectacles and peers in close, tracing the curve of the tail with one finger and examining where the girl's upper body joins the grotesque fish tail. Where the natural turns unnatural. He feels his lip curl in disgust, but he cannot tear his eyes away. Disgusting. And yet fascinating.

He dips one finger in the blackwine and smears it across the creature's tail, blotting it out and watching the paper crinkle and distort, until nothing remains except the upper body of a girl.

As though it were a human, and not demonspawn at all.

Chapter Twenty-five

'Is this it?' asked Joseph. 'It's a bit . . . er . . .'

'It stinks,' Tabitha finished for him.

Their shadows stretched out in front of them on the stone floor as they stood in the doorway, surveying the warehouse. If he craned his neck, Joseph could just make out rotting rafters disappearing into the gloom, several storeys up. Two tiny windows provided a little light, enough to see gigantic stacks of barrels towering on either side. The whole place reeked of griffin bile – a musty, sickly stench that sat somewhere between fresh vomit and rotten fish. Joseph peered into an open barrel and saw sludgy black dregs still clinging to the sides. A deep waft of the smell hit him, and he jerked backwards, trying not to gag.

It wasn't the ideal place to hide out. First they'd tried to go back to Bootles', but bully boys had been loitering at the end of the street. Next they'd ducked into an abandoned grogshop for a while, until Tabs spotted more of the Boy King's men in the tavern across the road. They'd moved to a grotty stables, then to a velvethouse on the edge of the Crosstree Quarter. Nowhere felt safe. At last Jeb had suggested his griffin-bile warehouse. And with nowhere else to go, here they were.

'It's only till tomorrow morning, when the ship sets sail,' said Jeb. 'I thought it was the fish girl who was supposed to be the princess?'

Pallione scowled at him. 'Look who's talking. *Oh, my beautiful yellow jacket, we can't possibly leave it behind!* If you ask me, we did you a favour.'

'All right,' said Tabitha. 'It'll do for now. What time does the ship leave? We'll need to go to an island near Illon.'

'An hour after dawn,' said Jeb.

Pallione's scowl grew darker. 'So we'll have to spend a night here, with this filthy griffin snot? Did I mention how much I hate this town?'

Tabitha rounded on her, cheeks flushed.

'Just shut up about Port Fayt, all right? You nearly

got us killed on the docks, so maybe you could stop moaning for half a minute.'

'*I* nearly got us killed? *I* did? Who was it who insisted we go down Mer Way? You heard the elf. His fairy spotted us.'

'Now hold on,' said Joseph. 'Let's all just—'

'Joseph told you,' interrupted the mermaid. She was still glaring at Tabitha. 'He told you not to take the biggest street in town. I told you too. We both did. But did you listen?'

Tabitha's face was red now, and her fists were clenched.

'We would have been fine if you hadn't thrown a fit at Harry.'

'That made no difference.'

'Tabs,' said Joseph. 'I . . . Maybe we should—'

'And you . . .' Tabitha turned on him, eyes blazing. 'You're always taking her side. We're supposed to be working together, aren't we?' She pulled up her sleeve, showed him her shark tattoo. 'Watchmen, see?'

'I'm just trying to—'

'You're just trying to be difficult!'

She stood fuming at him, looking so unfriendly he thought she might be about to punch him.

Jeb chuckled. 'Trouble in paradise, eh?'

'Shut up,' snapped Tabitha. 'We've got guns,

remember? So maybe you should keep your opinions to yourself.'

'Tabs—' Joseph began.

'And you too. Just . . . wait here. All of you. I'm going to get some food.' She sounded as though she was struggling not to yell at them. Or cry. Or both.

'But—'

'I said I'm going out. You're in charge.' She grabbed hold of Joseph's hand and pressed the pistol into it, without meeting his eyes.

'Are you—?'

'I told you, I'm fine.'

Joseph searched for something to say, but came up with nothing. He watched, helpless, as she strode out through the double doors.

Jeb gave him a wink and swaggered off towards a row of barrels, counting along until he found the one he was looking for, and began to remove the lid.

'The blue-haired girl is cross with herself,' said Pallione. Her arms were folded, and her tail tapped against the side of the wheelbarrow like a man drumming his fingers. 'She just needs time alone.'

'Maybe.' But Joseph wasn't sure he believed it. He'd never seen Tabitha so upset, and it didn't feel good.

'If my father was here, he would get us out of this

mess,' said Pallione. 'If we were in the ocean, I mean.' She sighed, and her eyes glazed over. 'I cannot wait to feel the water's embrace again. I came so close today . . .'

Joseph took hold of the wheelbarrow and pushed it further into the warehouse, towards a corner where some dirty old sackcloth littered the ground.

'So was it Harry who caught you?' he asked. Hopefully the mermaid could distract him from thinking about Tabitha.

Pallione shook her head.

'That pointy-eared fop does no dirty work himself. But it was one of his dinghies. They use nets like fishermen, but metal, so you can't escape. If I'd had my bonestaff with me . . .' She tailed off, lost in thought. 'When I get back, I'll never leave the King's Rock again.'

She turned to him as he wheeled her to a halt.

'Where's *your* father, Joseph?'

'He's not around any more.' *But where is he?*

Pallione frowned at him. 'I don't understand. He abandoned you? Like my father?'

Out of nowhere, Joseph felt a warm surge of anger. Anger at Tabitha, anger at himself, and anger at the mermaid. How dare she talk about his father like that?

'No, that's not it at all,' he said. 'And the King didn't abandon you. You swam too close to Fayt, remember? He told you not to. And you know he can't come here to rescue you himself. For Thalin's sake, he's pledged all his people to fight a war on your behalf, so you can't say he doesn't care about you.'

Joseph had never seen the mermaid look so surprised. Then again, he was pretty surprised himself. He was just opening his mouth to apologize when Jeb ambled over with an armful of blankets and a couple of lanterns dangling from his fingers.

'Keep this lot for emergencies,' he said. 'Now look lively, mongrel, and help me make the beds for later.'

For once, Joseph was glad the Snitch had made an appearance. He took the blankets, spread some over the floor and passed a couple to Pallione, who wrapped herself up inside the wheelbarrow.

He tried not to meet her eyes, but all the same he noticed she was watching him.

'I am sorry,' she said. 'I didn't mean to upset you.'

'It's all right.'

'Do you want to talk about it?'

Joseph shook his head hurriedly.

Pallione looked uncertain. 'Well then,' she said finally. 'I'm going to take a nap. Maybe I can forget where I am for a few hours. You?'

'I think I'll just wait. Keep watch. Until Tabs comes back.'

'Very well.'

She frowned at him, then shrugged and rolled over, her tail flopping against the side of the wheelbarrow. Within a few moments she was snoring.

Joseph envied her. There was no way he would get to sleep so easily tonight.

'Fish-tail's off to dreamland, eh?' said Jeb. Joseph looked up to see him standing a little way off, smiling. 'Which means you and I can have a little chat. What do you say?' He dragged two empty barrels out of the shadows and sat down on one, motioning for Joseph to take the other. Then he hunted around in his pockets, pulled out a pipe and tobacco and began to smoke.

Waiting.

Joseph cast a glance at the door. No sign of Tabitha. He closed his eyes and counted to ten in his head, breathing slow and even. Then he moved quietly away from Pallione and sat on the spare barrel, resting the goblin's multi-barrelled pistol on his knee. Just in case something went wrong. His palms were slick with sweat.

Jeb puffed out a smoke ring and fixed him with his pale eyes.

'So,' he said. 'Your pa's alive.'

Joseph's fingers closed around the handle of the pistol. *Breathe. Slow and even.*

'According to you,' he said.

'Aye. I ain't surprised if you don't believe me. So how about a little proof?'

He reached into his pocket and drew out a small metal object, holding it out in his palm for Joseph to see.

It was a pocket watch – old, battered and tarnished. It had been silver once. The hands ticked around the metal face, echoing Joseph's heartbeat.

'What does this mean?' But he already knew.

'Take it. Turn it over.'

Joseph did so. The back had a design etched around the edge – swirling flowers, poorly executed. It was clear the watch was cheap. But it was the engraving in the middle that stole his breath away.

TO MY DEAREST ELIJAH,

WITH ALL MY LOVE,

ELEANOR

Breathe. Slow and even. But the whole warehouse seemed to be spinning. *Elijah. Eleanor.*

His parents.

For years, all he'd had to remember them by was the silly song his mother used to sing. And now this.

As he ran his fingers over the engraving, he began to remember. It had been a birthday present. Must have cost his mother a month's wages. And his father had snatched her up in his arms and grinned and hugged her till Joseph was frightened he'd squash her.

His heartbeat outpaced the ticking of the clock.

He'd helped wind it up sometimes, and his father had taught him to tell the time. Once he'd dropped it. And when his father picked it up and found that it wasn't broken, he'd been so relieved he'd burst into tears.

Breathe.

'Lucky I had that on me,' said Jeb. 'Your father gave it to me. Had to. Times are hard nowadays, and a goblin's got to do what he can to make ends meet.' His pipe glowed as he inhaled.

Joseph looked at him. *Wait. Think straight.*

'This isn't proof,' he said. His voice came out hoarse. 'You could have stolen it.'

Jeb shrugged. 'Suit yerself. I know it ain't easy to trust me.'

Joseph licked his dry lips. He wanted to believe the goblin so badly. Even if it wasn't true, the Snitch knew *something*. He'd recognized his mother's song. The song she only sang to Joseph and his father. And now this . . .

'Why doesn't he come for me? If he was alive, he'd come and find me.'

Jeb leaned in through the coiling trails of smoke from his pipe.

'Now listen, mate. There's a good reason for that, and I'll explain. I'll tell you all about your pa. I'll even take you to him. But I want something in return. See, the ship ain't leaving Port Fayt tomorrow, like I told the girl. It's leaving tonight. We'll be on it, out of this place and away from the Boy King. Just you, me and that mermaid. We head off when it's your watch, nice and quiet, and we leave your friend behind. We take the fish girl to that island. Then I get my reward. Understand?'

The warehouse was spinning again. Maybe it was the smoke from the Snitch's pipe. Maybe not.

'What do I get?'

'The ship'll sail on to the Old World, and when we get there I'll take yer to your pa. That's where he's holed up.'

Pipe smoke hung above them. Silence. The goblin waited.

Joseph turned the silver watch over and over in his hand. *To my dearest Elijah, with all my love, Eleanor.*

'I've had it a while,' said Jeb. 'Worth a fair few ducats, that. You keep it, though. Little gift. Sign of my . . .what do you call it? . . . good will. I'll take you to him, if you help me. He's living across the ocean, doesn't know if you're dead or alive. And you can change that.'

Joseph felt a lump form in his throat. He took a deep, ragged breath, tucked the watch away in his pocket, still holding onto it. *I will not cry. Whatever happens, I will not cry.*

'I can't do it,' he said, his voice cracking. 'I can't leave Tabs on her own.'

Jeb let out a long sigh. 'She can't come, mate. She's a troublemaker, and she'll try and stop me getting my fair reward. You know that.'

Silence again. The metal of the watch was cold under Joseph's fingers.

'One thing about your father,' said the goblin at last. 'He always does what's best for other folk. Anyone's got a problem, they know Elijah will help them out. Seems you're like him, and that's all well and good. Trouble is, he never does a thing for himself. And that's you all over, ain't it, mongrel? Running around with the Demon's Watch trying to help them save a town that ain't been good to you. Look at that skin. All pink and grey and blotchy. You can't tell me life's been easy here. Not in Fayt. And that girl – when's she ever given you a kind word? You should stand up for yerself for a change.'

Joseph thought of all the times his uncle had hit him. All the customers who'd yelled at him, called him a mongrel. It was true that Fayt hadn't always been good to him. And maybe, sometimes, Tabs wasn't either. But that didn't mean he could turn his back on her.

He looked into the goblin's face, as if it might give some clue, some hint that this was all lies. But there was nothing. Just those pale eyes watching him, waiting for an answer. And somehow, he knew. *It was true.* The goblin was telling the truth.

'Tell me, please,' he said. It sounded pathetic, but he didn't care. 'Just tell me how to find him.'

Jeb shook his head.

'You have to tell me,' he said again. 'It's my father. Tell me or . . .' He raised the pistol with both his trembling hands. 'Tell me or I'll shoot. I will.'

'Don't be ridiculous.'

Joseph's ears burned with shame and anger. He was the one with the gun and yet, somehow, he was powerless. The goblin still sat there, smirking, saying nothing.

'Look, mongrel,' said Jeb. And suddenly his tone

was different – hard and cold. 'I can't sneak that mermaid out without your help. So yer'd better get smart. You've got until tonight to think about it. If you breathe a word to the girl, the deal's off. And if yer don't help, just have a little think about what might happen to your pa. What I might do to him.'

Something snapped. Before Joseph knew what he was doing, his left fist thudded into Jeb's face, knocking the pipe out so that it skittered away across the warehouse floor. His right foot slammed into the goblin's barrel as hard as he could kick. It was just enough to tip it backwards, and Jeb was already off balance, leaning away from the punch. He went toppling head over heels.

Joseph was upon him in an instant, trying to get the pistol up into Jeb's throat. But the goblin grabbed hold of his wrists. Joseph struggled on top, pinning Jeb down. And the next thing he knew there were hands on his shoulders and he was dragged away, flailing uselessly. There were tears in his eyes, but he could see a blurred image of the goblin scrambling to his feet. He was filled with a fresh urge to lash out. But the hands that held him were stronger than he was.

'What in Thalin's name are you doing?' hissed Tabitha.

'It's— He's—'

She grappled his arms behind his back and forced him down until he was sitting on the floor. Out of the corner of his eye, he saw Pallione, sitting up from her wheelbarrow, blinking and trying to make sense of the scene in front of her.

'Called him a mongrel one too many times, I reckon,' said Jeb, straightening his coat. 'He flew off the handle.'

'That's not— I . . .'

'It's your father again, isn't it?' said Tabitha. She was still angry, Joseph realized. Maybe even angrier. 'Look, Joseph, you can't believe a word he says, understand? Your pa's dead, just like mine. Forget it!'

She let go and stepped back. He turned to look up at her and saw that her eyes were just as red and swollen and full of hurt as he knew his own were. When she spoke again, her voice was quiet, brittle with emotion.

'We're not going on that boat. I'll find another way. I don't care how.'

'Tabs, I— We need to get out soon, or the Boy King will—'

'I don't know what's got into you. First you pull that stupid trick with the blackwine. Then you believe the Snitch's lies about your father—'

'Now see here,' said Jeb. 'There's nothing to—'

'*Shut up!*' Tabitha ran her hands through her hair, paced up and down. 'We'll have to keep this bilge rat here for now. He's too dangerous if we let him go. I just wish . . . I mean, for Thalin's sake, Joseph, I'd be better off on my own.'

The words stung him, and fresh tears threatened to well up.

Silence. Even Pallione said nothing; just watched, wearing a slight frown.

Joseph's fingers found their way into his pocket and closed around his father's watch.

Better off on my own. Maybe she was right.

Maybe they would both be better off on their own.

Chapter Twenty-six

Hal woke with a jolt. It was night, and the fire had died down to a few glowing embers. Everyone was asleep except for a single smuggler keeping watch.

He shivered and rolled over, tried to rearrange the seaweed he was sleeping on and get comfortable among the rocks. It was no good. He lay back, listening to the snores of the Bootle brothers, staring at the stars and clamping his teeth together to stop them from chattering.

He'd dreamed of the King. Of his strange throne of rocks. Of those liquid green eyes, ever changing, like the sea itself. And of his words.

My powers are at their strongest, magician . . . and now I am returned.

It should have reassured him, but instead it made him anxious. Joseph and Tabitha had been gone for three nights now. They'd had no word of Newton or the Fayter fleet.

And there was nothing they could do about it.

Distant thunder sounded.

Except, no – that wasn't thunder . . .

Hal staggered to his feet, picked up a spyglass and looked out across the sea to where the sound had come from. But it was too dark.

He fumbled on his shoes and picked his way through the sleeping bodies to the shore. The rolling booms sounded again, and again he scanned the horizon. This time a distant orange glow lit up the sky.

'Do you hear, magician?' said a voice close by. It was the mermaid who'd first brought them to the island. She was sitting on a rock a little way out to sea, her spiky fair hair just visible, her eyes gleaming in the night.

'Cannons,' said Hal. His mouth was dry, and he swallowed.

The mermaid laughed her strange, barking laugh.

'My people call this island The Claw. You know why? Because it rises above the waves like the hand of a beast. But tonight there are greater dangers than imaginary monsters.' She gestured to the distant orange light. 'The men in white like to practise.'

Another volley of booms carried across the water.

'Do you think we can defeat them?' asked Hal.

'You Fayters, on your own? You might as easily ask the sea and the sky to switch places.'

Hal swallowed again. 'What about you? If you fought with us?'

The mermaid was silent for a while. At last she shrugged.

'Perhaps.'

Perhaps. It wasn't the answer he'd been hoping for.

'Go, four-eyed man. Sleep. You might need it.'

'What do you mean?'

The mermaid's teeth flashed in a smile. 'The Fayters are approaching the big island now. The one you call Illon. Tomorrow they will reach it. Then the battle will begin.'

Newton leaned over the gunwale, watching the prow of the *Dread Unicorn* cut through the dark water. Derringer had dismissed him from the *Wyvern* the moment they'd caught up with the fleet, and that suited him fine. Now there were just a few crewmen still on deck, and the sounds of the ship filled his ears.

The rattle of rigging. The creaks and groans of the deck. The slapping of the waves against the hull.

He looked up and took in the rest of the fleet, sailing through the night, bound for Illon and the enemy armada. Not long now. He shivered and turned up the collar of his coat.

Newton was glad of those ships keeping them company. The sails, deep blue against a black sky dotted with stars. The yellow glimmer of candlelight from the stern cabins, and the odd lantern strung up on deck. He'd never liked the dark. Wasn't scared of it – not much seemed to scare him any more. But it reminded him of the mines.

The thought jolted him, as it always did. A wound that smarted when he touched it and never seemed to heal. Still, he kept going back to it. Especially since seeing Alice.

The mines. Every morning, kicked awake, and opening his eyes to the half-light. Breakfast – a thin soup and hard bread. The leftovers would reappear at lunch and at dinner time, if you were lucky. Then onto your hands and knees, scrabbling at the rocks, hunting for the precious gleam of zephyrum. The magical metal.

When Newton was a boy, before all that, his grandfather had told him stories of heroes who fought with zephyrum swords, and damsels wearing magical zephyrum brooches. There was no magic to the work though.

At noon they were driven up above for a few minutes to eat, the sunlight making their eyes throb. Then back into the dark again, working the rock face until they almost collapsed. Some did. And when that happened the pale forms of the whitecoats would appear out of the darkness, pick up the fallen miner and take him away. They would never see that person again.

No. Newton didn't like the dark.

He focused on the horizon ahead. Not long now. Not long before Illon appeared, a bump above the line of the sea, and then the League's armada with its fluttering white banners. He closed his eyes for a moment, tried to picture it all. Tried to stem the hot rage that threatened to surge up again and engulf him.

The memory of the zephyrum mines still hurt. The memory of his family, and seeing each of them, one by one, for the last time in the gloom beneath the earth. But it had been a long time since it had made him angry. The League had taken everything from him. And, worse, they'd taken that little girl, Alice Turnbull, and made her one of them.

Suddenly Newton realized that he didn't *want* to

control his anger any more. He wanted to unleash it on his enemies. He wanted to take revenge. For his grandfather. For his family. For every single one of the miners.

He reached down for the bundle that leaned against the gunwale, laid it flat and unwrapped the blanket. The Sword of Corin glinted in the moonlight. Newton's staff, the Banshee, remained in his cabin, and there it would stay until after the fighting was done.

He traced one finger along the groove of the fuller that ran the length of the blade. The Sword of Corin was ancient, practically a relic. But what better weapon to carry against the League than that of their own hero, Corin?

He'd let himself into the library before they set sail, while the governor was busy meeting Colonel Derringer. Taken the sword and whisked it away. It wasn't like him. But he'd felt, somehow, as though he'd needed to do it. And now he was going to hunt down the Duke of Garran and kill him.

A sword is just a sword. And tomorrow he was going to prove it.

Footsteps on the deck behind him. He flipped the blanket back to conceal the blade and turned. Old Jon was hobbling towards him, every wrinkle of his face thrown into shadow by the lantern he held.

'Evening,' said Newt.

Old Jon came up next to him, gazing out over the ocean. They stood like that for a while, in silence – but a comforting kind of silence. That was Old Jon all over.

'Newt,' said the elf at last. His voice was deep, soft and calming. 'You ain't yourself.'

'Aye.' There was no getting anything past Jon. 'I'm angry. What do you expect?'

The elf nodded slowly. 'Little bit of anger's fair enough.' He turned for the first time to look Newton in the eye. 'But don't be too hard on yourself. Don't lose your head.'

'Hmm.'

They stood a while longer, listening to the chop and slap of the waves against the ship's hull. Then Old Jon turned and limped away across the deck, lantern creaking as it swung in the breeze.

As the light went, Newton's rage returned, burning through him.

He drew aside the blanket again, lifted the sword out and stepped back. The stitches in his arm nagged at him, but it was no more than a flesh wound and it was healing fast. He swung the sword, once, twice, enjoying the soft hum of the blade as it cut the night air. His swordplay was rusty, but a little practice would soon bring it back. And he had strength on his side. *Yes*. He was almost looking forward to it.

Not long now.

Tabitha dreamed. She was out at sea, in a mist, treading water. The mermaid floated opposite her, holding something behind her back. Something that belonged to Tabitha. She wanted it more than anything, but when she reached for it the fish girl twisted away, smirking.

'It's mine!' she cried.

There was a sound behind her – oars, dipping in and out of the water. She turned to see the shape of a dinghy, and she floundered towards it.

'Joseph,' she gasped. He was rowing the boat closer and closer. But his eyes were fixed on the mermaid, his face blank, as though he hadn't heard her. 'Joseph!' She screamed it this time. Still nothing. 'Help me. Please. Help me get it back.' But he kept rowing. When he reached Pallione he lifted her out of the sea as though she was as light as a feather, set her down in the boat and kept rowing.

There was a strange scent in the air, rich and musty and sickening.

'Wait!' howled Tabitha. 'Wait for me!'

Sea and sky had turned dark now. She rose and fell with the waves, higher and higher, lower and lower. Thunder rolled overhead and rain began to fall.

'I'll drown!'

But the boat just kept moving away, into the mist. As it went, Pallione watched, still smiling. She held out her hand, but when she opened her fingers there was nothing there.

'You're better off on your own, remember?' said the mermaid.

And now the sea was surging as something rose up in the space between Tabitha and the dinghy. A vast, terrible form, water cascading off it. Its body was the colour of seaweed, its back curved, covered in spines. Its limbs were like spiders' legs – long, slender and pointed. A demon of the ocean. *The Maw.* And it was too late for Tabitha. *Alone*. She would die here, all on her own.

The Maw threw back its head and screamed.

Tabitha's eyes flicked open and she sat up, the stink of griffin bile hitting her nostrils instantly. Sweat drenched her brow, and her breathing came fast and heavy.

She pushed the thin blanket away from her as her eyes adjusted to the dim interior of the warehouse.

A nightmare. It was just a nightmare.

She yawned and stretched. Shouldn't Joseph have woken her already? Surely it was her turn at watch by now? She turned to check on Pallione.

The mermaid wasn't there.

Tabitha rubbed her eyes, looked again.

Still not there. And no wheelbarrow either.

She looked round at the barrel where she had left Joseph sitting, keeping first watch. There was another barrel next to it, the two of them like empty chairs. But no sign of Joseph. No sign of Jeb. No sign of Pallione.

They were gone.

Chapter Twenty-seven

Pallione was a deep sleeper, and it was only once they'd trundled her up the gangplank and onto the deck that she woke up. Her tail flicked round and caught Joseph a stinging blow, sending him staggering away. She writhed, knocking over the wheelbarrow and falling out. Immediately four big sailors dived onto her, two holding down her tail while the others pinned her arms to her sides.

'Fiery little fish girl, ain't she?' remarked Jeb.

Joseph couldn't let this go on any longer. He stepped forward, rubbing his arm where the mermaid had struck him.

'Pallione.'

'Joseph,' yelled the mermaid. 'What's going on? Where are we going?'

'It's all right,' he said. He crouched down beside her. Her eyes were wide with fear and fury, and his heart ached to see it. 'No one's going to hurt you. We're taking you to the King.'

Pallione stopped thrashing, her face full of uncertainty. She glanced around, taking in the hobgoblin junk – the polished black lacquer of the deck, the low gunwales and furled battened sails. Above, the sky was still dark. Morning was a good few hours off yet. 'Then why didn't you wake me sooner? And where is your friend Tabitha?'

'She . . . well . . . It's complicated.'

It hadn't felt good, leaving her there in the warehouse. Tabitha frowned even in her sleep, as if she knew what they were doing and disapproved of it.

Pallione narrowed her eyes. 'You left her behind?'

The words twisted his gut. Yes. He had left her behind. That was what she'd wanted, wasn't it? *I'd be better off on my own.* He'd go back for her, just as soon as they'd taken Pallione to her father. And in the meantime Tabs would be fine. Wasn't she always saying she could look after herself?

'Take that mermaid down below,' said Jeb.

The four sailors picked up Pallione and began to

carry her away. She struggled again as they took her across the deck to the square hatch that led below.

'Wait!' she cried. 'I don't understand, I don't—'

'It'll be all right,' said Joseph, but the words sounded hollow. Unconvincing.

Don't worry, he told himself. He was doing the right thing. Tabitha didn't need looking after. Pallione was going to see her father again. And the merfolk would fight for the Fayters.

This isn't just about me.

At the stern, the gleaming black cabin door opened and a hobgoblin strode up onto the deck. He was tall, grey-skinned and thin, dressed in sailor's clothes, with eyes and ears larger than those of a normal goblin.

'Captain Lortt,' called Jeb. 'We're ready to make sail.' The hobgoblin nodded and began to shout out orders.

Jeb leaned down to squeeze Joseph's shoulder, grinning in a way that made Joseph want to punch him in the face. 'You've made a smart move here, lad,' said Jeb. 'We'll get this fish girl to her father. Then I'll get my reward, and you'll be off to see your pa again.' He leaned down to squeeze Joseph's shoulder, grinning in a way that made Joseph want to punch him in the face.

This isn't just about me.

* * *

Tabitha raced out of the warehouse, her boots pounding the cobblestones. *Faster. Come on, faster!* She pushed hard, her lungs burning with the chill of the night air.

Was it possible that the Boy King had taken them? No. He would have taken her too. So they must have gone themselves. Jeb the Snitch, Joseph and the mermaid. If this had anything to do with that bilge about Joseph's father . . . Somehow, she had a feeling it did.

The streets were empty save for a snoozing drunk sprawled in a doorway and a few beggars sleeping out under awnings. Not even a Dockside Militia patrol. Tabitha sucked more air into her lungs and ran on through the darkness. The Boy King's men might spot her, but she didn't care about that any more. There was no time to worry. Whatever Jeb the Snitch was up to, it wasn't going to be good. She had to stop them.

That was the funny thing. She'd *known* they were ganging up on her. But now that she had proof of it, she actually felt better. At least she'd been right. And at least she knew what to do next.

She veered into a shipyard, stopping to root through its rubbish dump until she found what she was looking for. A hand saw, half rusted, with several teeth missing. But it would get the job done.

She ran on, out of the town, climbing the path up to the eastern cliffs, beyond the lighthouse, then down to the beach. The sand soaked up the last of her energy, each step exhausting. The night was almost over and she could see things clearly now – the deep blue shape of the Brig, crouched on the shoreline against the azure sky, waves lapping at its hull.

Dawn was coming. But she couldn't rest yet. If Jeb, Joseph and Pallione had taken the Snitch's ship out of Fayt, there was only one way she could go after them. It was a risk, of course. But it wasn't as though she had a choice. If that princess didn't get back to her father, the merfolk wouldn't fight. And if the merfolk didn't fight, Port Fayt was doomed, along with all the watchmen. Hal, the Bootle twins, Newt . . .

The surface of the Brig was covered in cemented seagull droppings, old seaweed and barnacles, so encrusted that there were plenty of foot- and handholds. And Tabitha had always been a good climber. She clambered along the length of the vessel, out above the sea, peering in at the tiny barred windows. It seemed to take for ever, but she knew she was getting closer all the time.

At last she found the right window. She tapped at the wood beside it, pushed her face up against the bars. Beyond, the dawn light picked out gentle ripples on the surface of the water in the merfolk tank.

'Wake up,' she hissed. 'Come on, wake up!'

A face appeared at the window, so suddenly that Tabitha almost lost her grip and fell. A merman, glaring at her from between long damp strands of black hair plastered to his face. *It's all right*, she told herself. *He can't hurt you. Not until he's out, anyway.*

'You,' growled the merman. 'I remember you. You came to the Brig. Two days ago. What do you want?'

So they can speak. Or at least, this one can. Good.

Tabitha reached for her belt and pulled out the hand saw.

'Shh,' she murmured. 'You'll wake the troll. I'm getting you out of here.'

The merman's eyes narrowed. 'Why?'

Don't lose your temper.

'Do you want me to explain,' asked Tabitha, 'or do you want me to saw?'

Chapter Twenty-eight

'Out of the way, mongrel!'

Joseph's eyes flicked open, and he rolled aside just in time to avoid the heavy boots. The sailor stomped by, coiling up a length of rope.

Already the blankets the crew had slept on were rolled up and stowed away, and the junk bustled with activity. Joseph sat up, clutching his own blanket to him and blinking. It was a glorious golden morning, gulls crying, sunshine slanting across the water, making the tips of the waves sparkle. Still, it wasn't exactly welcome. He'd barely slept. Couldn't stop thinking about Tabs, all alone in Port Fayt . . .

Sleeping under the stars hadn't helped, of course.

Jeb had taken the guest cabin and left him out here on deck – and there was nothing he could do about it. Back in the warehouse he'd been the one with the gun, and the Snitch had to do what he said. But here, among the hobgoblin's crew, he wasn't so sure. These were Jeb's friends, not his. And from the looks they gave him, he was starting to realize they didn't like him very much.

He took a deep breath to calm himself. *No need to worry*. Everything would be all right, just as soon as they got to the island. What had he expected, after all? A cosy warm bed and friendly faces?

Not that. But not this, either.

He rolled up his blanket and made his way across the deck, ducking and dodging to avoid the busy sailors. Once or twice he got in the way, and that earned him curses and even a clip round the ear. He felt like he wasn't wanted here. And he hadn't seen Jeb or the mermaid since they'd left port.

Of course, there was a reason why he hadn't gone down below to see Pallione. She'd ask him questions. She'd want to know why he'd abandoned Tabitha. *Not abandoned. Left behind*. No. That sounded even worse.

He joined a shuffling line and collected breakfast from a skinny young hobgoblin serving from behind a pair of barrels. A plate of salted fish with a slab of rockbread on the side. He hesitated a moment. He still didn't really want to see her, but she'd be hungry, and she deserved some breakfast at least. *Can't put it off for ever.* With a heavy heart, he climbed down the steps into the hold.

It was dark below, but as his eyes adjusted Joseph could make out the shape of the mermaid, seated and tied to the base of the mainmast. It made him feel sick. Why had they done that? It didn't make sense. It wasn't as though she could run away, was it?

Pallione struggled against her bonds and tried to spit out a dirty rag that had been stuffed in her mouth. Joseph dreaded what she was going to say, but he couldn't leave her like that. He wove through the crates and kegs, crouched down and pulled the gag away from her face.

'I'm so sorry,' he told her. 'I didn't know they'd tied you up. If I had, I'd have . . . well . . .' *What? What would I have done?*

She was silent, just looking at him. 'Why are you doing this?' she said at last.

Joseph set the plate on her lap and tried to feed her some of the fish, but Pallione just shook her head.

'There must be a reason.' She'd been trussed up in the hold for hours, but for once, she didn't seem angry

– just curious. 'You're a terrible singer, and any shark would make mincemeat of you. But you're a good person. So why are you helping the goblin?'

'We're taking you back to your father,' said Joseph lamely. He broke off a bit of rockbread and offered it to her, but again she shook her head.

'I'm not hungry. And you're not answering me. What do you get?'

Joseph put down the food and glanced around. The hold was empty. Up above he could hear the gulls and the shouts of the sailors keeping the junk on course.

'All right,' he said. 'Jeb says my father is alive, somewhere in the Old World. He told me that if I helped him get his reward, I'd see him again.'

'You believe him?'

Joseph reached into his pocket, brought out the tarnished silver pocket watch and showed it to her. 'This belonged to my father. Elijah. And Eleanor was my mother.'

The mermaid frowned, scrunching up her nose. 'How do you know the filthy goblin didn't steal it?'

'I – I just . . . know.' It sounded ridiculous. 'Anyway, even if there's a chance it's true I have to take it. Otherwise Jeb said he'd do something bad to him. I can't let that happen.'

'It's all right,' said the mermaid. 'I don't blame you.' Her green eyes sparkled. 'But then, I am not the blue-haired girl.'

Joseph felt as though he was dangling from a cliff, losing grip with every word Pallione spoke.

'You don't understand.'

'You're right, I don't.' She bit her lip, brow furrowed in thought. 'You know what *my* father told me?' she said at last. '*Always do the right thing*. He says you know, deep down, what the right thing is. And you have to do it. Even if it's not the thing you want to do. Even if—'

She stopped and took a deep breath.

'Are you all right?'

Pallione shrugged. And then, suddenly, the tears came.

For a moment Joseph forgot about his own father.

'You'll see him soon,' he said gently. 'I promise. And I bet he cares about you more than you think.'

'Really?' Joseph was startled by the tone of her voice. Anxious. Pleading. 'I was thinking about what you said. In the warehouse. I ought to have listened to him. I should never have swum so close to Port Fayt.'

A shout came from above. 'Land ahoy!'

Their eyes met for a moment.

'I'll be back,' said Joseph, his voice no more than a croak. The mermaid sniffed and nodded. He hurried across the hold and climbed the steps to the deck.

The wind was up, and Joseph had to fight against the tilting of the deck as he made his way to the gunwale. He shielded his eyes and looked out over the shining sea.

There was the island where they'd left their fellow watchmen – a rock in the distance. The thought of seeing them again should have made him happy, but instead he felt ill. *Where's Tabs?* they'd ask him. *She's still in Fayt? You did what?*

Movement caught his eyes in the surrounding water, and he gasped. Heads were dotted amongst the waves. Merfolk. Hundreds of them – maybe more. It was impossible to tell. The surface was endlessly breaking as they breached, dived down, arced through the air, twisting and flicking water at their friends, signing to one another with rapid hand movements.

More merfolk than he'd ever seen. Each one ready to fight.

'Hold course,' called someone from amidships. Joseph turned to see Jeb the Snitch swaggering over. He popped a last morsel of fish and rockbread into his mouth, licked his fingers and winked. 'Morning, mongrel. Sleep well?'

Joseph felt a sudden rush of anger. He shook his head. 'Never mind that. Why did they tie her up? She's not our prisoner.'

'Now, now,' said Jeb, leaning over the gunwale and picking his teeth. 'No need to get yer breeches in a twist. It's just a little precaution. This is Captain Lortt's ship, remember, so what he says goes.'

'And why are we holding course? We need to turn north. If we carry on east, we'll pass the island.'

'Why, so we will.' Jeb grinned.

Something's wrong.

'We have to drop the mermaid off,' said Joseph. 'Her father's waiting for her. I thought . . . I mean . . .'

Jeb put an arm around his shoulders, as though he was sharing a secret. 'Now listen, mate. Might be I wasn't entirely straight with yer back in Port Fayt. Thing is, see, we're still going on to the Old World. But we're not taking the mermaid back to her pa. We're taking her to Illon.'

Something's very wrong.

'Illon? What do you—?'

'Truth is, the Duke of Garran got wind of your little deal with the merfolk pretty sharpish. So a couple of days ago his people got a message to me, asked me if I could get hold of the mermaid for him. For a price, of course. That way he can hang onto her, make sure the King keeps his nose out of the battle.'

Panic gripped Joseph's chest so tightly he could barely breathe. *He's the biggest liar in Port Fayt*. That's what Tabitha had told him. And she'd been right.

'You're working for the League?'

'It's just business, mongrel. It's always just business with old Jeb. The mermaid won't come to no harm, so long as the merfolk don't fight. And you'll get to see your pa again. Makes no odds to you. Remember what I told yer, back in the warehouse? Do something for yerself for a change. Who knows, maybe the Fayters'll win the battle anyway.'

Joseph looked out to sea, and an image came into his head of Newton's fleet, blown apart by enemy gunfire. Sailors screaming for help. Newt would fight to the end, of course, even as his men fell around him.

A cold weight settled in his stomach. He wouldn't let it happen. He couldn't. How could he look his father in the eye, if he'd betrayed his friends? If he'd kept Pallione and the King apart? She'd saved his life, twice. Was this how he was going to repay her?

What was he doing?

What, in Thalin's name, was he doing?

The deck juddered, and Joseph had to grab hold of the gunwale. Shouts went up. He looked around and saw the other sailors staring at each other, eyes wide, uncertain. Jeb's pale eyes darted nervously to the prow. 'What the—?'

The deck gave another shudder, longer and harder this time, and the hull groaned.

The cabin door banged open and Captain Lortt strode out.

'Sky's sake!' barked the hobgoblin. 'What's going on?'

'Don't know, sir,' said a sailor.

'Maybe a rock?' suggested another.

Lortt frowned. 'We're too far from shore for—'

A third time, the vessel shook. A barrel came loose from its moorings and rolled across the deck, banging against the side.

'What's going on?' shouted Lortt. 'Answer me, someone.'

And in the silence which followed, a voice floated up from the waters below. A voice Joseph would have known anywhere.

'Ahoy,' Tabitha called. 'Surrender the mermaid, or we attack.'

He peered over the edge of the gunwale. There were three haggard merfolk bobbing in the waves, none armed, but all looking desperate and determined. *Where did they come from?* Tabitha sat on the shoulders of one of the mermaids, pale and tired, her wet blue hair clinging to her head, her brown coat soaking wet. Knives glittered in both hands, poised to be thrown. She met Joseph's eye, and a cloud passed across her face. He felt his stomach lurch as she looked away again.

'Come on!' yelled Tabitha. 'You're surrounded. We haven't got all day.'

Joseph turned back to the ship, his heart weighing him down with such a swell of emotion that he didn't know what to do. 'We should give them the mermaid,' he said.

But no one was listening. Jeb had scurried away towards the cabin. Captain Lortt was reeling off orders, and already sailors were rushing up from below carrying muskets, crossbows and blunderbusses. They lined up along the sides of the ship, nocking bolts, pouring out gunpowder, taking aim. Joseph found himself pushed back, away from Tabitha.

'Ready,' shouted Lortt. 'Aim . . . FIRE!'

But as he spoke the last word there were splashes on either side of the junk, and several shapes arced overhead like dolphins, casting shadows across the deck. Joseph had never seen merfolk leap so high or so far. Gunfire erupted from the crew, but they were too late. A pair of them were seized and dragged wailing over the gunwale into the sea. Joseph caught a glimpse of Tabitha in mid-air, her mouth open wide in a battle cry, held tight by her mermaid companion. One of her knives flashed down and struck Captain Lortt's foot. The hobgoblin yelped and hopped, screaming abuse at the merfolk.

'Reload!' yelled Jeb the Snitch.

Captain Lortt pulled the knife out of his foot and began hobbling back towards his cabin.

Do something. Do something now.

Joseph scrambled after the discarded blade, wiped the blood off on his breeches. He raced across to the hatch as more gunfire sounded and more merfolk arced overhead, back the way they'd come, snatching more sailors with them as they dived into the sea.

You know, deep down, what the right thing is.

He clattered down the steps into the darkness of the hold. Pallione was struggling against her ropes, trying to get free.

'Stay still,' he told her.

'What are you . . .?' Then something changed in her face, and she stopped moving. She smiled at him, and to his surprise, Joseph found himself smiling back. 'I knew you were a good person,' she said.

Joseph didn't know what to say to that, so instead he hacked at the rope, sawing and chopping until it frayed into nothingness, then tugged the rest away as fast as he could. He was scared. But at the same time he was buzzing with energy. He felt good. Like he'd been locked away in a dusty room and was finally emerging into fresh air. And all he'd had to do was make the right choice. *Do the right thing.*

He bent down, straining his muscles to lift her over his shoulder. She wasn't heavy, but then, Joseph wasn't strong either.

'Careful!' she snapped. 'I'm a princess, remember.'

He staggered with her, climbing the steps into the open air.

'Oi!'

Joseph turned and saw Jeb the Snitch striding across the deck towards them, snarling and brandishing a pistol. 'Drop that mermaid, mongrel.'

'Don't you dare,' said Pallione.

More gunfire, and Jeb crouched down along with the rest of the crew as the merfolk flung themselves above the deck once again. 'I got one,' shouted a crewman. Joseph hoped in the name of Thalin that he hadn't.

He kept going, stumbling across the deck to the side of the ship near the prow, which was empty of sailors. The crew were too busy fighting off the merfolk to worry about them. All except Jeb.

'One more step, mongrel,' said the goblin. 'We had a deal.'

Joseph didn't even look back. He should have known better than to trust Jeb the Snitch. And now he wasn't going to listen to another word from him.

A pistol crack, noticeable even amongst the other gunshots, and in front of them splinters flew from the deck. Joseph's heart hammered inside his chest. He set Pallione down on the gunwale, placing himself in front of her so that she was out of harm's way.

Jeb was fumbling to reload. 'What about your father, boy?' he yelled. 'You'll never see him again. I'll make sure of it.'

'Leave me,' said Pallione suddenly.

'What did you say?'

The breeze whipped the mermaid's white hair across her face. Her green eyes were wide and filled with doubt. Were those fresh tears forming in them or was it just the wind?

'I don't . . . What if he's right?' There was panic in her voice. 'What if you never see your father again? Because of me.'

'It doesn't matter,' said Joseph, and as he spoke he

knew it was true. 'Remember what you said? I have to do the right thing.'

He clambered up onto the gunwale, took hold of Pallione's hand and pushed off over the edge. He barely noticed the crack of the second pistol shot.

Chapter Twenty-nine

'Come on, mate,' said Frank. 'Is it a League ship or Fayters?'

Phineus Clagg peered through the spyglass, his tongue sticking out of the side of his mouth as he concentrated.

'Beats me, matey. But either way I wager they'll have a drop of firewater on board. Saved at last!'

Paddy rolled his eyes and took the spyglass from him. 'It's a hobgoblin junk,' he said. 'See those battened sails? So the odds are good.'

'Then why are those merfolk attacking it?' asked Frank.

'Something's changed,' said Hal. They all looked

back at the ship. The gunfire had stopped and the merfolk had disappeared into the water. There was still movement on deck though.

'Looks like they're arguing about something,' said Paddy, adjusting the spyglass. 'Now the crew are heading to their stations.'

Slowly but surely, the ship turned, tacking away from the island and back out to sea. East. The sails filled with wind.

'Maw's teeth,' muttered Hal. He didn't often swear, but it was unbearable being stuck here on the beach when the ship was so close. If he had to watch the twins play another hand of cards . . . Well, he didn't like to think what he'd do.

Phineus Clagg raced across the sand and into the surf, waving his arms, his coat flapping behind him.

'Wait! Come back – I can't take it here any more!'

Frank chuckled.

'There's something strange about this,' said Hal. 'Why would they come so close to the island and then turn back? It doesn't make—'

'Hold on,' said Paddy, pointing as he held the spyglass. 'Look over there, closer to shore.'

They all squinted at the ocean. And then they saw it. Six shapes moving fast through the water towards them. Merfolk. And three of them had passengers clinging to their backs.

Frank's enormous hand fell on Hal's shoulder, squeezing so hard he winced.

'Three,' said Frank. 'Joseph, Tabs and Pallione?'

Hal shrugged himself free of the troll's grip and shook his head. 'Pallione is a mermaid. She wouldn't need to be carried. Unless . . .'

'Oh no,' said Paddy. 'Oh, Thalin, no.'

'What?'

Paddy lowered the spyglass, his jaw hanging open. Hal gently took it from his hand and peered through it.

The merfolk were moving too fast for him to make out much. But he saw a flash of blue, which had to be Tabitha's head. Then a blur of grey skin – Joseph, surely. *Thank Thalin.* Then he saw the third passenger and the breath left his body. A mermaid, not much older than Tabs.

Behind her, the water was stained red.

The sea bed rose up below, visible at last through the shallows. Tabitha slid off the merman and stumbled into the water. Her feet found rocks and she steadied herself, looking around for the princess. There she was, slumped on the back of another mermaid. Pallione's eyes were closed and her skin was as white as her bedraggled hair. The sea around her clouded with blood as they came to a stop.

Tabitha felt sick as she fought her way through the surf, lifted one of Pallione's arms over her shoulder and floated the princess free of the mermaid who'd been carrying her. Joseph appeared on the other side, his face frozen in shock as he took Pallione's other arm over his own shoulder. He tried to meet Tabitha's eyes, but she couldn't look at him. Not yet. Together they waded onto the beach.

The Demon's Watch were racing towards them. The two hulking troll shapes of Frank and Paddy in the lead; Hal, hanging onto his hat and spectacles as he ran. Then the smuggler Phineus Clagg, wild-eyed and pale. She should have been pleased to see them, but she could feel nothing but fear for the mermaid.

Please hang on. Please. Don't . . . Don't be . . .

Tears pricked her eyes. Paddy put his big green arm around her shoulders, tried gently to move her away. But she wasn't leaving Pallione. She took hold of the limp tail, shouldering it as Joseph, Frank and Hal stumbled to hold up the rest of her. They made their way out of the surf and along the beach. Blood dripped onto the sand, even more now that they were out of the water.

Pallione was breathing, but in weak, choking gasps. Her face was becoming whiter by the minute and her eyes were still closed. Tabitha would have given anything for her to open them. She bowed her head so that she wouldn't have to look at the red that stained Pallione's seaweed tunic. *Why couldn't I have been nicer to her?* Thalin knew, she didn't like the mermaid. But Pallione had been trapped in a town she hated, all on her own, and Tabitha had made it even worse for her.

What's wrong with me?

As they stumbled on round the curve of the island, a strange rock column came into sight – giant boulders balanced improbably in the shallows, one on top of the other. On the highest boulder sat an old merman. He wore no crown, but Tabitha knew at once that this was the King. *Pallione's father*. Thousands of heads bobbed up and down close to the shore. No more leaping or playing. Each and every one of the merfolk was still, floating with the waves, watching and waiting.

They waded out into the surf, holding the princess above the water and struggling for a footing on the rocky bottom. The waves lapped at their knees, then their waists, then their chests. As they came closer, Tabitha saw the breeze buffet the King's long white hair and beard. His pearl-studded bonestaff trembled in his hand.

They came to a halt several feet from the column of boulders, with the water almost up to their necks. 'Your majesty,' said Frank, and his voice was hoarse. 'Your daughter, Pallione.'

The King blinked as though he couldn't believe what he was seeing.

'Pallione?' he said at last. His voice was barely a whisper, but it broke Tabitha's heart. When he spoke again it was an anguished cry, like that of a wounded man. 'Pallione!'

He pushed off from the boulder with his tail, diving into the water and sending up a plume of spray. A moment later he surfaced, his long hair slicked back, his eyes red.

'Let her go,' he growled, and there was thunder in his voice. 'Her place is here. In the ocean.'

The watchmen stood aside and let Pallione float free, her hair fanning out like a living thing. The King took her in his arms, clinging onto her as though she might escape at any moment. 'Pallione,' he whispered again. 'My daughter.'

'I'm sorry,' said Tabitha, but it sounded pathetic. Inadequate. As if she was apologizing for treading on someone's foot. 'I'm just so sorry.' This time it sounded as if she was an actor trying too hard with her lines.

Out of the corner of her eye, she saw Joseph lurch forward.

'It was my fault,' he said. Hearing his voice, Tabitha suddenly felt sorry for him. 'I was selfish. I was stupid, and I—'

Frank laid a hand on the tavern boy's shoulder.

'Joseph, that's enough.'

'No, it's not enough. It's not—'

A sudden gasp went up from the merfolk all around them, and Tabitha's eyes snapped back to Pallione. Her heart beat wildly. The mermaid's tail was twitching, her eyelashes fluttered, and at last she opened her eyes. They were still a vivid green but glassy, lifeless. The King cradled his daughter's head and pushed the tangled hair away from her face.

'I'm sorry,' said Tabitha again, but no one was listening. She was choking, and she could no longer see the mermaid's face through her tears.

'Father,' said Pallione, and drew a shuddering breath. 'Father . . .'

'I love you,' said the King. 'My daughter. You must know I—'

'I'm sorry,' murmured Pallione. 'I should have . . .' She paused to take a breath which twisted her face with pain. 'Should have listened. You told me . . . told me not to . . .'

The King laid a finger on her lips.

'You mustn't be sorry. Pallione. My daughter. My seraph. Forgive me.' He was rocking her gently in his arms. 'Please forgive me. I don't think I ever told you enough . . . Or I didn't show you . . . I didn't . . .'

Pallione smiled.

'I love you, Father.'

She drew another deep breath, and it seemed to rack her body from her head to the tip of her tail. When she let it out, it was as though she had been half awake, and was relaxing back into sleep.

Tabitha waited, but there were no more breaths. The breeze stung her tear-stained cheeks.

The King combed his daughter's hair with trembling fingers.

'Stand aside,' he said quietly. 'All of you.'

Tabitha felt it before she saw it: a shuddering through her very bones. Then the shimmer of the air around them. No, a *tremor* – that's what Hal called it. The sign of a spell being cast. In an instant her knives were in her hands.

'No,' said Hal. 'It's all right. We're safe.' His eyes were wide behind his spectacles as he watched the merman and his daughter. Tabitha didn't think she'd ever seen him look so astonished.

The tremor grew so that the King and Pallione were nothing but a blur. Tabitha pushed away, trying to escape the strange shuddering sensation. She stumbled out of the water and onto the beach, turning to look back in awe. It was one of the strangest things she'd ever seen – as though someone had cast a great rock into the ocean, but the ripples were moving through the air as well as the water.

The other watchmen had made it onto the beach too, and were open-mouthed in wonder. All except Joseph. He had sunk to his knees in the sand, his grey-pink face turned away as though he couldn't bear to watch. Again Tabitha felt a pang of pity for him. Despite what he'd done. Or maybe because of it.

'You must leave,' said a fair-haired merman. 'All of you. There is no place for you here.'

'We can't,' said Tabitha. 'We can't go now.'

'What about Pallione?' said Frank. 'What's happening to her?'

The merman shook his head. 'There is nothing more you can do.'

Tabitha felt a chill run through her body, right to the tips of her toes. They had come so far, but they had lost the one thing that mattered. *Pallione*. And now the merfolk would never fight. Why would their King join the Fayters when, instead of rescuing his only daughter, they'd got her killed?

'Back home then, eh?' said Phineus Clagg, laying a hand on Tabitha's shoulder. 'To Port Fayt. Where there's food and firewater and peace and quiet.'

Paddy shook his head.

'There is no home. No peace neither. Not until the League's defeated.'

'Aye,' said Frank. 'Only one place to go now. To Illon. To the battle.'

He spears another morsel of fish with the gleaming silver fork, slices it away with the knife. The delicate fried crust yields easily to the soft white flesh beneath.

'Still no word from the goblin?'

Major Metcalfe shakes his head. He and the other commanders are standing to attention as best they can in the cramped cabin, but they have to bend to fit under the low ceiling. The day is already hot, and they are sweating in their uniforms. 'Nothing, your grace. And our scouts' latest report is that the merfolk remain gathered near their island.'

'Interesting.' So the Fayters have not yet found the mermaid princess.

The Duke of Garran dabs at his mouth with one corner of his thick white napkin.

'There is one thing, your grace,' says Major Garrick. 'An hour ago our lookouts on the starboard flank spied a hobgoblin junk sailing due east, towards the Old World – too far north to intercept.'

More interesting still. Fayters abandoning their fleet? But if so, they would surely go west. Or Jeb the Snitch . . . ? But why should he run?

The answer comes to him at once. The goblin fears the wrath of the League. Fears it because he has failed.

Could it be that the mermaid is dead?

The Duke of Garran cuts off another piece of fish, conveys it to his mouth and chews, savouring it.

It is not perfect. He wanted her alive. A prisoner. Then the King would surely not dare to fight. But it makes little difference. The merman will not lead his hosts into battle now. Not if his daughter is lost.

'Very well,' he says when he has swallowed. 'We shall delay no further. Majors, ready your vessels and attend my signal.'

The men salute and leave the cabin. Only Major Turnbull remains. She is leaning against the door frame, her blue eyes shining in the gloom, her long blonde hair let free for once, falling over her shoulders. She looks so innocent and beautiful, it is easy to forget the things she can do. The things she has done.

'A chance to test out your blade on the demonspawn,' says the Duke of Garran. 'You must be delighted.'

She says nothing, of course. Not even a shrug.

He smiles.

'You will stay with me, Major, aboard the Justice. *As we agreed. And make certain there are no mistakes.'*

She nods and leaves the cabin, the sword on her back gleaming as she steps out through the doorway.

The Duke of Garran sets down his knife and fork and lays his napkin on the half-finished plate of food. He reaches across the table and picks up his brace of pistols, so encrusted with silver and gold filigree that the wood beneath can barely be seen. He stands and stows them at his belt, ready for use.

It is time.

Time to bring light into the darkness.

PART FOUR
The Battle of Illon

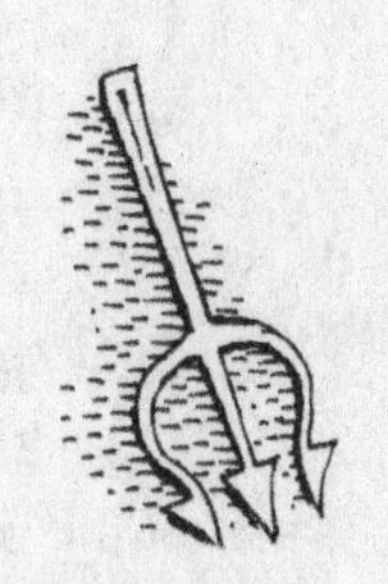

Chapter Thirty

It was a fine morning, all right. A couple of wisps of white cloud in a sky so blue it looked unreal. The sun shining overhead, its light gilding the waves and making them sparkle. The island of Illon, a distant green mound rising from the sea off the starboard bows of the Fayter fleet. Even the wind was perfect – steady and strong as it carried their enemies towards them.

As death came closer, and closer.

The first League vessel had been spotted a quarter of an hour ago, a white shape against the horizon, growing steadily larger. Then more ships. And more. Now they cluttered the ocean, flags flapping proudly, sails full as they approached.

'Shall I go again, mister?' asked Ty. The fairy sat on the gunwale beside Newton, kicking his feet over the edge.

Newton shook his head.

'No point, Ty.'

He glanced at the rest of the Fayter fleet. The vessels were strung out prow to stern in a ragged battle line, ready to deliver a broadside blast of cannon fire as the League came at them head on. With this wind, though, they'd have no time to reload before the League broke through. Then the real slaughter would begin.

In the centre, the *Wyvern* rose above the other ships. The signal flags fluttering from the masthead still carried the same message: *Hold the line*. Newton had already sent Ty to ask Colonel Derringer for further orders, and the fairy had returned with the news that the colonel had clearly indicated to hold position. That was that. There had been no council of war, no plan beyond those three words: *Hold the line*.

Derringer might be an expert swordsman, but he no more knew how to command a fleet than a griffin knew how to make a sandwich.

Still more League vessels appeared over the horizon. Those at the front were clearer now. In the lead was the *Justice* – heading up a wedge pointed towards the centre of the Fayter line. Towards the *Wyvern*. The *Justice* was the biggest ship Newton had ever seen. Each pristine sail was embroidered with the League's Golden Sun, and the white hull gleamed in the sunshine.

Newton realized that he was rubbing at the scars on his wrists again, and forced himself to stop. Old Jon stood quietly smoking at his side, and that calmed him a little. He reached down for the hilt of the sword propped against the gunwale – the Sword of Corin – and ran his fingers over the cool metal of the pommel. Whatever happened, he wouldn't go down without a fight.

'Um, excuse me? Sir?'

Newton sighed before he turned round.

'You don't have to call me "sir". You're the captain, remember? I'm just Newton. Or Newt.'

'Yes . . . Sorry, Mr Newton.'

The young imp, captain of the *Dread Unicorn*, still wore the red velvet jacket he'd had on when Newton first met him a few days ago. This time, though, his face was as pale as an imp's pink skin would ever go. No, not quite – Newton watched it go paler still as the captain caught sight of the enemy fleet beyond.

'The thing is,' said the imp, 'the gun crews are all ready.'

'Aye,' said Newton.

'But most of them don't know how to, er—'

'How to what?' Newton's spirits were sinking again.

'How to fire the cannons.'

Newton closed his eyes and took a deep breath.

'Er . . . Mr Newton, sir?'

He opened his eyes.

No more playing dead.

No more doing what he was told.

It was time. Time to fight.

'Jon,' he said, laying a hand on the elf's shoulder. 'Go below. Teach them how to work those guns.'

The elf nodded, knocked out his pipe and hobbled off.

'And you . . .' Newton turned to the imp. 'Weigh anchor. Make sail and steer us hard a-starboard.'

'Starboard?' said the imp uncertainly. 'Isn't that – towards the enemy?'

'Aye. This is a battle, remember?'

The imp's eyes darted in the direction of the League.

'Um, you did say I was the captain. And that you were just—'

'Not any more.'

Newton was pretty sure the imp looked relieved.

'Aye-aye, Mr Newton, sir,' he said, saluted, and turned on his heel to deliver orders to the crew.

'What about me, mister?' came Ty's tiny, tinkling voice.

'Fly to Colonel Derringer. Tell him we're engaging the enemy, and if he has any sense he'll strike those signal flags and do the same.'

Ty grinned, sprang off the gunwale and shimmered away across the water towards the *Wyvern*.

Only Newton remained on the poop deck as the anchor was hauled up and the sails unfurled, his eyes fixed on the *Justice* as she sailed closer still.

All right, you scum. Now we'll show you what Port Fayt is made of.

'A Fayt vessel's breaking the line, your grace.'

Major Turnbull turned from the prow, her blonde ponytail whipped out over her shoulder by the breeze.

'It must be Captain Newton,' she said. Even her voice was beautiful, the Duke of Garran reflected. He settled back into the gilded chair set up for him on the forecastle.

'We shall see.'

Turnbull drew her double-handed sword from its sheath. It was so ugly compared to its owner. Big and brutal, the metal dulled from long use, a couple of chips marring the blade. A tool, nothing more. Not like the Sword of Corin.

'Engage that vessel, and signal that it belongs to the *Justice*,' said the Duke of Garran. The order was picked up by the sailors nearest him, transferred in shouts towards the stern. 'We will make an example of her.'

They surged through the water, swimming close to the surface. Joseph clung onto the merman who carried him, trying not to shiver with cold every time they leaped up above the waves, where the breeze bit into his sodden clothing.

Whenever he was able to steal a glance, it seemed as though the ocean was moving alongside them – flashing tails of merfolk on both sides, sending up a constant rush of spray as they made their way fast towards Illon. Tabitha's merfolk – the ones she'd rescued from the Brig – had agreed to carry them into battle. But once they arrived, the watchmen would be on their own.

Joseph patted his coat, checking that his father's watch was still in place. Probably waterlogged and broken by now, but that was what he deserved. *It wasn't your fault*, the troll twins had told him. But they didn't know the full story. How he'd been so obsessed with finding his father that he'd betrayed Port Fayt. Tabitha hadn't told them. Not yet, anyway. In a strange way, he hoped she would – they had a right to know.

They dived under the waves again, and Joseph held his breath as they streaked along underwater. It felt safer here, with the sea filling his eyes and ears, protecting him from the world.

Once, a long time ago, he'd sat with his father on the docks watching for merfolk. That was when he'd first heard the story of how the Old World began. How the very first people were made by demons and seraphs. *There's a little bit of demon and a little bit of seraph in everyone,* his father had told him. And now he'd found that little bit of demon in himself.

There was nothing he wouldn't give to bring Pallione back.

Suddenly the merman kicked upwards, jolting Joseph out of his thoughts. They sprang up above the waves and came to rest, bobbing there in the water. All around them the merfolk had stopped. Joseph rubbed the seawater from his eyes, peered ahead and took in the scene that lay ahead.

Ships. More ships than he'd ever seen before. To their right, a motley line of vessels – galleons, wavecutters, junks and dhows, strung out end to end, all flying sea-green flags with silver shells stitched on. The Fayter fleet, he realized. One of the ships, a frigate, had broken the line and was sailing out across the sparkling water. Two impish dhows were following. Heading towards . . .

Joseph caught his breath. To the left was the League armada in full sail, heading towards the Fayter battle line. In the lead was an enormous white ship, the Golden Sun shining from each of her sails. It was the ship he'd seen three days ago, through his spyglass, from the crow's nest of the *Sharkbane*. And at that speed she would engage with the Fayter frigate within minutes.

The battle was about to begin.

In the centre of the tiny band of merfolk, Paddy Bootle turned, caught Joseph's eye and nodded at him. No cheery smile. Not today.

'Come on then,' said Frank. He swept off his tricorne hat and pointed it, dripping, at the fleets. 'What are we waiting for?'

'Faster!' roared Newton from the prow.

'Can't go any faster,' squeaked the captain.

Newton glanced over the side of the ship. The *Dread Unicorn* was nippier than he would have given her credit for. But now a League vessel was pulling past them to starboard. One good volley of cannon fire from the enemy, and they could be finished. He licked his lips.

'Very well. Deliver a broadside on that vessel. And don't let the *Justice* get into position to fire on us.'

'Aye-aye.' The captain scurried below. Moments later, the ship shook as her starboard cannons thundered into life. At least half of them by Newton's reckoning. Better than he'd expected; Old Jon had taught them well.

The League vessel splintered in a few places, but there was no serious damage. The range was too great. She just carried on, ignoring the *Dread Unicorn* entirely.

Probably for the best.

Newton strode across the deck, down into the darkness of the lower levels, where the imp captain stood by Old Jon, watching the gun crews reloading and dabbing at his brow with an expensive-looking handkerchief. Smoke hung heavy in the air, along with the smell of gunpowder.

'Are there any magicians on board?' barked Newton. 'Anyone?'

'But Mr Newton . . .' said the imp. His cheeks were flushed now. 'Magic isn't permitted in Fayt without a warrant.'

Newton had all but lost his patience. 'We're

not in Fayt now,' he pointed out. 'Any magicians?'

Hesitantly, three figures stepped forward from among the gun crews – a nervous-looking woman with scraggly grey hair, a fat bald man with several teeth missing, and a tall, gaunt elf with hollow eyes.

'Perfect. Follow me.'

He led them up the steps and across the deck to the prow. More cannon fire was sounding now, making them duck with every volley. The faces of the three magicians paled, just as the imp's had, when they saw the towering *Justice* approaching them. Newton didn't have time to reassure them.

'We need to get onto that ship.'

The bald man and the elf shook their heads.

'It's too high,' said the elf.

'We could lift a person up onto it,' said the man. 'But not a whole crew.'

Newton was just wondering if knocking their heads together would help, when the woman spoke up. 'What if we go through? Instead of up? If we all work on one small area of the hull, we could smash a hole – some simple arboreal manipulation. Then we could jump across onto their gun decks.'

Slowly, her two companions nodded. They looked a little disgruntled that they hadn't thought of it themselves.

'Aye, s'pose we could do that.'

'Then do it,' growled Newton.

A shape dropped out of the sky towards them and they all ducked again. But it was only Ty. The fairy alighted on Newton's shoulder.

'Colonel Derringer's not too happy, mister. Called you some pretty bad names, if I'm honest.'

'He can take a dive into the ocean for all I care. Get everyone armed and ready to board the *Justice*.'

'Aye, Captain.' The fairy's wings blurred back into life. He took off, saluted and darted down below decks.

The three magicians stood side by side, staring at the approaching ship and holding hands. Newton stepped back, not wanting to break their concentration.

The *Justice* was close now. Very close. He could see the cannon poking out of the gun ports, four ranks deep. But still the enemy flagship made no attempt to steer away and expose the *Dread Unicorn* to her fearsome gunnery.

Then he spotted a figure up on the enemy deck, silhouetted against the sails. A second joined him. A third. They wore white uniforms with red symbols embroidered on their shoulders.

Fireballs.

'Look out!' he roared, but even as he spoke the

League magicians raised their arms, and three streaks of unnatural fire tore through the air.

Newton dived onto the Fayter magicians, bundling them to the deck. A wave of heat passed overhead. But when he looked up, he saw that they hadn't been the targets after all. The *Dread Unicorn*'s sails were ablaze, smoke billowing from rapidly widening holes scorched in the mainsail and two topsails.

Behind, there were shouts of dismay as Fayters saw the damage.

Newton grabbed hold of the magicians and pointed them towards the *Justice*.

'Best get going. And quickly.'

The woman nodded and took the other magicians' hands. They stood shakily, working up their power again.

Newton watched the League magicians raising their hands for a second time . . .

Cannon fire, to port. The *Justice* shook, and the League magicians stumbled, turned to see what was happening. Newton turned too. *What in Thalin's name was that?*

Two small vessels had sailed out from behind the *Dread Unicorn* – low-lying, with elegant triangular sails. Impish dhows. One had smoke rising from her cannon. The other fired a broadside as Newton watched, red flashes racing along her gun deck, booms rolling out across the waves. The *Justice* shuddered for a second time as cannonballs smashed into her hull.

In spite of everything, Newton smiled. The imp captains had remembered his plan from their first encounter with the League. And it was working.

The nearest dhow had strung up a set of signal flags: *Good luck.*

The *Dread Unicorn* was on a collision course with the *Justice*. Just a few more moments . . .

'Now!' roared Newton.

The three Fayter magicians threw their hands out as one. The air shimmered and there was an almighty *CRACK!* as a section of the enemy ship's hull broke apart, crumpling like paper, planks splintering inwards to leave a gaping hole big enough for two men to enter side by side. Inside, Newton saw wide-eyed League marines stumbling backwards in surprise.

At the same instant, the two vessels collided with a bump, throwing everyone off balance as the hulls ground together.

Newton stepped up on the gunwale and leaped into the enemy ship, raising the gleaming Sword of Corin high above his head.

Chapter Thirty-one

Cannons blasted into life, and the merfolk dived down deep as the shots thundered overhead. Tabitha got a mouthful of seawater and spluttered as they came up for air. She clung onto her mermaid carrier with one hand, rubbing salt from her eyes with the other.

Whatever happened, she couldn't let go. She was just as helpless here in the sea as Pallione had been on the land. *No, don't think about her. Not now* . . . There were other things to worry about.

One of the League scout ships had sailed out ahead of the armada, uncomfortably close.

'Turn!' yelled Paddy, pointing with his cutlass. 'To the Fayter fleet!'

But it was too late. The League ship seemed to shimmer for a moment, and a ripple raced through the air towards the merfolk.

'Down!' Tabitha heard Hal shouting. 'Down again!'

She spotted one of the mermaids leaping out of the waves, carrying a smuggler on her back. The pair of them caught the full force of the magic bolt and were hurled backwards, coming apart and smashing into the sea like cannonballs.

Her heart was pounding as they dived.

The first of us to die, she realized. *Probably not the last.*

They surfaced moments later, and Tabitha saw that the League ship had tacked back towards the battle. But now a Fayter vessel had broken the line and was steering towards them. A small wavecutter, keeping watch over the flank. Signal flags were raised. *Come aboard.*

Good. They needed to get onto a friendly ship fast. Tabitha did not want to be floundering around in the ocean amid the enemy fleet.

The merfolk turned like a shoal of fish, streaking towards the wavecutter at incredible speed. The ship loomed larger and larger, and Tabitha saw rope ladders being flung overboard. As her own mermaid reached the hull, the troll twins were already there, heaving themselves out of the water, dripping wet. They clambered up the side of the ship to the welcoming arms of Fayters in sea-green armbands. Next went Phineus Clagg. Then Joseph, Hal and the remaining smugglers.

Tabitha was the last to go. She grabbed hold of the rope ladder and pulled herself out of the water. 'Thank you,' she called over her shoulder. 'On behalf of the Demon's Watch.'

'You rescued us,' said a mermaid with thick black hair and a broken nose. 'Now the debt is paid.'

Tabitha nodded and watched as they disappeared beneath the waves. She'd hated them at first. But the more she knew of these merfolk, the more she liked them.

No. Don't think about her.

She began to climb. Hal was ahead, scrambling up over the gunwale, helped by a man wearing a Fayter armband, with ginger hair tied back in a ponytail and a ginger beard and moustache.

She'd seen him somewhere before. Somewhere recently. Where was it?

'Hello there, miss,' said the man, holding out a hand. As Tabitha reached up, she saw that there was something wrong with it. The hand had only three fingers.

A man with a ginger ponytail . . . and three fingers . . .

With a sickening jolt, she knew exactly where she'd seen him. She pulled her hand away, but the man snatched her wrist and held on with an iron grip, tugging her towards him.

'Let me go,' she yelled, but it was no good. She sounded pathetic. Tommy just grinned, and a dwarf joined him, heaving her up over the gunwale and onto the ship.

The Demon's Watch were kneeling on the deck, hands on their heads, weapons piled in front of them. One of the crewmen was inspecting Hal's wooden spoon with suspicion, before finally throwing it onto the pile. Joseph caught Tabitha's eye for a moment before she looked away.

Ranged around the prisoners were the ship's crew, armed with crossbows, blunderbusses and pistols. They wore the sea-green armbands of Fayt, but up close she saw that their faces were hard, cold and cruel. In the centre stood a tall man dressed in black, wearing a hammered ducat as an eye patch and smoking a pipe. At his side was a much smaller figure. A child dressed in gold, from his buckled shoes to the tip of his cockatrice feather plume. His hand was outstretched, and in his palm sat a fairy, swinging his legs and smirking at Tabitha.

Slik.

'You fools,' sneered the Boy King. 'Did you really think you could get away from me?'

Smoke everywhere. Newton didn't know where it had come from, but it engulfed him, along with the noises of battle: the clash of steel, the cries of the dying and the boom of distant cannon.

He stalked across the gun deck, almost tripped over the sprawled, bloodied body of an imp. No time to stay and see if the fallen Fayter was dead or alive. He pressed on, a pistol in one hand, the Sword of Corin in the other.

Old Jon moved behind him, stealthy and silent, his cudgel poised to strike.

Always got my back, Old Jon.

A glimpse of white coats through the smoke, and Newton veered away from them. He didn't want to get bogged down here below decks. The man he wanted would be up above, overseeing the battle from the foredeck.

A dwarf appeared out of nowhere, roaring with all his lung power, and Newton had to sidestep to avoid being chopped in half by a whirling axe.

'Sorry,' grunted the dwarf, and disappeared back into the smoke, roaring again.

At last they came to the steps that led to the upper deck. Newton took a deep breath and flexed the fingers of his sword hand. His grip was too tight – no good for fighting. But anger and the adrenaline of battle did that to you. He tucked the sword under his arm and shook out his hand, looking back at Old Jon to check that he was ready. The elf nodded. They set off up the steps.

Above, more smoke. None of the Fayters had made it this far yet, and the only figures to be seen were white-coated League sailors scurrying about, and a couple of snipers trying to sight through the smoke, looking for targets on other ships.

One turned at the sound of their footsteps, swinging his musket round. There was a gunshot and the man collapsed like a puppet whose strings had been cut. Old Jon dropped a smoking pistol, drew another from his belt.

Newton peered through the smoke. There, on the foredeck, was an ornate golden chair, its back to them. It could only belong to the Duke of Garran. He broke into a run, cleared the steps and leaped forward, boot first, connecting hard.

The figure sitting in the chair went into a roll as it tumbled forward. Newton landed off balance, and staggered back. It wasn't the Duke of Garran at all.

Instead, he found himself glaring into the blue eyes of Alice Turnbull. Her white coat was pristine and her blonde hair was tied back in a ponytail, as before. She held her huge sword in both hands, relaxed but ready. Her face was expressionless – no trace of fear.

A pistol crack from behind him.

Old Jon, again.

But the woman didn't fall. Instead her eyes flicked momentarily to Newton's left. He spun round and his heart jolted.

Old Jon was on his knees, one hand still holding his cudgel, the other clasping his throat. Blood bubbled through the elf's fingers. His face was as white as a sail and his eyes bulged. He raised the cudgel slowly, pointing it at something.

'Mr Newton,' said a familiar voice. The Duke of Garran stepped out from behind the foremast, holding an ornate pistol. He blew away the smoke, pulled back the hammer and began to reload. 'I suspected we might meet again.' He pointed a white-gloved finger at the Sword of Corin. 'A beautiful blade for a mongrel.'

The Boy King took a sugar lump from his pocket and tossed it to Slik. The fairy caught it and tucked in, gnawing like a rat.

'You did, didn't you?' said the boy, and his voice

was a sneer of triumph. 'You thought you could beat me. Me, the Boy King! Lord of the Marlinspike Quarter! Terror of Port Fayt! How absurd. How . . . funny!'

His crew chuckled.

'Yes, very amusing. But I hear everything, you idiots. Everything! This fairy found out about the hobgoblin captain, and your little plan to sneak away in the night. My ship's *much* faster than his stupid junk. And now I'm angry. Very, very angry. You, Tommy. You know what happens when I get angry, don't you?'

Tommy held up his three-fingered hand.

'And you, Gargunnock.'

Another crewman stepped forward, a goblin, lifting off his hat to reveal that he had no ears.

Joseph couldn't stop trembling. He cast a quick glance at the other watchmen, and that settled him a little. The troll twins looked icy calm. Tabitha too. Only Hal looked halfway scared.

'But this is different,' the Boy King went on. 'You spilled wine on me. You failed to entertain me. You spoiled my special punishment and you stole my mermaid from me. And now you've forced me to chase after you. In the middle of all this!' He flung his arm out, indicating the battle.

Cannon fire sounded somewhere close by, making half the crew jump and turn round. There was too much smoke to see what was going on, but every now and again there was a flash of guns, or the shape of a vessel looming in the distance. The wavecutter was cruising at the fringes, safe from the fighting.

'And what's more,' said the Boy King, 'it's my birthday! So you see, it won't just be a couple of fingers or a pair of ears for you, you disgusting, foul-skinned mongrel runt. And you, you filthy girl with your stupid hair.' He spat on the deck in front of Tabitha. 'Oh, no. You see, my papa was Lord of the Marlinspike Quarter before me. And every year, on my birthday, he used to hold a party for me. There were cakes and jugglers and music. But my favourite part was the piñata.'

The crew shifted, anticipation in their eyes. They knew what was coming.

'Oh yes. A big ball made out of cloth, hung from the ceiling, with sweets inside. And every time you bashed it, sweets fell onto the floor. I used Papa's mace for it. It was the only time he let me touch it. Bash. Bash. Bash.' He grinned, and his eyes grew wide. 'So now we're going to bash you and see if any sweets come out.'

Chapter Thirty-two

Newton snarled and threw himself forward. In a split second Alice was there, raising her sword to parry his swing. A clash of metal on metal. Newton stepped back, his sword juddering in his hand, trying to calm himself. If he lost his temper this woman would butcher him. He had no doubt of that. She stood in a fighting stance, blue eyes fixed on his, her sword held steady in front of her.

The Duke of Garran calmly poured powder into the barrel of his pistol, as if he was nowhere more dangerous than a shooting range.

'Coward!' growled Newton. 'Why don't you fight me yourself?'

The Duke didn't even look up from his pistol. 'Because, Mr Newton, I might lose. And I only enjoy the games I know I will win.'

Behind him, Newton heard Old Jon slump onto the deck. He wanted to look so badly, to go and help the old elf. But that was out of the question. One slip-up, one waver of his attention, and Alice would carve him into pieces. No. He had to deal with her first.

Best get on with it then.

She was fast, he knew that. But he had ogre blood in his veins. *So use your strength.*

He sprang forward, unleashing a torrent of heavy blows. She stepped back, deflecting each one with calm, precise movements, allowing the Sword of Corin to slide off her own blade and never meeting it full on. All the power of his swings counted for nothing. He would only wear himself out.

He paused, panting. The wound in his arm was playing up but he scarcely noticed it. Alice waited, watching him, offering no attack of her own. She had fought in total silence, Newton realized. It was eerie.

The Duke of Garran had loaded his pistol now, but he didn't fire. Just stood there, enjoying the spectacle with a half-smile dancing on his lips.

At the sight of that, Newton threw himself into

another attack. He swung his sword once to keep the woman at bay, then crouched, grabbed hold of one leg of the golden chair and flailed it round at her.

If you're so clever, try parrying a chair.

Alice moved with incredible speed. Newton hadn't realized what she'd done until he saw the chair go crashing across the deck. In his hand he held only the severed stump of its leg.

For Thalin's sake . . . If she could pull off a move like that, she could just as easily have taken his arm off. She was playing with him. He looked up at her again, and saw that she knew what he was thinking. A small, tight smile formed on her lips, with no emotion behind it. As though she smiled only because it was expected.

What has she become?

He lunged at her and she sidestepped, fast as a mermaid in water. He lunged again and she repeated the move, not even bothering to touch his blade with her own.

Why hadn't he brought the Banshee? The weapon he knew best how to fight with in the whole world. *Idiot.* He'd been so fixated on killing the Duke with the Sword of Corin that he'd become foolish. Lost his head.

Why hadn't he listened to Old Jon?

And now at last the League officer stepped forward for her own attack. She darted in under his guard, swiping away his blade. Newton stumbled backwards, trying to bring the sword back to protect himself, but she struck again, a twisting blow that sent the Sword of Corin spiralling out of Newton's hands. His eyes followed it, saw it land with a thud in the foremast. Just like Tabitha throwing knives at a target. Then something struck his chest and he tumbled backwards, floored by a kick more powerful than a woman that size should have been able to deliver.

Joseph tried struggling, but it was no good. Lord Wren held him firmly in place as Tommy tied a thick rope around his wrists and ankles.

'Nice and tight,' said Tommy, with a wink. 'Don't want you coming loose before his majesty is finished with you.'

The crew were shouting at him, calling him greyskin, mongrel and worse. It all blurred together into one torrent of hate. That was fine though, because Joseph hated himself. It wasn't enough to get Pallione killed. Now he'd brought the whole of the Demon's Watch to their deaths.

'You bilgebags,' yelled Frank, his voice rising above the clamour. He sprang to his feet, but immediately several of the biggest bully boys leaped forward, battering him with musket butts and forcing him back down.

Paddy tried to wade in and help his brother out, but there were too many of them, and he was shoved onto the deck as well.

'Don't listen to them, Joseph,' he called out.

'Shut your disgusting green face!' screamed the Boy King. 'Now hoist him up.'

There was a whirring sound as several crewmen pulled on a rope, taking up the slack, then a *swoosh* as Joseph's feet were pulled from under him, and the world turned upside down as he went whizzing up into the air. The insults turned to laughter as he bobbed, suspended from a spar, and the men at the end of the rope had their fun, letting him drop a short way before tugging him back up again. The blood rushed to his head and he spun; he was so dizzy he thought he might be sick. His clothes were still dripping from the sea, and salt water stung his eyes, mingling with his tears.

'Now the girl,' commanded the Boy King.

Joseph watched Tabitha fight, but she couldn't win. Lord Wren held her tight, just like he'd held

Joseph, as Tommy knotted the rope around her. And then there was a cheer as she was dragged across the deck and up into the air beside him. They were lowered so that crewmen could grab hold of them and push them, sending them through the air, right out over the ocean, before they swung back, just missing each other the first time, but colliding the second, unable to stop themselves. Tabitha let out a grunt of pain but said nothing. She hated him just as much as the Boy King's men. More, probably. Joseph didn't blame her.

The swinging slowed, and Joseph saw, in revolving upside-down images, that Lord Wren had brought something up from below. A long rectangular box covered in black leather. He knelt and opened it for the Boy King. In the red velvet interior lay a mace, the shaft as thick as an oar pole and studded, the head a lump of metal almost the size of Joseph's head, cruelly ridged and spiked.

'Happy birthday, your majesty,' said Lord Wren.

'Happy birthday,' echoed his men.

'Hmphy brmphdy,' said Slik, cramming the last of the sugar lump into his mouth.

Some crewmen had set up a raised platform on the deck – planks of wood lashed together and laid out on barrels. Hal and the smugglers watched, helpless, still on their knees. The troll twins fought to get upright again, but many hands held them down.

The Boy King snatched the mace out of the box. His eyes were glued to Joseph and Tabitha, as though he was a spider watching the flies caught in its web. Slik fluttered away to land on Lord Wren's shoulder.

'My father's mace,' said the Boy King, and grinned. It was clearly too heavy for him, but not so much that he couldn't lift it. He leaped up onto the platform and gave the mace an experimental swing. The crewmen cheered. One or two fired flintlock pistols into the air, the shots mingling with the cannon fire and noise drifting over from the battle. Smoke had billowed across the deck now, obscuring half the Boy King's men.

Joseph and Tabitha were lowered, inch by inch, until they were level with the boy on his platform.

'I'm sorry,' said Joseph, but Tabitha didn't answer.

'Ladies and gentlemen,' roared the Boy King, his legs wide apart, his cockatrice plume bobbing in the smoke. 'Behold the death of these scurvy sea slugs! Behold their punishment for defying me, the Boy King, Lord of the Marlinspike Quarter. Behold my birthday treat!'

He raised his mace amid the cheers.

'You first, you filthy mongrel,' he whispered.

Joseph closed his eyes.

Newton crashed down onto the deck, his head throbbing with the impact. Out of the corner of his eye he could see Old Jon lying flat, motionless, his eyes glazed over. He tensed, ready to crawl towards the elf, but before he could move, he saw the point of Alice's blade hovering above his throat. She was holding it in a stabbing grip now, like a dagger, ready to push downwards with all her strength. No flicker of emotion touched her cold blue eyes.

Beyond, the Duke worked the Sword of Corin free from the mast and held it up, admiring it. The noise of battle still surged all around them, but in the smoke it felt like they were alone.

'Do you understand me now?' asked the Duke. 'You could never have defeated Major Turnbull, Mr Newton. She is amongst the greatest swordsmen the Old World has to offer. A worthy bodyguard, I'm sure you'll agree.' He gestured with the sword. 'If you don't mind, I shall be keeping this. A little memento.'

He stepped across the deck, leaning down to inspect Newton like an explorer discovering some strange new species of insect. His colourless eyes narrowed, and his lip curled.

'You mongrels have always fascinated me the most. To have mingled blood – a little demonspawn and a little humanity. Extraordinary. Almost as though you were shaped by both seraphs and demons. But I know better.' The Sword of Corin snaked forward, poking at the wound on Newton's arm. He had to grit his teeth so as not to cry out in pain. 'The seraphs made us, Mr Newton. We humans. But a little demon blood is enough to corrupt any one of us.' He whipped away the blade, tucking it under his arm.

'And so it is farewell. Major Turnbull – kill the mongrel.'

Hal couldn't watch. He turned away from the Boy King, trying to focus on anything but Tabitha and Joseph.

Wait.

There. Out to sea, beyond the smoke of the battle, something was moving. No, a thousand things. Flashing silver shapes, racing towards them like the shadow of a storm cloud.

Merfolk.

Ahead of them the water pulsed with magic and a wave began to form, like no wave Hal had ever seen before. It grew higher and higher, lifting up the leading warriors until it was roaring forward, twice as tall as the Boy King's ship. The merfolk rode it in a ragged line, silhouetted against the sky. Each held a bonestaff high above their heads, the air around them hazed with magic. And in the centre, riding the crest of the wave, was a mermaid. Her white hair streaked back in the wind.

It can't be . . .

He blinked, took off his glasses, rubbed at them and put them back on again.

What in Thalin's name . . .?

She was still racing towards them, her bonestaff held aloft.

Out of nowhere, Hal remembered Paddy's words as they sat around the camp fire on the island, talking about the King.

I heard he's so powerful he can even bring the dead back to life . . .

The wave was roaring towards them, no more than a few ship-lengths away. Hal turned and saw that the smoke had cleared, and everyone was watching.

The Boy King's mouth twisted in a sneer.

'Kill the fish folk!' he screeched. 'They won't spoil my treat!' He turned, raised the mace one more time. Tabitha and Joseph twitched like fish on a line, desperately trying to swing themselves out of reach. But it was no good.

Hal caught Frank's eye, and the troll mouthed two words:

Do something.

He dived forward, snatched the wooden spoon from amongst the weapons piled on the deck. Maybe there was a better spell, but he couldn't think of one, and the spoon was there in his hands. The bully boys were too busy gawping to stop him.

Concentrate.

He gripped it tight, levelling it like a pistol at the boy.

At the Azurmouth Academy they taught you to forget yourself. *All that matters is the spell. To control reality, you must first step out of it.* Of course in those days the most he had to worry about was a rap on the knuckles from Master Gurney – no maniacs with cutlasses who might cut your head off at any second.

The Boy King tensed, ready to swing.

Concentrate.

Warmth coursed through his body, from his head down to the tips of his fingers and toes. It was amazing how easy it was. The warmth found the wand and surged into it, making it hum in his grasp. He locked eyes with the boy.

Your mind is mine.

Your mind is mine.

Your . . .

. . . *mind* . . .

. . . *is* . . .

And suddenly, he was Nathaniel Ketteridge. The Boy King; Lord of the Marlinspike Quarter. Ten years old today, and furious that his birthday might be ruined.

Nathaniel Ketteridge, who didn't want to hurt the children any more. Who wanted to put down his mace.

Nathaniel Ketteridge, hesitating . . .

Abruptly, Hal was Hal again. Something was flying at him out of the corner of his vision, and his concentration had gone.

Slik slammed into the wooden spoon, wrapping his arms around it. His eyes were lit up with greed and his wings blurred as he tried to carry it away. Hal clung on but the spell was broken. The Boy King blinked, shook his head.

'What in the Ebony Ocean was—?'

'Look out!' howled Tabitha, still dangling from the spar. 'Look out!'

And with a thunderous crash, the great wave broke. Water gushed over them, sending Slik sprawling away, then Hal himself. The last thing he heard before he went under was the war cry of the merfolk, their voices raised up as one, carrying above the mighty roar of the sea.

'PALLIOOONNEEE!'

Chapter Thirty-three

Newton rolled aside as Major Turnbull's blade slammed into the deck where his neck had been a split second before. She tugged at the sword. But in the instant it took her to pull it free, Newton leaped to his feet and barrelled into her, shoving her backwards. He picked up the nearest weapon he could see – Old Jon's cudgel – and swung it. She ducked away.

Newton glanced to his right, hoping to see the smile wiped off the Duke of Garran's face. But he was looking out to sea. Newton followed his gaze and saw shapes – glistening, flickering shapes – moving fast below the surface of the water and streaking towards the *Justice*.

What the—?

Alice's sword blade sliced towards him, catching the cudgel with a glancing blow. *Idiot. Pay attention.* He charged again, staying close so she wouldn't have a chance to lunge at him. As she darted away, he caught a glimpse of something red on her shoulder. A fireball. The mark of a League magician. Funny. He hadn't noticed that in the library at Wyrmwood Manor.

Major Turnbull sidestepped round him, slamming him in the back with the pommel. Pain burst across his shoulder blades. And now she was raising her sword, ready to swing . . .

The deck jolted, throwing both of them off balance. Newton reached out, clung onto the gunwale. Major Turnbull lost her footing and slid away from him as the ship tipped.

Somehow Newton found it in himself to grin. Those shapes he'd seen, racing towards the vessel . . . They could only be one thing.

He heaved himself up and peered over the edge. The *Justice* was listing in the water and merfolk warriors crowded all around, shaking their bonestaffs, signing to each other and diving below. He'd be willing to bet they were heading for the bottom of the hull, pushing at it or using magic to capsize it.

'Kill him,' barked the Duke of Garran. For the first

time, Newton heard a note of anger in the man's voice.

He spun round, saw Turnbull leaping at him, her sword raised over her head. She was fast, that was for sure. But she was light too. Newton dropped the cudgel and dived, low and hard. She faltered, unsure what to do. *Weren't expecting that, were you?* And by then it was too late. He crashed into her legs, gripping them tight and sending her toppling to the deck. The sword skittered away but Newton reached out for it, caught it and swept it up, the blade resting against her neck.

Do it. Do it now.

Old Jon lay no more than three paces away. And here she was. The daughter of Governor Turnbull, the man who'd run the zephyrum mines of Garran. Black Turnbull, they'd called him. The man who had destroyed his family.

Ten years spent toiling in the dark, eating slop, seeing his friends die, while Turnbull and his daughter lived in a fancy townhouse with servants at their beck and call. Ten years. And now she was back, a full-grown woman, to enslave his new family and friends. The people of Fayt.

Newton snarled. The rage was back, surging through him, overwhelming him.

Do it now.

* * *

Cold water broke over Tabitha, knocking the breath from her body and setting her spinning wildly out over the sea, her stomach churning. She opened her eyes as she began to swing back, and saw a figure surging towards her, riding an unnatural column of water as though it was a galloping horse. Tabitha knew she must be seeing things. A slim, white-haired figure, holding out a bonestaff in her outstretched hand. *Could it be . . . ? No, no, it couldn't* . . . The bonestaff twitched, the ropes around her hands and ankles came free and she was falling.

She cried out, and a calm voice spoke in her ear:

'Don't be afraid.'

It was *her*.

How in all the—?

They plunged into the ocean, and a moment later strong hands had her by the shoulders and tugged her, gasping, above the surface.

Tabitha rubbed water from her eyes. The wave-cutter's deck faced her, as though she was seeing it from above. She saw men clinging to the rigging, a few falling into the sea, cannons crashing across the deck. She heard orders, screams, the groaning of the vessel itself, then a slap of spray as the masts hit the water. Merfolk swarmed all about the capsized ship. Two small groups sped round the prow and the stern, latching onto the masts like leeches and tugging them down, so the ship kept rolling over. Meanwhile others made for the deck, where the Boy King's men floundered, some trying to escape, others – the braver ones – drawing weapons and snarling insults at the merfolk.

She spotted Slik, his wings spraying water in all directions, flying away from the battle for all he was worth.

'Wait here,' said her rescuer.

Tabitha turned. The mermaid was pale, but her green eyes sparkled. Her powerful silver tail shimmered below the surface, rippling as it bore her up in the water. She looked strong. Like a princess. She was home at last.

'How did—? Why did—?'

Pallione shook her head impatiently. 'It doesn't matter,' she said. 'Not now.' She raised her twisted bonestaff, studded with pearls, and pointed at the ship. 'I have work to do.' With that she upended, showering Tabitha with water as she darted towards the wavecutter.

'Tabitha,' came a big, booming voice from nearby, and she turned to see the troll twins striking out towards her. Frank was supporting Hal, who looked as though he barely knew how to swim. His glasses were spotted with droplets, and he was clutching the wooden spoon. Later she'd have to thank him for saving her life. But now wasn't the time.

'Joseph!' she shouted. 'Where is he?'

'I've not seen him,' Paddy called back.

They bobbed together in the water, scanning in every direction. Tabitha's heart was thumping. *Please, no. Don't let him be—*

'There,' Frank yelled, pointing a big green finger.

Tabitha's racing heart stopped dead.

Riding the waves was a wooden raft loaded with bully boys, and in their midst the Boy King, his golden clothes waterlogged, his cockatrice plume drooping. It was the platform he'd been standing on when the wave hit. Two of the bully boys were pulling a bedraggled figure out of the water. A scrawny boy with pointed ears and mottled skin.

'Joseph!'

Major Turnbull was breathing fast. Even if she was a magician, like that red fireball suggested, there was no way she could focus enough to cast a spell with a blade at her neck. She closed her eyes. As if she knew what was coming next and was readying herself for it. Newton readied himself too. He was going to kill this woman.

Except she hadn't always been a woman. Not back then.

Just do it. His grip tightened on the hilt. One quick movement and it would be over.

Out of nowhere, Newton was struck by a memory. A sunny day just like this one. She was playing in the garden as the miners marched by the governor's house. Her eyes were scrunched tight, her hands covering them, and she counted down from a hundred as her nursemaids scattered. A game of hide and seek. And she'd opened her eyes, peeking through her fingers. Just for a moment. Enough to see Newton watching her as they trudged past.

For Thalin's sake, do it. Black Turnbull had killed his uncle, run him through for stealing bread. And there were countless others, the inglorious deaths in the mines, the forgotten souls who were simply worked until they dropped. *Revenge.* If they could see him now, they'd all be crying out for it.

Do it now. Do it for them.

That day in the garden he'd smiled at her, and she'd covered her eyes quickly, as though he might give the game away.

Do it.

But the rage was gone. Instead he felt weary. Tired of being angry. He flexed his fingers, loosened his grip on the hilt. He staggered to his feet, fighting the listing of the deck.

'Go,' he said, his voice hoarse.

Major Turnbull's eyes flicked open, and she glared at him like a cornered animal.

'Quickly. And take your sword.' He flung it away.

She scrambled to her feet, racing after it.

Newton stumbled across the foredeck to where Old Jon lay. The elf's face was white and his eyes were glazed, and Newton knew at once that it was over.

No time for tears. Not yet.

He slung Old Jon's frail body over his shoulder. The ship jolted until it was almost side on in the water. No chance of clawing his way back up to the top side of it now.

Newton glanced around one last time. Major Turnbull was gone. So was the Duke, and the Sword of Corin.

He took a deep breath and tightened his hold on Old Jon. Then he closed his eyes and leaped out over the sea.

They dumped him, shivering and dripping, on the wooden platform.

'You!' screeched the Boy King. 'You ruin *everything*!'

He grabbed Joseph's ears and pulled him to his knees.

'Someone give me a weapon!' he howled. 'I've had enough. I want him dead.'

A bully boy passed him an axe. It looked like it was made for chopping wood, but Joseph knew it would have no problem chopping mongrel boy instead. *Saved from a mace to be killed by an axe.*

He closed his eyes. This was what he deserved. As he waited for the blow to fall, he was almost glad. At least after this he couldn't disappoint his friends. Couldn't betray his town. Couldn't get anyone killed.

'Let him go,' said a voice from behind.

Joseph turned. Bobbing in the water was a mermaid with long white hair, green eyes and a bonestaff.

No, no, no. His mind was playing tricks on him. Horrible tricks. He'd seen her die . . . hadn't he? He blinked, but the mermaid was still there. He felt as though his heart might burst.

'You,' snarled the Boy King. His eyes bulged and his face was bright red. 'You sneaking, backstabbing, fish-tailed *witch*! I hate you! Someone give me a gun.'

'Don't you dare,' said Pallione. Her eyes burned with fury, and her bonestaff was raised and pointed at the raft. 'This is not your court, *child*. It is mine. And my powers are returned. I will ask you one last time. Let him go.'

'You can't tell me what to do,' shouted the Boy King. 'No one tells me what to do!'

'Then don't say I didn't warn you.'

She disappeared, slipping below the waves with a flash of her silver tail. The bully boys edged backwards, raising their muskets and scanning the water.

'Where's she gone?' demanded the Boy King. 'Where's she—?'

CRRRASH!

The wood below their feet erupted in a shower of splinters. Bully boys lurched in all directions, and the raft rocked as several fell into the sea. Pallione rose up through the shattered planks like an avenging seraph, gripped the Boy King by his collar and lifted him up into the air. Joseph forgot to breathe. She hovered there in a haze of magic, long tail gently pulsing like a snake's coils, as though she was treading water. The Boy King dangled from her hand like a marionette.

'The rest of you can go,' she said.

The bully boys didn't need to be told twice. They dropped their weapons and dived into the sea, striking out in all directions. Anything to escape from the flying mermaid who had just punched her way through six inches of solid wood.

'Cowards!' yelped the boy. 'Come back . . .' He struggled weakly, but he'd dropped his axe and had nothing to fight with.

Only Joseph stayed on the raft, still on his knees, still staring at Pallione.

It was her.

It really was.

'How shall we kill him?' said the mermaid.

The Boy King's eyes went wide, and all of a sudden he was no king at all. Just a child squirming in the grip of someone stronger and more powerful than he was. For an instant, Joseph thought of his uncle, Mr Lightly, hitting him for getting the customers' orders wrong, or for not cleaning the tankards properly.

He tried to speak, but no words came. In the end he just shook his head.

Pallione raised an eyebrow, hesitating for just a moment.

'Please,' whined the boy, and all the arrogance was gone from his voice. 'Please, let me go.'

The mermaid flung her arm out, tossing him into the ocean like an unwanted catch. They watched as he floundered amid the debris, bodies and broken bits of ship. He looked even younger than before, small and helpless as he paddled away. His golden hat floated nearby, the plume soaked and sagging.

Maybe they should have killed him. But Joseph was glad they hadn't.

He stared up at the mermaid. The gunshot wound was gone. So was the blood and the deathly pallor. He had so many questions he didn't know where to begin.

'Look, Joseph,' said Pallione, and she pointed out to sea with her bonestaff.

Most of the smoke had cleared now, and Joseph saw ships in the distance. League vessels sailing away, rounding the coast of Illon. Fayter vessels in pursuit. Merfolk everywhere, swarming through the water. As he watched, a League galleon was tipped onto its side in a great crash of spray, and warriors raced to attack its crew.

Something about the sounds of battle had changed too. Joseph had been too distracted to notice it until now. Screams of rage and pain mingled with yells of triumph. An impish dhow slid past, the crew jumping up and down on the deck and cheering, the sea-green banner of Fayt fluttering from the mainmast. Some of the fleeing League ships were nothing but dots in the distance now.

'The Fayters have won,' said Pallione. She smiled, but it was a weary smile, full of sadness as much as joy.

'What did . . . ?' Joseph began, but tailed off.

'How . . .?' he tried again, but he couldn't get any further.

Pallione floated down through the air and came to rest, sitting on the edge of the raft with her tail submerged and her bonestaff laid across her lap. She looked suddenly exhausted. The effort of the fighting and the magic had clearly taken its toll.

'Do you remember what you said on the hobgoblin's ship?' she said, in a quiet voice. 'You told me that when I saw my father, I'd see he cared about me more than I thought.' She bit her lip. 'I was so close to death. I could reach out and touch it. But he brought me back. He saved me with his magic.'

Joseph said nothing. He could tell there was more to come.

'But a spell like that comes at a great price for the magician who casts it. The greatest price there is.'

Silence. The breeze stirred her damp hair, but nothing else moved.

'Pallione, I'm just— I'm so—'

She raised one hand. 'No, Joseph. When it counted, you tried to save me.'

Silence again. Joseph didn't know what to say. There was one question he wanted to ask more than anything else, but he didn't know how. Pallione seemed to sense it.

'I didn't have to come. I could have stayed on the island. Done nothing while the League defeated your fleet. But I came. I came because . . .' She paused for just a moment. 'Because it was the right thing to do.' She smiled at him, a weak smile, but her eyes sparkled like tropical seas. 'Goodbye, Joseph. We'll meet again.'

In one swift movement she was gone, disappearing deep below the surface. Joseph watched her go, until all he could see was the silver glimmer of her tail below the waves.

And then nothing at all.

PART FIVE
The *Dread Unicorn*

Chapter Thirty-four

The flames leaped up high, sending sparks dancing into the night sky. Tabitha gazed into the fire, holding her hands out for the warmth. She was dimly aware of the feasting, drinking, singing and dancing going on around her, but no more than that.

It had taken an hour for her clothes to dry out after the battle. Now they were stiff and uncomfortable, encrusted with sea salt. Not that Tabitha cared. There was so much more to think about. Old Jon. Pallione. And Joseph.

He was an idiot for believing Jeb the Snitch. And even more of an idiot for trying to help him. But when she remembered what she'd said in the warehouse, she felt horribly guilty. *I'd be better off on my own.* What had she been thinking? She hadn't really meant it. Surely he knew that. It was obvious, wasn't it?

A large man strolled round the edge of the fire towards her, half in shadow. The orange glow lit up Newton's shaven head and the shark tattoo on his cheek. He sat down on the sand next to her, reached out to ruffle her hair, then remembered she didn't like that and let his hand drop. They gazed into the fire together.

Tabitha stole a glance at him. It was only now they were together again that she realized how much she'd missed him. He wasn't her father. Never was, never would be. But he was the closest thing she had.

'I'm sorry,' she said. 'About Old Jon.'

Newton nodded. 'Aye.'

'You knew him for a long time, didn't you?'

'A long time. Not long enough.'

Tabitha didn't know what to say to that, so she went back to staring into the fire. She felt so safe with Newton by her side. After all that had happened, she would have liked him to put his arms around her and hold her, like when she was little. Of course, if he had done that, she'd have squirmed away and told him off for treating her like a baby. But still.

She hugged her knees up close and scanned the ocean, trying to spot the flash of merfolk tails among the moonlit waves. But they'd all gone. Disappeared almost as soon as the fighting was over, taking their dead with them. It made all this celebration seem hollow, Tabitha reckoned. After all, it was Pallione who'd really won the battle.

Pallione. The Queen of the Merfolk.

'I still don't understand,' she said out loud. 'Why did she help us? After everything that happened?'

Newton didn't reply. Tabitha glanced at him and saw that he was looking uneasy, rubbing at the red marks around his wrists. Clearly he had something on his mind.

'Tabs,' he said at last. 'Something's up with Joseph. Do you know what it is?'

Tabitha shrugged.

He turned to her with that expression on his face – the earnest look that showed he was trying to act like a good father but didn't have a clue what he was doing.

'Thing is, Tabs, friends are worth hanging on to.'

'I know. What do you—?'

'And I think, right now, Joseph needs somebody to talk to.'

Tabitha was about to argue, but then for some

reason Old Jon came into her mind. Old Jon and Newton sitting in the corner of Bootles' Pie Shop while the others played triominoes, just sitting together and smoking. Not even saying a word to each other, but content. From now on, when Newton smoked in the corner of the pie shop, he'd be smoking alone.

She got to her feet, using his shoulder to steady herself.

'All right,' she said. 'I'll go.'

'. . . and if I never eat fried fish again, it'll be too soon!' finished Frank. The others around the fire laughed, and Joseph smiled along with them. It helped, somehow, having all this energy and happiness around him. Helped him think, without anyone noticing that something was wrong.

The Fayters all seemed so relaxed, as if this was over. But for him it wasn't. He remembered his last sight of Jeb the Snitch, snarling and pointing a pistol at them. That last threat too. *What about your father, boy? You'll never see him again.* If there was even a chance that Jeb meant to hurt his father . . .

Pallione's face came to him, her white hair slicked back and dripping with water as she sat hunched on the raft, telling him how the King had died to save her life. *Always do the right thing,* she'd told him.

At last he was starting to see what the right thing was.

Joseph looked around at his friends and noticed Hal, sitting cross-legged on the sand next to him, cradling the wooden spoon and frowning through his spectacles at it.

'Thank you,' he said. 'For saving us on that wavecutter.'

Hal flinched and looked up, as if he'd just been woken from a deep sleep.

'Oh. You're welcome.'

'How does it work? The wooden spoon, I mean.'

Hal's whole face lit up, as if he'd been waiting for someone to ask him that.

'It's a question of mental focus,' he said. 'Very little more than that. That's the genius of it. Most wands require a kind of specific thought process achievable only by the most talented of magicians. Or a verbal trigger to unlock the wand's potential. But in the case of this wooden spoon none of that is needed. You merely have to be in contact with the wand, with a clear line of sight to the target, then concentrate on your intention to take control of their mind. Extremely sophisticated.'

Joseph frowned at the wand as Hal held it up. Half

of the spoon lay in shadow from the fire; the other half glowed orange.

'Are you saying you don't even have to be a magician?'

Hal frowned. 'It would be unwise for a layman to use it. Only magicians have the necessary mental focus and—'

'But you wouldn't *have* to be.'

'Well. Technically, I suppose not. Although it could be highly dangerous if used incorrectly. I read about wands like this when I was studying at the Azurmouth Academy, but I had no idea there were enchanters still capable of creating them.'

'And if you take control of a person's mind, you can make them do anything you want?'

'Naturally. That's what mind control is.'

'So you could make them tell you something they didn't want to tell you?'

Hal's eyes darted from the spoon to Joseph's face, narrowing slightly.

'I suppose so. Why do you ask?'

'Just wondering.'

The magician relaxed and turned his attention back to the wand. At this angle his spectacles were two solid orange discs in the firelight.

'Well, I'm glad. No one else in the Watch has an

appreciation for the art of magic. Except Newt. And he doesn't talk about it much.'

'No,' said Joseph absently.

You could make them tell you something they didn't want to tell you.

'Hey.'

They both turned at the voice. Tabitha was standing there, her face lit up from below so that strange shadows danced across her features, and Joseph couldn't quite tell what expression she wore.

'Tabs,' he said cautiously.

'Can we talk?'

He nodded and scrambled to his feet. Hal went back to his wand without a second glance.

They set out across the beach, away from the firelight, music and drunken songs. They passed a pair of trolls, stripped to the waist and wrestling while spectators cheered them on; a dwarf with a bandaged leg telling tales of the battle to a circle of friends; scores of folk smiling, laughing and dancing. Further up the beach, Joseph made out the shadowy figure of Governor Skelmerdale. He had arrived an hour before to congratulate the fleet, and now stood drinking firewater with Colonel Derringer and a group of blackcoats, smiling and laughing. Joseph watched him pat the colonel on the back before moving on to another group.

Their feet sank deep in the sand, still warm from the day's sunshine. As they got further from their fellow Fayters, Joseph began to notice the surge of the sea, and the cries of the birds that lived inland. One took flight from a nearby tree, the blue and yellow of its wings still just visible in the dusk. It was a perfect evening on a beautiful island that, just a year ago, he could never have even imagined visiting. For a moment it made him forget everything. Made him feel sad and happy at the same time.

Tabitha stopped and sat down on the sand. She hadn't said a word yet. Joseph lowered himself down beside her.

'Tabs,' he said, and his voice shook. He took a deep breath and tried again. 'Tabs. I'm so sorry. About leaving you in Fayt. And . . . and about *everything*.'

'That's all right.'

'You must be really angry with me, and you're right to be. I was—' He broke off, realizing what she'd just said. 'Did you say "that's all right"?'

Tabitha nodded. She still wasn't looking at him, but something about her had softened.

'I think I just want to forget about it.'

Joseph could barely believe what he was hearing.

'Besides,' she went on, sifting sand through her fingers. 'The truth is . . .' She sighed. 'Well, I'm sorry too. When we were in the warehouse, and I said . . . I said I would be better off without you.'

'It doesn't matter,' said Joseph. He tried a smile. 'I mean, I suppose you were right.'

She smiled back at him, and it was the best thing he'd seen all day.

There was a silence, but a comfortable one.

'There is one thing though,' said Tabitha finally. 'I want to know what happened. Why did you help the Snitch?'

Joseph hesitated. He didn't want to talk about it. But after everything he'd put her through, he owed her an explanation at the very least.

He reached into his coat pocket. There it was, nestled next to his heart. He pulled out the watch and handed it to her. Against all the odds, it was still ticking.

'It's a watch,' said Tabitha. 'So what?'

He turned it over in her hands so that the engraving was face up. 'See? Elijah. My father. Jeb gave it to me. He was going to take me to him. To the Old World.'

Tabitha stared at the engraving. Then, slowly, she shook her head.

'Bilge,' she said.

Joseph felt as though she'd slapped him. His ears twitched.

'What do you mean, bilge?'

'This is Jeb the Snitch we're talking about. Listen to yourself! I already told you, he made it up so that you'd help him.'

'You don't know that,' said Joseph, as calmly as he could.

'He tricked you, Joseph. He got someone to make that watch for him. Or maybe it *was* your father's, but that doesn't mean he's alive. Look, don't feel bad – he even tricked Newt into trusting him, before he betrayed us all to Captain Gore and his pirates. I know how hard it is not having a ma and a pa. But that doesn't—'

'That's not what this is about.'

Tabitha raised an eyebrow. 'Really? Are you sure about that?'

He wasn't. Not at all. But he wasn't going to tell her that.

'Forget it,' he said unsteadily. 'Forget I said anything.'

'Even if it was true, and even if you helped him, he still wouldn't tell you. Why would he?'

'I'd make him.'

There was a pause. Something about the way he'd said that had thrown her. He swallowed. 'I mean, I'd—'

'Hey,' said Tabitha. She smiled at him and punched his arm. 'I'm sorry. Let's just forget about it, all right?'

Joseph looked back at the Fayters sitting around their fires, celebrating, and for a moment he felt like he was looking at them from outside. Like Pallione and her father, bobbing in the waters of the bay and wondering at the strange way these land dwellers behaved. He thought of the mermaid princess hunting for shells and chasing shoals of fish. Fighting in the shark pits. Singing for the Boy King. And he thought about her father, waiting for her, and dying for her.

Forget about it.

No. That was the one thing he couldn't do.

Chapter Thirty-five

When Newton woke, the snoozing figures all around him were just dim blue shapes dotting the beach. In the distance a soft orange glow ran along the horizon, staining the clouds. Dawn.

He sat up, pushing the thin blanket aside. He ignored the ache in his back from sleeping in the wrong position, the twinge in his arm from the butcher's sword and the pain in his chest from where Alice Turnbull had kicked him.

It hadn't been a restful night. That little red fireball on the League officer's arm had kept reappearing in his dreams, like an itch he couldn't scratch. Perhaps there was a completely ordinary reason why she hadn't worn it the day before, in Wyrmwood Manor. Perhaps not.

And that wasn't all. What was it the Duke of Garran had said? *I only enjoy the games I know I will win.* Well, he'd lost the battle. The merfolk had turned the tide and the League ships had fled. But Newton had a feeling that there was something else going on, and the more he thought about it, the more certain he was. The Duke had insisted on the parley in Port Fayt, but why? He must have known Skelmerdale would never bargain with him. So what had he got out of it?

Only one thing. *The Sword of Corin.*

Newton rubbed at his stubbled chin and sighed. He didn't know why the League wanted that sword. But he knew he shouldn't have let the Duke get to him. Shouldn't have become so angry. Should have taken the Banshee into battle, instead of that relic.

Out of nowhere, Old Jon's voice came into his head.

Don't be too hard on yourself.

Newton pictured the elf's face, rugged, weather-beaten and kind. Jon would have wanted him to stay strong, for the Demon's Watch.

He took a long, deep breath. He felt calm. Calmer than he'd felt in days.

Whatever it meant – and whatever happened – he would be ready for it.

'Newt!'

Around him, several of the sleeping figures stirred.

'Newt! Get up!'

Tabitha's voice. He turned and saw her stumbling towards him across the sand. Judging by her pale face and hollow eyes, she'd had as sleepless a night as he had. But he knew at once that it was more than that. Something was wrong.

'It's Joseph,' she said breathlessly, before he could speak.

'Keep it down,' muttered one of the Fayters.

'Some of us are trying to sleep,' grumbled another.

Tabitha ignored them. 'I was talking to him last night, and he was being really strange. It's not as if I said anything bad. I was just trying to be nice. And now this morning—'

'What is it, Tabs?' asked Newton gently.

She ran her hands through her tangled hair and swallowed.

'He's gone.'

All right. Think.

'Just Joseph? Or is anyone else missing?'

Tabitha shrugged.

He got to his feet, laid his hands on her shoulders.

'Tabs. Is there anything he said last night – anywhere he might have gone?

She chewed her lip, frowning. At last she looked up at him.

'Yes,' she said. 'He did say something. Something about Jeb the Snitch.'

There was a shout from further down the beach, making more of the Fayters groan and roll over. Newton turned to see Cyrus Derringer striding towards him, fully dressed in his black uniform despite the hour. Following him, half scurrying to keep up, was an imp in shirtsleeves. Newton recognized him at once.

'You!' Derringer called out. He didn't sound happy. Didn't look it either. 'Mr Newton. You're responsible for that filthy smuggler, aren't you?'

'Phineus Clagg? Why?'

'Mr Newton, sir,' said the imp, who was only just catching his breath. 'It's my ship. The *Dread Unicorn*. He's . . . Well, he's stolen it.'

The wind was good and the *Dread Unicorn* had left Illon behind, a dim shape in the distance. Gulls circled above. Ahead, there was nothing but the open sea.

'Not much to look at, this ol' tub,' said Captain Clagg. 'Fast though, ain't it? Even with them burned up holes in the sails. That imp and his crew'll be hopping mad when they wake up, I'll wager. Eh, lads?'

His crew chorused their agreement.

'And you,' he called as he strode across the deck. 'Knew yer'd see sense. Bunch o' do-gooders like the Demon's Watch. You're much better off here with me, out on the Ebony Ocean.'

The smuggler clapped Joseph on the back, nearly making him spill the bucket of water and soap suds he was holding. He carried on scrubbing the cannon, trying to ignore Clagg's running commentary. It felt good to do some cleaning, just like he used to in the Legless Mermaid. Something familiar to hang on to. Something to stop him from looking back at the rapidly disappearing island of Illon, and the Fayter fleet that lay at anchor there.

'Yer'll make a fine cabin boy, just you wait and see,' said Clagg. 'You've come a long way from that scrawny, scared little tavern runt I met back in the Legless Mermaid. Maybe one day you'll even—'

'Just till Azurmouth, remember?' Joseph interrupted. He sat up and dropped the sponge into the bucket. 'I'm only your cabin boy until then. After that I'm leaving you. That was the deal.'

Clagg tapped his nose. 'Aye-aye, matey. Don't you fret, I'm a man of my word. Yer'll regret it though. A mongrel boy in Azurmouth! Only say the word and yer can stick with me and my crew. It's back to smuggling for us. Just like old times, aboard the *Sharkbane*.'

There was a quaver in his voice, and Joseph looked up to see that the smuggler's eyes were filmed with tears.

He didn't know what to say. But thankfully Clagg was already striding off, whistling to himself and pulling a bottle of firewater from his pocket. 'Nice drop of firewater . . . How I've missed you, my darling . . .'

Joseph put down the bucket and reached into his coat. There it was, at the bottom of his inside pocket. The silver pocket watch. And next to it his fingers found the wooden spoon. Hal had been fast asleep when Joseph took it from under his pillow. What was it the magician had said? All you had to do was point the wand at the target, then think the right thoughts.

How hard could that be?

He remembered the last glimpse he'd had of Captain Lortt's junk, heading east. If Jeb was going to the Old World, then Joseph was going too. He'd make the Snitch tell him the truth about his father. And more than that, he'd get his revenge. *Two dragons with one fireball,* as the old saying went. It was Jeb who'd tricked him into betraying his friends. Jeb who'd sided with the League. Jeb who'd shot Pallione, before the King died to save her.

Finally Joseph knew what he had to do. And he was going to do it, even if it killed him.

He knelt back and breathed in the fresh sea air. He felt calm at last. Almost content. And best of all, this way he wasn't putting Tabitha or any of the other watchmen in danger. It was all up to him.

Always do the right thing.

He rested one hand on the hilt of his cutlass and gazed out over the prow, across the sparkling Ebony Ocean, towards Azurmouth.

Epilogue

Azurmouth. The greatest city in all the Old World.

The white carriage is waiting on the docks, emblazoned with the Golden Sun, drawn by four white horses puffing out clouds of mist in the cold morning air and stamping their hooves on the cobblestones.

He pauses a moment on the quayside before climbing inside. It is so good to breathe Azurmouth air again. His eyes wander over the brickwork of the giant warehouses that line the docks, each one as big and imposing as the governor's manor house in Port Fayt. Below, sailors and stevedores go about their business. So many human faces. Not an imp, elf, goblin or troll in sight. A dwarf hobbles into view from behind a warehouse, rattling a tin full of coins. The Duke of Garran frowns, turns and points out the beggar to a revenue official.

'Have that taken care of.'

'Yes, your grace.'

Strange. He almost misses those creatures. Clearly there is some sickness in his soul that drives him to seek out demonspawn. To probe at the darkness within them.

And yet someone must.

He steps into the carriage as two soldiers head over to the dwarf.

Major Turnbull follows him, settling on the plush red velvet seat opposite. She carries the Sword of Corin wrapped in a leather sheath, laid over her lap. Her delicate fingers clasp it tight as the carriage moves off.

'An unfortunate loss, the Justice*,' he says mildly. 'Expensive.'*

She nods.

'But a worthy sacrifice, nonetheless.' His eyes return to the chased silver hilt of the sword, encrusted with white star-stones. It is beautiful. 'What spell did you use in the library, I wonder? A little emotional manipulation, perhaps – intensifying his anger and binding it to the sword? Hardly required. The only pity is that we could not crush them all at Illon. The captain of the Demon's Watch, that mongrel—'

'Filth,' says Major Turnbull. She spits the word out like a mouthful of rotten apple. 'Demonspawn.'

The Duke of Garran smiles. Since the battle, Turnbull has been even more quiet than usual. This is the first thing she has said all day, and he knows he has made her furious to get that much out of her. It amuses him.

'Filth, you say? Perhaps. But a worthy enough opponent for you on this occasion. You let him beat you. And with nothing more than a wooden club. Are you not ashamed?'

Turnbull does not rise to the bait, just turns to glare out of the window at the people passing in the streets.

'No matter. I do not doubt that you will have another opportunity to cross swords with him.'

Turnbull carries on glaring, and the Duke of Garran smiles again.

He leans forward, takes the leather sheath from her lap and places it on his own. The blade slides out easily, just a little way, so that he can admire the craftsmanship. It has stayed with him all the way from Illon, in the wavecutter he commandeered from one of his scout captains, locked up in a chest in his cabin.

The Sword of Corin the Bold.

The most powerful blade in all the Old World. Imbued with a magic so deep and ancient that scarcely any still remember. They will be reminded though. And from this day forward, he will not let it out of his sight.

Soon, perhaps, the Fayters will realize what it is they have lost. The price they have paid for their little victory.

Perhaps they will even try to take it back.

The Duke of Garran smiles and slides the blade back into its sheath.

Let them, he thinks.

Let them try.

HERE ENDS BOOK TWO

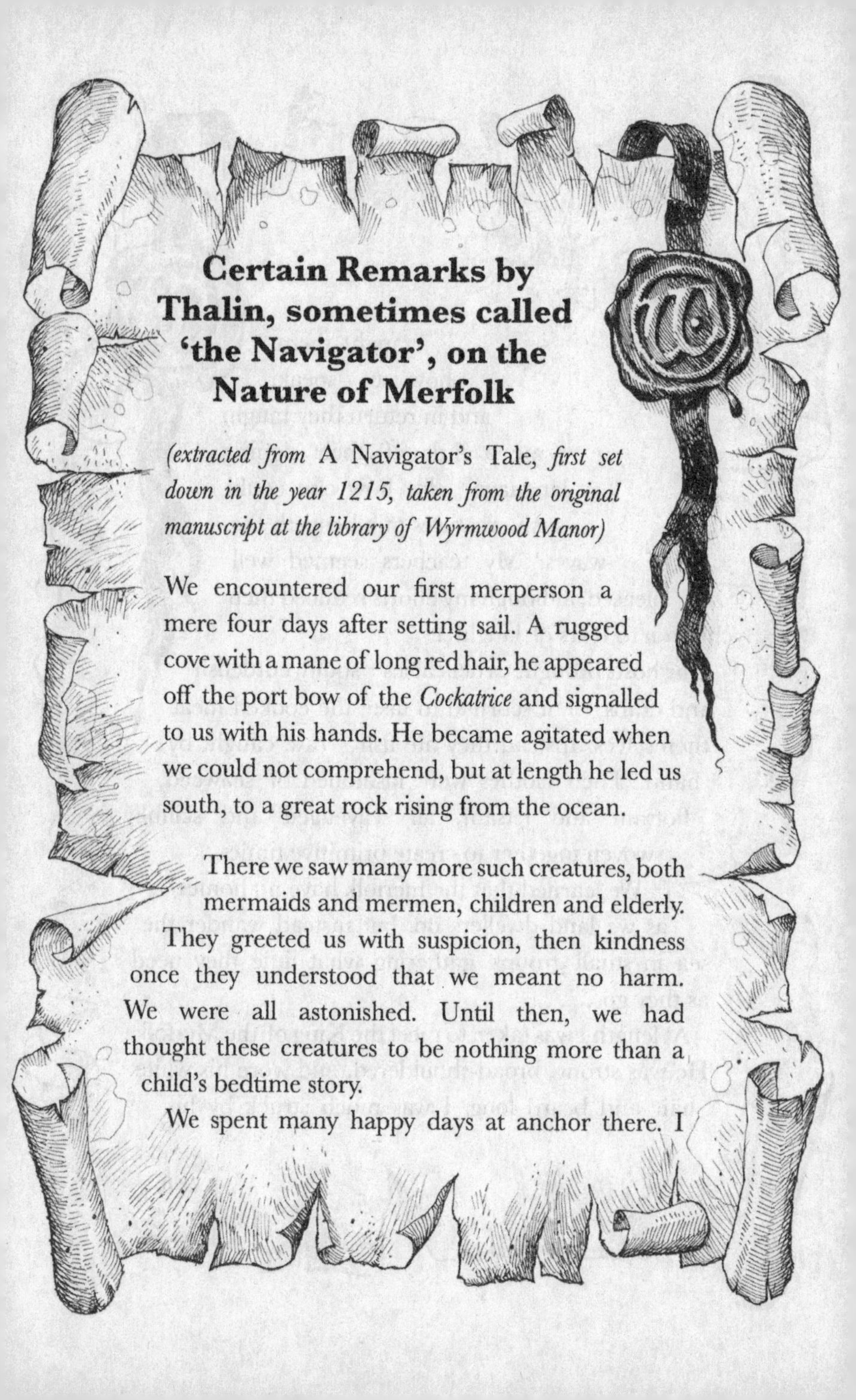

Certain Remarks by Thalin, sometimes called 'the Navigator', on the Nature of Merfolk

(extracted from A Navigator's Tale, *first set down in the year 1215, taken from the original manuscript at the library of Wyrmwood Manor)*

We encountered our first merperson a mere four days after setting sail. A rugged cove with a mane of long red hair, he appeared off the port bow of the *Cockatrice* and signalled to us with his hands. He became agitated when we could not comprehend, but at length he led us south, to a great rock rising from the ocean.

There we saw many more such creatures, both mermaids and mermen, children and elderly. They greeted us with suspicion, then kindness once they understood that we meant no harm. We were all astonished. Until then, we had thought these creatures to be nothing more than a child's bedtime story.

We spent many happy days at anchor there. I

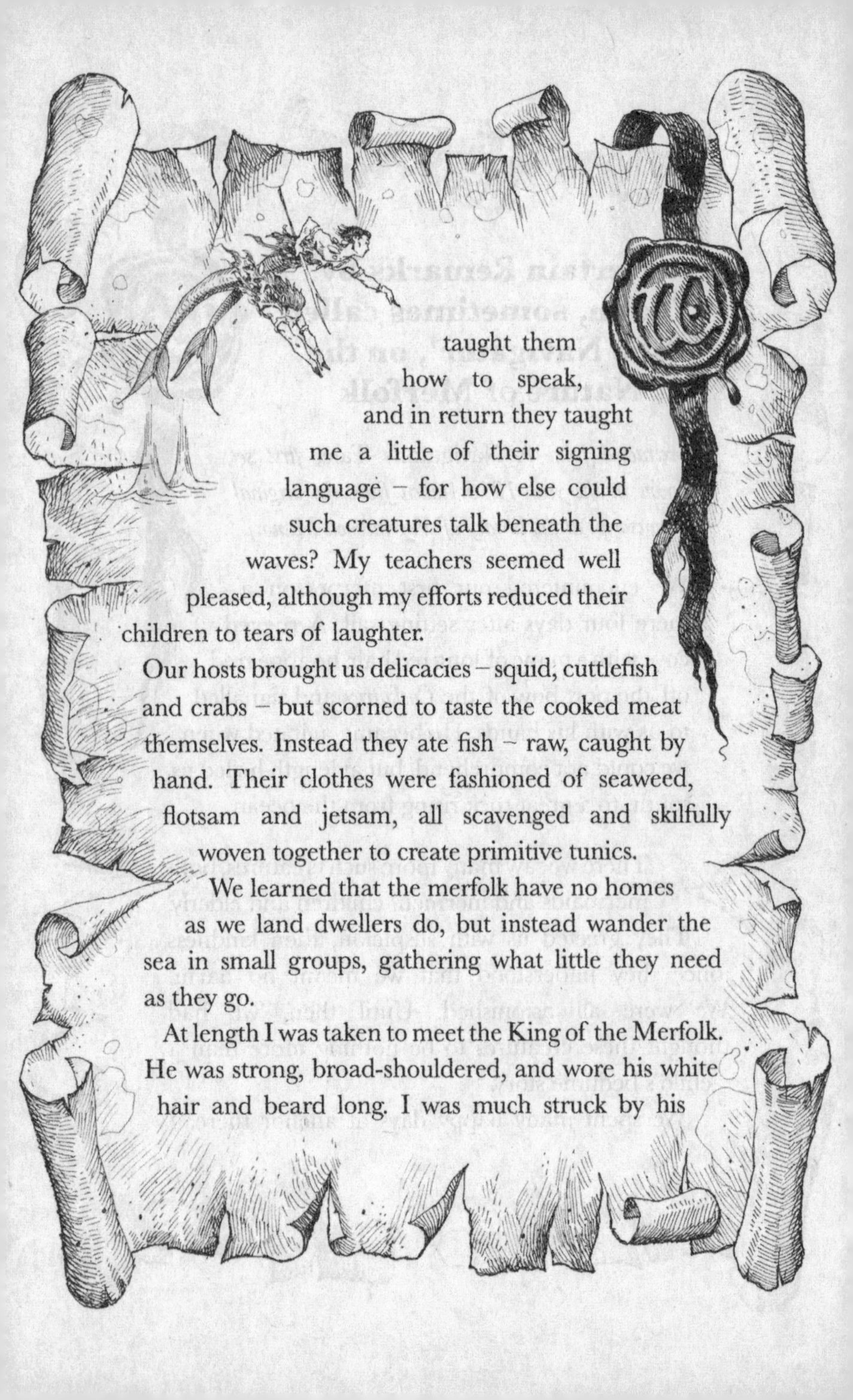

taught them how to speak, and in return they taught me a little of their signing language – for how else could such creatures talk beneath the waves? My teachers seemed well pleased, although my efforts reduced their children to tears of laughter.

Our hosts brought us delicacies – squid, cuttlefish and crabs – but scorned to taste the cooked meat themselves. Instead they ate fish – raw, caught by hand. Their clothes were fashioned of seaweed, flotsam and jetsam, all scavenged and skilfully woven together to create primitive tunics.

We learned that the merfolk have no homes as we land dwellers do, but instead wander the sea in small groups, gathering what little they need as they go.

At length I was taken to meet the King of the Merfolk. He was strong, broad-shouldered, and wore his white hair and beard long. I was much struck by his

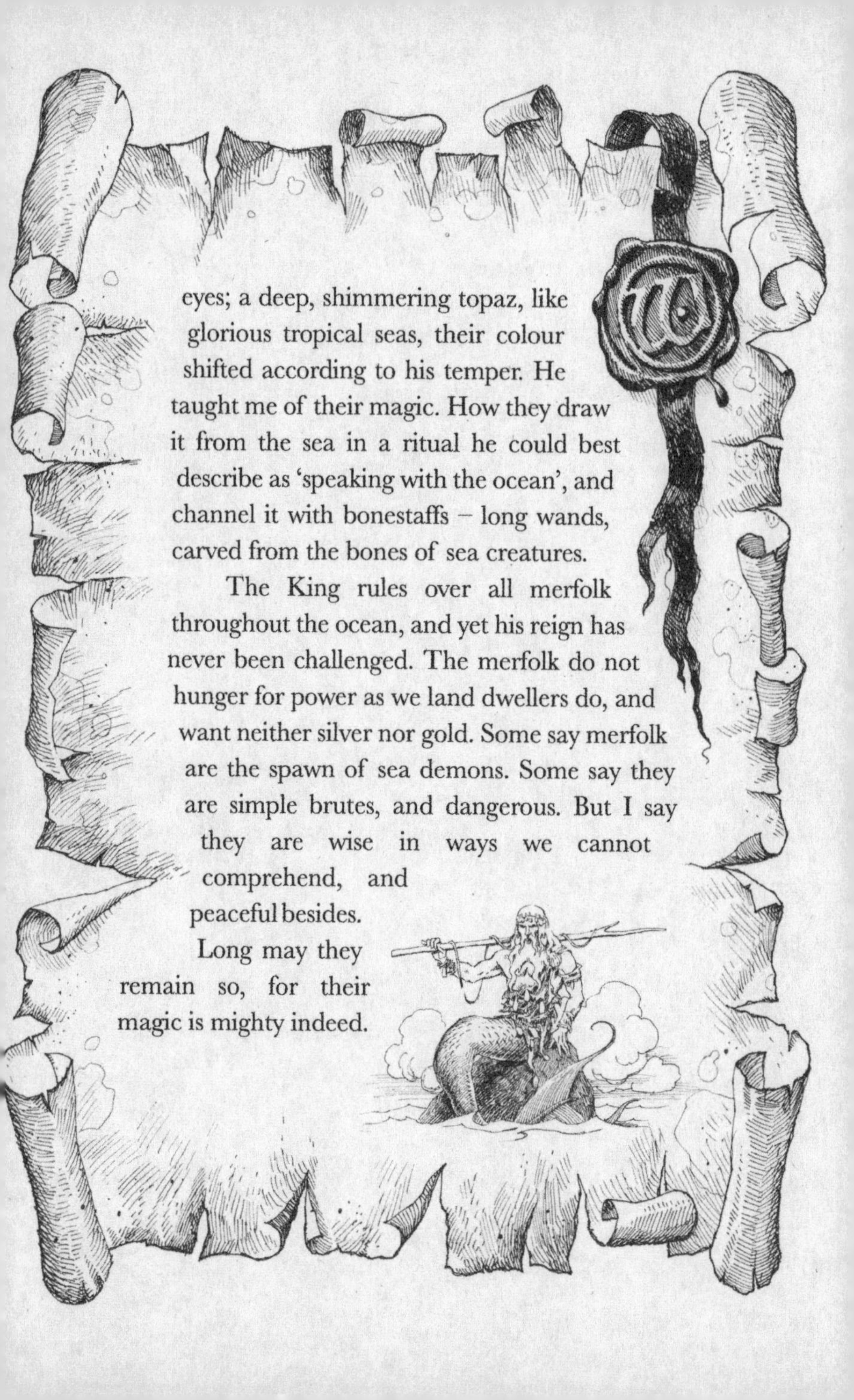

eyes; a deep, shimmering topaz, like glorious tropical seas, their colour shifted according to his temper. He taught me of their magic. How they draw it from the sea in a ritual he could best describe as 'speaking with the ocean', and channel it with bonestaffs – long wands, carved from the bones of sea creatures.

The King rules over all merfolk throughout the ocean, and yet his reign has never been challenged. The merfolk do not hunger for power as we land dwellers do, and want neither silver nor gold. Some say merfolk are the spawn of sea demons. Some say they are simple brutes, and dangerous. But I say they are wise in ways we cannot comprehend, and peaceful besides.

Long may they remain so, for their magic is mighty indeed.

Acknowledgements

Huge thanks once again to Jane and to everyone at Lutyens and Rubinstein. To my superstar editors Hannah and Bella, and to Simon, Tilda and David. To Lauren and everyone at RHCP, and to cover wizards Alison and David. To all my wonderful supportive friends and colleagues, particularly Hugh for comments on the manuscript and Simon for trailer-making skills. A special thanks to Henry for his Latin expertise. And as ever, thanks to Mark, Verity and Katrina, who've read this book almost as many times as I have.